WANDERERS

SUSAN KIM & LAURENCE KLAVAN

WANDERERS

An Imprint of HarperCollinsPublishers

HarperTeen is an imprint of HarperCollins Publishers.

Wanderers
Copyright © 2014 by Susan Kim and Laurence Klavan
All rights reserved. Printed in the United States of America.
No part of this book may be used or reproduced in any manner whatsoever without written permission except in the case of brief quotations embodied in critical articles and reviews. For information address HarperCollins Children's Books, a division of HarperCollins Publishers, 10 East 53rd Street, New York, NY 10022.
www.epicreads.com

ISBN 978-0-06-211854-7

Typography by Michelle Gengaro-Kokmen
14 15 16 17 18 LP/RRDH 10 9 8 7 6 5 4 3 2 1

First Edition

To my parents, who—among other things—gave me lots of books
—Susan

To Mina Gruber, who put up with me in childhood
—Laurence

PART ONE

ONE

A RAVAGED STREET RAN THROUGH WHAT WAS ONCE A BUSTLING SUBURB. There were no signs of life; even the treetops were motionless, etched in black ink against a dirty-yellow winter sky.

A flicker of movement broke the stillness.

It came from a hedge by the side of the road, overgrown and dying, its tangled branches spilling onto the sidewalk. The foliage trembled again, and a moment later a girl in battered sunglasses and a torn red hoodie emerged from its depths. She wore a leather quiver across her thin chest and a fiberglass bow dangled from her hand.

It was a January morning and so the air was relatively cool.

Even so, Esther's throat was parched and she could feel sweat trickling down her back. She had been tracking her prey for nearly two hours, and it was painstaking work. This kind of patience, careful and focused, had never been her strength. She preferred action, and as unskilled as she was at killing, she was tempted to rush forward now and attempt an attack. Yet there was too much at stake to fail, so she forced herself to remain still.

Her target was across the street. It was a large animal, shaggy with gray, bristled hair, a feral pig that was making its way past the abandoned houses that lined the street, grunting as it rummaged for food.

This was a rash choice, the girl knew. Even to an experienced hunter, a pig was formidable prey, surprisingly fast for its size and dangerous when cornered. But such a beast could feed her family and friends well for weeks. And what Esther lacked in hunting skill, she could make up for in stealth.

Or at least she hoped.

Moving noiselessly in her shredded sneakers and staying upwind so the animal wouldn't catch her scent, Esther managed to keep distant pace as the pig continued to root its way through the trash that spilled from open doorways and abandoned cars. She only moved when the animal was distracted, when it paused to nose through the sections of broken pavement that exposed tree roots and red clay. At such moments, she tried to imitate one of the many cats owned by her friend Joseph: moving in tiny yet swift increments, freezing after each time.

Even so, it seemed impossible to get close enough to draw an accurate bead on her target, much less get off a good shot. Esther had only three precious arrows with her, spindly feathered shafts that were so weightless, she had to keep checking her quiver to make certain they were still there. She would likely need all three to finish the job, and that was only if she was lucky enough to immobilize the animal with her first shot. And arrows were growing rarer by the day.

As if it could hear her thoughts, the pig now raised its head and Esther again froze. She could see its tufted ears twitching as it gazed around. Its obsidian eyes seemed to slide over her, unseeing. Then, with a grunt, the creature turned and ambled past the overgrown yard and into the woods that lay behind the house.

Across the street, Esther swore under her breath.

But there was perhaps still hope. The pig was trotting, not galloping. That meant it wasn't frightened; clearly, it hadn't seen her. Gritting her teeth, Esther took off across the street in pursuit.

The small forest was carpeted with dead leaves and household trash, piles of moldering clothes, and filthy and broken bits of furniture and plastic. It was as if the garbage had leaked out of the house it surrounded, like putrescence oozing from a dead thing. In addition, the woods were choked with vines and fallen branches, making it difficult to navigate.

Still, it wasn't hard to guess where the pig was headed. Esther could hear the steady sounds of its progress in the distance: twigs snapping, leaves swishing. Feeling reckless, she put on speed; and it was a pleasure to move swiftly, to hurdle dead trees and push past branches that whipped her face. Then she stopped short.

To her surprise, she found she was much closer to the animal than she had thought; it was no more than a few body lengths in front of her, partly hidden by a mound of leaves. It had its head down and appeared to be rooting, too immersed in whatever it had found to notice her, to even look up.

Inwardly rejoicing, Esther forced herself to slow down as she approached the leaf pile from behind a tree. To lose this advantage due to overeagerness would be terrible indeed. Barely daring to breathe, she drew even closer, and the pig had still not moved away.

She was almost upon it.

Esther took an arrow from her quiver and fit it to the bow. Then, in one swift movement, she raised the weapon to her shoulder as she pulled the bowstring back past her cheek and stepped around the tree, aiming downward.

The pig did not see her. Its head was turned away, butting something with its snout as it made a soft sound that was half grunt, half chuckle. Beneath it, nuzzling its underbelly, was a smaller version of itself, faint stripes visible on its still-soft fur.

The pig was a female, a mother nursing her child. And even as Esther took aim at the animal's heart, so close she swore she could see it beating beneath the shaggy pelt, she was shocked to find herself trembling, her aim wavering.

She hesitated, confused. Then she steeled herself, trying to shake off the feeling. But it was no good.

Esther had no false sentimentality about the wild animals that roamed the streets of Prin. And she needed no reminder of the urgency of her situation. Until recently, it had been disease that everyone feared. The illness, carried in water, was both invisible and inevitable; it meant no one lived past the age of nineteen.

But in the past few weeks, it was hunger that threatened to kill them all. And it would strike, regardless of age.

Even now, Esther knew her loved ones awaited her at home, starving a slow yet certain death—as was she, as was everyone else in the town of Prin. Yet for reasons she could not explain, Esther felt her grip on her weapon weaken. Then she lowered the bow.

Trembling, Esther stepped behind the tree, out of sight. She was about to stumble away when she sensed someone watching her.

Several yards away, a figure stepped into a shaft of sunlight. Androgynous and small of stature, the person had sun-darkened skin and a bald head that were covered with an ornate pattern of scars and primitive tattoos that acted as a kind of camouflage. The bulging lavender eyes placed far apart crinkled as the creature smiled, revealing a mouthful of tiny teeth.

It was Skar.

Esther was about to exclaim, surprised as she was to encounter her oldest friend, whom she had not seen in many weeks. But the other one silenced her with a finger to the lips, first gesturing toward the nursing sow, then indicating that they should leave the woods. Esther understood and fell into step behind her.

As they walked, Esther's joy at seeing Skar was tempered by the shame she felt knowing that her friend had most likely witnessed her inexplicable cowardice. The variants, after all, were skilled trackers and hunters; and while Skar was never cruel, she would surely tease her friend about her odd behavior. Esther tried to explain her jumbled feelings once they had made their way to the street, but the other girl cut her off.

"You were wise to leave that one alone," Skar said. Her voice was unusually somber. "There is nothing more dangerous than a mother. If you attempt to kill one, you must do it in a single stroke, without hesitation. Otherwise, she will take advantage of your doubt and kill you instead."

There was a pause. Then, her lecture over, Skar smiled. "It's so good to see you, Esther."

Yet when Esther tried to hug her, Skar flinched and drew back. At first, Esther was puzzled, then hurt, as a familiar wave of sadness washed over her.

The two girls had been best friends since early childhood, their relationship flourishing in spite of the tension between their two communities. It was a tremendous relief to both when the variants and the "norms" had reached a sort of truce in the past few months. Real distance between them had only come about recently, seemingly overnight, and for reasons more personal than either could have anticipated.

It happened when both girls became partnered.

It was to be expected, Esther now thought with a pang. *After all, they weren't children anymore; she and Skar were both well into their middle years, fifteen, and so they had both chosen mates. Life wasn't meant to be the same after you were partnered.*

Or was it?

After partnering with Caleb, Esther felt the same as ever, only stronger and happier. The love she felt for Caleb was still new and remarkable, constantly astonishing her with its depth and power. Beyond that, nothing had changed; she was still the person she had always been.

It was Skar who seemed different, who had become remote and formal after partnering with Tarq. It was she who had broken off the relationship with Esther, without warning, and who until now had avoided her oldest friend.

Esther shook off her misgivings. Skar was here and there was no telling when the two would see each other again. It seemed foolish to waste any of their precious time together on hurt feelings. Instead, she clasped Skar by the hands.

"It's good to see you, too."

Although Skar squeezed her hands back, Esther again sensed a slight awkwardness, something unspoken that confused her. While the variant girl seemed happy to see her, there was an odd restraint to her manner, a formality that seemed strange compared to her usual affectionate behavior. But as they walked through the familiar and desolate streets, Skar began to relax and soon seemed more like her old self.

The two talked of family and friends, and of the terrible famine that was gripping the area. The shortage was starting to affect even the variants, who had never before needed to rely solely on hunting for food. The situation had grown so dire that Skar's partner, Tarq, had allowed her to leave the variant camp that morning in search of game. On an impulse, she had decided instead to visit Prin.

As Skar talked, Esther noticed something odd. Skar, like all variants, wore nothing but a short, sleeveless tunic. Other than a few bangles, wristwatches, and a necklace made of braided leather, her ornamentation consisted of the elaborate scars and designs etched on her skin with pigments pounded from rocks and rubbed into fresh cuts. But now, there was something different about her throat and upper arms. They were heavily daubed with what looked like dried and cracking patches of red clay.

"What's that?" Esther interrupted, reaching out.

But again Skar flinched, ducking away before Esther could touch her.

"It's nothing." Then she changed the subject. "Here," she said, nodding at the weapon Esther still held in her hand, "you need help with that. If you like, I can teach you how to shoot better."

The girls spent the afternoon practicing how to aim, draw, and release the bow. For a target, they used a sodden and stained mattress they found in the gutter. It was soft enough not to blunt the tips of Esther's precious arrows, which they retrieved and wiped off after each use. Then Skar took her into the woods and taught her how to identify rabbit warrens and squirrel nests and opossum scat.

"If you're hunting something," she explained, "it's usually better to lie in wait than to try chasing it down."

By the time the sun was low in the winter sky, Skar had managed to shoot three quail and a rabbit. She took her time aiming the shiny black bow that was half as tall as she was, never wasting any of her arrows. After many failed attempts, Esther also managed to kill one squirrel, something that felt at the moment like an enormous achievement. Yet now, as she weighed the small body in her hands and imagined attempting to feed four people with it, she was filled with a feeling of utter hopelessness.

Skar must have thought the same thing, for without speaking, she handed over the two fattest birds. And while Esther normally would have refused such charity, she now bit her tongue and accepted them, nodding her thanks.

As the two girls said good-bye, Skar promised she would try to visit again soon. Yet despite her generous gift and warm words, the variant girl once more kept her distance, avoiding Esther's embrace. This made Esther wonder whether Skar, who she once thought incapable of lying, was telling the truth. Such conflicting thoughts filled Esther's mind as she watched Skar mount her bike and take off, pedaling powerfully until she disappeared from sight.

Esther was brooding about Skar when she sensed rather than heard someone approaching her from behind. Before she could whirl around, she felt a quick tug on the back of her hair, where it was the shortest and spikiest; and she broke into her first real laugh of the day.

"Hey!"

Caleb had pulled up next to her on his bicycle, smiling. He

stopped so he could gather Esther into his arms for a kiss. Then she pulled away to look at him.

Even though they had been partnered for several months, it was astonishing how he still looked new to her, like she was seeing him for the first time: the hazel eyes, the dark, tousled hair. It was, she decided, a little like falling in love again each time she saw him, although she would never say it out loud. Even so, she could not help but notice with a fresh pang his terrible gauntness, the shadows that hollowed his face and made the underlying bones protrude so painfully.

But he had already seen the game hanging from her belt and gave a low, admiring whistle. "You catch all those yourself?"

"Only the one," Esther admitted, indicating the squirrel. "Skar came to visit and helped me with my shooting. Then she gave me these."

Caleb nodded as he handled the birds. "She's a good friend. I just hope it don't get her into trouble at home."

Esther didn't ask how Caleb's day of Gleaning had gone; she didn't need to. His backpack seemed almost as flat as it had been that morning. Still, he had had some luck; he had Gleaned a dusty box that read DOMINO SUGAR on its faded label.

Gleaning was what they used to do, what everyone did in Prin, in the old days. It entailed breaking into abandoned buildings and searching them for anything even remotely of value. You would bring whatever you found—old tools and clothing, as well as books, weapons, and strange objects of plastic and metal whose purpose no one even pretended to know anymore—to the Source in exchange for clean water and food. It was the only way they knew how to feed themselves and the only sustenance they ever had: packets and jars of dried beans, flour, coffee, honey, salt. But the Source had burned to the ground two months ago. Since then, the people of Prin had been forced to Glean to feed themselves.

Of course, it was pointless. There was little to be found anywhere and most of that—the rare can of vegetables, soup, or fish—had long since rotted to poison. Everything in Prin, every house and office building and store, had been picked clean months, even years ago. But the habit of Gleaning proved hard for people to break. *It gave them the feeling*, Esther thought, *of doing something besides waiting for death.*

When they reached home, the shattered building at the end of the main street called STARBUCKS COFFEE, Esther held the bicycle and waited. Caleb scaled the fire escape and then the gnarled tree in front, checking the squirrel traps he had set that morning. It was more ritual than anything; the traps were useless because there was never any food with which to bait them.

But at least for now, there would be fresh meat for dinner. If they were sparing in their portions, they might even save one of the quail, which would keep for another day. For there was no telling when and where their next meal would come from.

Caleb dropped back to the ground as Esther pushed open the front door, hanging crookedly on broken hinges. Upstairs, she could hear Caleb's son, Kai, crying; as always, the sound made her insides clench with anxiety. She could also hear the murmuring of their friend, Joseph, who was trying to soothe him. Joseph was an awkward soul with more good intentions than talent for nurturing. She could picture him holding Kai in his arms, rocking him while trying to get him to suck on his favorite toy, the ring made of clear rubber with tiny plastic fish bobbing inside. It was the only way any of them knew to distract the child from his hunger, even for a short while.

By the time they made it upstairs, Kai's cries had subsided to hiccups. Joseph, flustered, was pacing, the baby held close to his shoulder.

"Please," Esther said. "Let me take him."

Relieved, Joseph relinquished the child, and Esther took him in her arms. Kai was soft, warm, and surprisingly heavy.

"There," she whispered into the baby's neck. "That's a good boy."

But it was a mistake. The boy's eyelashes, long and dark and dappled with tears, fluttered open. He opened his mouth and despite Esther's best efforts, he began to wail once more, his face turning red.

How could anyone calm a hungry baby? she wondered, stricken.

It seemed impossible.

It was so hot.

Esther was bound, her arms and legs crushed close to her body, struggling to break free. Around her, the walls of her prison pulsated in a powerful rhythm. She could not breathe and was filled with panic, fighting for breath; she would suffocate from the heat.

She tried calling for help, but it was no good. When she shouted, her voice was inaudible, like the mewing of a kitten, and her words were sucked away from her.

The redness behind her eyes seemed to bloom into an obliterating brightness as Esther sensed the walls around her start to give. Her lungs exploding, she fought her way through the shimmering wall in front of her as she broke free.

And then she was safe. As she took in shuddering gasps of air, she was enveloped in arms that were warm and gentle. Far above her, she sensed a face gazing down at her own, a face that was both kind and strong.

Esther wanted to see who it was. She needed to see for herself, once and for all, the face of her rescuer.

Her mother.

But she could not make out her features.

Esther jolted upright. In the moonlight, Caleb lay next to her in bed, awake. He was propped up on one elbow, watching her.

"What were you dreaming about?" he said.

Already, the images of her dream were rushing away. "I think it was my mother," Esther said. "I never knew her. But I guess nobody does."

Caleb nodded and Esther realized too late that he might be thinking of his first partner, Miri. She had been murdered the year before when her son, Kai, was only an infant. But Caleb gestured for her to keep talking and, after a moment, she did.

"I wonder who she was." Moonlight streamed in the cur-tainless window, casting shadows on the bed. "Just a girl, I reckon. Nobody special. I bet she wanted to take care of me. Protect me from bad stuff. Keep me fed. The only one who did that for me was my sister."

At the mention of Sarah, Caleb spoke up. "You were lucky."

Silence filled the darkness between them. Esther knew he was thinking about his older brother, Levi: ruler of the Source, provider of Prin, and his enemy. She had never learned what happened between the two boys on the day of the fire that destroyed the Source and killed Levi; Caleb never spoke of it. But it was clear it still haunted him.

She touched his cheek, cradling it in the warmth of her hand. It had been forever since they had last spoken like this, just the two of them. The apartment had become so crowded, it seemed, with so many things and people to look after.

"We'll take care of each other now," Esther said.

He seemed to have the same thought, for they turned to each other at the same time. Caleb kissed her cheek, then her lips. She responded, her hand moving beneath the sheets, caressing him.

"I love you," he whispered.

It had been so long, too long, since they had last touched each other; they both missed it too much to say. Esther clung to his shoulders, shifting to be beneath him. Caleb yanked the sheet from her, pulling her oversize T-shirt above her knees, and higher.

Then he stopped.

"What is it?" she whispered, her arms around his neck. But he was alert to something she did not understand.

Then Esther became aware of it, too.

It was smoke.

* * *

Joseph had thought the cats were just being friendly.

As he lay asleep, Stumpy had begun kneading him, digging her claws into his leg. Then Malawi stood on his chest and started to scream.

Groggy, he had tried to shoo away and silence them, to no avail. Then he attempted to ignore them, burying his face into his pillow.

This had been the first night Joseph had managed to get much sleep in Esther and Caleb's apartment. Following the destruction of his home, he'd found out that living with other people took getting used to: It was certainly more difficult than just existing alongside animals. His first nights on Esther and Caleb's lumpy living room couch had been miserable bouts of tossing and turning, as he thought longingly of his cluttered rooms in the deserted hotel, full of his books, clocks, home-made calendars, newspaper clippings, and, most precious of all, his solitude.

Naturally, he was grateful to Esther and Caleb for taking him in, along with his ten cats and the few books he had been able to save. Still, he mourned the loss of his old life.

Now, even as his breathing slowed and he began sinking into his first real dream in what felt like months, Joseph was dragged back to consciousness, almost literally, by Stumpy's insistent scratching and pummeling.

"Mahhh!" Malawi yowled, not giving up, either.

At last, Joseph sat up, exasperated, his hair standing on end as if awakened, too. Stumpy held on to his thigh, undeterred.

"What is it!" he exclaimed.

Then he smelled it. Something was burning.

His eyes already stinging, Joseph remained upright in bed for a few moments, stunned and immobile. Then he kicked off the covers, scattering his cats.

Moonlight revealed that smoke was billowing across the floor in dense waves. Caleb and Esther had already come in, Esther holding a lit candle as she carried the still-sleeping Kai. Caleb was going from room to room, looking for the fire. When he returned, his face was grim.

"It's downstairs," he said.

Esther was at the window, opening it to the night air. In her arms, Kai had awoken and was beginning to whimper. Coughing, Joseph began shepherding his cats across the windowsill and onto the fire escape, but they needed little encouragement. Soon, everyone was outside on the rickety metal staircase, climbing down toward the sidewalk.

Caleb had already dropped to the ground and entered the front door. Once Esther was able to hand the baby to Joseph, she joined him. Inside, a small but smoky fire was burning in the back of their storefront, at the foot of the stairs. Large pieces of soot blew through the air.

Puzzled, Esther stood by Caleb's side. The fire was nothing more than damp paper and twigs, which explained all the smoke. As a result, it hadn't burned very hot and was in fact dying, unassisted, at their feet.

"Who would do this?" asked Esther.

Caleb shook his head, bewildered. Then there was a shout from outdoors.

On the sidewalk, Joseph was so agitated, he could barely get the words out. With Kai in his arms, he pointed at the open window above them and then down the street.

"A boy. Someone. He jumped down and ran!"

Understanding dawned on Caleb's face.

"He must've been hiding in the stairs," he said. "When he set the fire, he figured we'd go out the window. That gave him time to go upstairs."

"To do what?" Esther asked.

"Steal."

Esther was uncomprehending. It made no sense that some-one would go to so much trouble.

Caleb shrugged. "All he got was flour. And it's mostly rot-ted. There's nothing to do but go back to bed."

Indignation flared in Esther's breast. "But it's wrong."

Caleb placed a hand on her shoulder. "Let it go."

But she would have none of it. Then another thought struck her. "The extra quail we saved. The one Skar gave us." After all the time she and her friend had put in that day, the thought of anyone stealing their supplies, as meager as they were, made her doubly furious. She turned to Joseph.

"Watch the baby," she said. "Please."

And with that, Esther took off in the direction her friend had indicated, still barefoot and wearing only her oversize T-shirt. Unable to stop her, Caleb had no choice but to follow.

Esther sprinted down what remained of the central street of Prin, Caleb close behind. Clouds darkened the sky and made it hard to see; still, they barreled past the devastated storefronts that served as makeshift homes for the rest of the town.

Esther stopped and, after a moment, Caleb caught up with her. He had never fully recovered from the old arrow wound in his chest; and now he had trouble breathing.

Then they both heard it.

It came from the side of the street, in the shadowy wreckage of DEL'S FROZEN YOGURT: a faint rustling and the unmistakable sound of breathing, quick and shallow. Esther turned and cocked her head, as if locating its source through hearing alone. Then, without a word, she sprang into the darkness, a vengeful hawk after a mouse. There was a cry, and a moment later, she dragged a struggling figure onto the street.

The bag of flour dropped from the thief's hands and broke open, its contents spilling in a faint cloud of white by their feet.

The crook glanced up, helpless, as the clouds shifted and the moon shone down. It was a boy, perhaps eight years old. He was emaciated, and the features of his face, already sharp, were made even more distinct by the shifting shadows.

His expression was a mixture of defiance and terror. Then despair seemed to overtake him; his eyes briefly closed and reopened. When he spoke, his voice was fatalistic, as if coming from one much older and wearier.

"My shoes," he said. "They ain't no good."

Esther and Caleb glanced down at his filthy feet. They saw the remains of what had once been sport sandals, the reason he was unable to run any farther.

They knew who he was, of course. Silas lived in the remains of the library, near the end of Main Street, with several others his age. They were scavengers, living off garbage and whatever else they could scrounge. Now he and his colleagues had apparently turned to thievery as well.

Still gripping him by his collar, Esther shook him once, hard. "You got anything to say?"

"Not much."

"No?"

He shrugged. "Everybody got to eat."

"Where's the bird you took?"

The boy just shrugged again. "Musta dropped it."

He was too tired to care, and too young to be up so late in the first place. But his reaction infuriated Esther. As she raised her hand, the boy wrapped his arms around himself, bracing for her attack. Then Caleb grabbed her from behind.

"Okay," he said, as she bucked in his arms. "That's enough!"

Esther stopped struggling. She stayed still, panting, her head against Caleb's chest.

"Go on," Caleb said to the boy. "Get going."

Silas glanced up, surprised. Then he turned and within moments, melted into the darkness.

"You should have let me at him," Esther said after a pause. Her voice was hoarse.

Caleb shook his head. "We're done with fighting. I am, anyway."

Unexpectedly, he let her go, and she almost stumbled. Then he picked up what remained of the flour and started for home, without waiting for her.

Esther stood alone, breathing hard.

Caleb's words stung. Only recently, he had spent months immersed in violence and revenge, hunting down the variants he believed had murdered his partner and stolen his son. If he was able to renounce all of *that*, what was wrong with her?

Esther wasn't proud of the fact she had always been impulsive and hotheaded. True, some of it had burned off when she learned how to love first Caleb, and then Kai. But the terrible times they were living in brought out the worst in everyone.

Moments earlier, she had nearly beaten a starving child. Two months ago, it was an act Esther would have not only despised but been incapable of. That Caleb had kept her from doing so made her both proud of him and ashamed of herself.

As Caleb reached their building, a penitent Esther ran to catch up with him. Then they climbed the stairs together, in silence.

Joseph was sitting in their bedroom, next to the cradle Caleb had fashioned for Kai from an old shopping cart. The baby had gone back to sleep, and Joseph, too, was fighting to stay awake.

"Thanks," Esther said. Joseph gave an awkward wave and then trudged to the living room, a cat at his heels.

Caleb and Esther got into bed, still not speaking. Then she touched his arm. "I—" she began, then stopped.

He glanced at her. It was clear the mood had been broken; there was no recapturing their interrupted intimacy. But that was not what she wanted.

"There's no staying here no more," she said in a rush. "We got to leave."

For a moment, Caleb didn't understand. "Leave?" he repeated. "What do you mean?"

"Prin."

He didn't respond, but neither did he pull away when she draped her arm across his chest. After a few minutes, he rested his hand on hers.

They remained like that, silent and awake, until the sun rose.

TWO

THE NEXT DAY, CALEB LOOKED OUT UPON A SEA OF FACES. THE NOISE
was deafening.

The people of Prin were in the town meeting place, the
glass and brick building at the end of the main street with the
mysterious yellow arches outside. This was where impassioned
yet orderly gatherings used to take place, where public business was done. But soon after the destruction of the Source,
the assemblages had begun to fall apart. As the famine had
grown more severe, they had degenerated into complete
chaos. Meanwhile, the boy Rafe, who had once enjoyed the
privileges of being town leader, had quietly relinquished the

position, leaving the town without any direction at all.

Today, Rafe sat with the others at one of the many plastic tables molded to the floor. He watched Esther and Caleb with open curiosity, as if to say, *let's see how well you can do.*

Neither Caleb nor Esther had ever called a meeting before and were unaccustomed to addressing so many at once. The townspeople were nearly anonymous in their sunglasses and hooded robes made of sheets and towels belted at the waist, worn as protection against the deadly sun. Amid the pastels, stripes, and floral patterns, Esther's red hoodie and Caleb's black sweatshirt stuck out. Bouncing Kai on her hip, she met his eyes and gave a brief nod.

"I know it don't feel good to hear it," Caleb began, and most of the room fell silent. "But there ain't nothing here for us now. We're at each other's throats, fighting over what little's left. Stealing from each other."

He had noticed the thief Silas against the far wall with his friends, who were as young and scrawny as he was. But the boy refused to make eye contact and so Caleb continued. "One of us has maps that could help us get somewhere. A place with more food." Joseph, already in obvious discomfort near the front door, squirmed at this indirect mention. "We can build wagons and pool all our supplies. It'll be safer if we travel together."

Esther and Caleb had disagreed about this. She wanted it to be just the four of them—her, Caleb, Kai, and Joseph.

"There's no one else in town I trust," she had told him. "If you knew them the way I did, you wouldn't, either."

In fact, Caleb understood the small-mindedness of the

townspeople all too well. Still, he had argued back, it was better to travel with a large group and not only because it was safer. He knew that on the open road, loneliness and exposure were as dangerous as floods and fire. They would eventually turn you into an animal.

Even after he had persuaded her, Caleb suspected that the real challenge would be getting the town on their side. And now, he feared he was right.

There was a brief pause as the meaning of his words sank in. Then the room erupted in noise.

Everyone was talking at once, and the response was clearly negative. Caleb and Esther were facing the worst-case scenario: not just skepticism, but open scorn.

One girl, thirteen or so, with eyes deeply ringed, stood up, her thin frame swallowed up by the billowing folds of her robes. In halting speech, she said what seemed to be on everyone's mind.

"You're wrong," she said. "Sure, they ain't much to eat. But we can always get more. We can find more houses and Glean. They ain't no reason to leave."

Esther's heart sank as the room broke into cheers and calls. She knew that if people still wanted to Glean empty houses in a depleted town, they were holding on to a past that was over. And that meant there was only one reason why everyone wanted to stay: fear.

"Besides," the girl added, "only water we got now is from the spring. You think of that?"

It was, Esther knew, a good point. Nearly all water in their poisoned world—rivers, rain, the dew that covered the yellowed grass each morning—was deadly; even a few drops splashed by accident into one's mouth, eyes, or an open wound could kill a healthy teenager in days. For years, the people of Prin had relied on the diminishing stores of bottled water from the Source. Then, two months ago, the discovery of an underground spring pumping clean, safe water came like a miracle, one that had saved their lives.

"We can bring all we need," Caleb replied. "And there's got to be other sources of safe water somewhere. We just got to find one, that's all."

His reply was met by a ripple of discontent and, worse, dismissal. From the corner of his eye, Caleb saw Silas and his comrades flee through the door, unnoticed. Sneaking out behind them was Joseph. Two boys, perhaps seven years old, now scrambled onto his chair and began punching each other as others watched them, laughing and shouting.

Esther decided to take a chance. "I know," she said, speaking over them all, "that you're scared. We all are."

For a second, there was no reaction. Then her words sank in, and all chatter dried up. Esther had succeeded in getting their attention, but not in the way she intended.

"*Scared!*" several exclaimed.

"You calling us cowards?" shouted one boy. In an instant, the mood of the crowd had turned ugly. People only quieted down when a pinch-faced girl rose to her feet. Close to eighteen, Rhea was one of the oldest people in town and well aware of the power that gave her. She was also someone who had routinely mocked Esther's sister, Sarah, and been instrumental in Esther's having once been Shunned from Prin.

"We all know what this is really about." The quiet viciousness of her words was at odds with her sweet voice. "This is just you trying to clean up the mess you made. The mess you both made."

Caleb didn't reply but saw that Esther, her face flushed with emotion, had turned to take in the speaker. Esther, he knew, had no love for the older girl.

"Go on," Caleb said to Rhea.

"Everything was fine under Levi. We got plenty to eat. We had a good way of working for it, by Gleaning, Harvesting, Excavating. If we did our part, we got what we were promised. Everything worked just fine."

By now, everyone in the room, including Rhea's partner, Sokol, was listening to her words with intent expressions, nodding in agreement.

"You two got rid of Levi," Rhea went on, her voice rising, "and look what it got us. We don't got to leave Prin to be in the wilderness. We there already."

Rhea's speech seemed to embolden those around her. A twelve-year-old got to his feet. Pushing his face so close to Caleb that Caleb was forced to step back, the boy spoke loudly enough for all to hear.

"It would've been better if you never come to town!"

A frightening restlessness fell over the room; ugly words had given way to the threat of real violence. Esther could see it on the scowling faces around her, the clenched fists, the angry whispers. As other boys jumped to their feet and moved toward Caleb, Esther gripped Kai so tightly, the child began to wail.

"All right," Caleb said in an even voice. Although surrounded, he wasn't going to give them the fight they wanted; he didn't even take his hands from his pockets. "I guess that's how you all feel then."

One who had been watching smiled to himself. *Now*, he figured, *was a good time to remind the others of his authority.*

"I think," said Rafe as he stood up, "this meeting is adjourned."

Feeling the hair stand up on the back of her neck, Esther took Caleb by the hand. *Surely*, she thought, *they wouldn't attack the two of us. Not while we're with our baby.* Then, with stiff and deliberate steps, she and Caleb picked their way through the hostile crowd.

When they made it outside, Esther breathed with silent relief. Yet Caleb refused to storm off, as she would have done if alone. Instead, he waited by the door as the others filed past. Most avoided his eyes; a few walked by with a contemptuous gaze or a nasty parting word. One or two even shoved him, hard, and, again, Caleb didn't respond. Yet more than a few were sympathetic, even though it seemed they had been too intimidated to say so in front of the others.

"I liked what you said," whispered Asha, a gentle fourteen-year-old with the mind of someone ten years younger. "It was good."

Right behind her was Eli. Caleb's former rival, now friend, lingered with his usual awkwardness. He seemed uncertain how direct to be.

"They're fools," he said at last, nodding at the others. Then he, too, headed off.

The only one remaining was Rafe. Both his swagger and his potbelly were long gone. Yet he still had the air of someone with ambition, despite how he had been humbled.

"Too bad," was all he said. Then he shuffled past them and down the sidewalk.

At last, Caleb and Esther were alone.

"So I guess that's it," Esther said. "We're staying."

"No," Caleb said. "You were right. Guess it'll just be us."

He was about to head inside to blow out the candles that lit the tables, but something stopped him.

Esther had wrapped her arms around him from behind, squeezing him tight.

Esther alone sat by the bedroom window, gazing at the moonlit street.

It was the middle of the night, yet she had been unable to sleep, torn by doubt.

Where would they go? How would they manage on their own? They had so few supplies as it was, here in town; how could they last on the open road?

Esther glanced at the bed, where Caleb breathed evenly, and the cradle, where Kai was punching out a little fist. From the living room, she could hear Joseph turning over, for what seemed like the hundredth time. In sleep, they all appeared so vulnerable. It seemed impossible that the four of them could travel anywhere, alone.

Were the others in town right? Should they stay?

Then, without warning, she felt the floor below her shudder.

At first, Esther had the irrational thought that their home was being robbed again. Someone else had come to steal their food and was trying a different trick to get them to leave.

But then the floor rocked again, and this time she felt something brush the top of her head. When she reached up and touched it, her hand came away chalky with plaster dust.

Confused, she glanced across the room. The entire floor of the bedroom seemed to be rippling, lifting the furniture it supported like leaves on the surface of a lake. With a cracking and popping sound, gaps opened and widened between its wooden planks. For a second, Esther was transfixed: It was like a vision from a dream.

Then something fell and crashed from a shelf in the kitchen.

She could hear the bookshelf that had belonged to her sister buck and tip in the living room, sending its contents tumbling to the floor. Esther heard a faint yell outside, down the street. She looked out the window and saw another uncanny sight.

By moonlight, a crooked line was working its way down Main Street as if drawn by a giant, invisible hand. Then the road itself began to separate, to crack open like a piece of broken plastic.

By now, Caleb had joined Esther, Kai in his arms. As the floor buckled beneath their feet, they both stumbled, clinging to one another. At the same moment, a wooden beam broke through the ceiling in an explosion of plaster and smashed onto the bed. Esther only had time to see Joseph, standing in the bedroom doorway, staring in total confusion. In the next moment, another beam came crashing down and the window behind her exploded, showering her with broken glass.

Somehow, they made it to the wooden table in the living room. There was no room for all four of them underneath and yet they managed to fit by huddling close together, while around them, the world seemed to end.

All they could do was wait.

When the sun rose, Esther saw that Prin was gone.

Most of the buildings on Main Street had vanished, replaced by piles of rubble and skeletons of frames that still drifted dust. The few storefronts left standing were in precarious condition, with bent metal rods protruding from fallen roofs. Glass from windows had exploded onto the sidewalks, crunching underfoot in glittering shards.

The crack that ran down the center of the street had opened into a jagged chasm. Long-dead cars that had been parked along the street had fallen in completely or stuck halfway out like toys, their hoods and windshields smashed.

As if in a dream, Esther headed down the street with Kai in her arms. Caleb was next to her; Joseph trailed behind. She sensed rather than saw that others were joining them: More than a dozen townspeople who had also survived emerged from the ruins in shock, still in their sleeping clothes.

And then she saw the first body.

A young boy lay facedown in a mountain of rubble, crushed by a metal beam. As her unbelieving eyes took in the sight,

Esther realized that she was surrounded by at least half a dozen more bodies, bloodied and motionless amid piles of rubble and brick.

And those were only the ones she could see.

A young boy was crouched by the remains of one building, clutching his knees as he rocked back and forth. His hair and face were white with plaster dust.

"My sister." He sounded strangely detached; he might have been commenting on the weather as he pointed at something brown that protruded from the wreckage. With a start, Esther saw that it was a slim bare leg, the toenails still painted a chipped blue. "That's her."

There was nothing to do; Esther and the others kept walking. The only sound was when a building shifted, raining fresh debris onto the street. But other than that, the four were enveloped by an eerie silence.

Movement caught Esther's eye. In the shadow of a ruined store, she noticed another boy who knelt, facing away. To her shock, she saw he was going through the pockets of someone who lay partly crushed by a wooden dresser; he had just removed a Swiss Army knife and was examining its blades. This he added to a pack of other tools he had obviously stolen.

It was Silas, the boy who had robbed their home. Sensing her gaze, he turned and caught her eye. Then he shrugged and went back to his business.

Suddenly, there was another sound, faint yet distinct.

"Help."

The sound snapped Esther from her torpor.

"Come on," she said to Caleb. There was a moment before he too emerged from a daze.

"Yes," he said. "Let's go."

Joseph took the sleeping baby. Then Esther and Caleb ran to the building from which the voice had come. Working as quickly as they dared, they managed to remove a section of roof, which allowed them to clear away the bricks underneath. In minutes, they uncovered a bed that was still intact, with blankets and pillows on it.

But there was no sign of survivors. And soon the cries grew fainter and fainter until they stopped altogether.

Caleb continued for a few more minutes before giving up. But Esther refused to quit. In vain, she tugged at a wooden beam that was twice her size, trying to gain access to more of the rooms.

Caleb watched for a while before he drew her away.

"It's all right," he said. "We did what we could."

As they continued down the street, still others joined them, one by one. While many had survived, at least a few dozen, most were injured, some of them badly. A girl, her face nearly unrecognizable under a blackening mask of dried blood, lunged at Caleb and clung to his arm.

It was Rhea.

"He's gone, my partner." Her mouth was a pitiable twist, and tears ran down her cheeks, leaving white streaks. "I tried to pull him out, but he was already dead." She turned to the others, her voice rising. "What did he do to deserve this? What did any of us do?"

She was nearly screaming. *If unchecked,* Caleb realized, *her hysteria would spread through the townspeople like fire.*

"Nothing," he said, cutting her off. "Can't you understand? No one did nothing."

Someone unexpected spoke up.

"Not now, anyway."

Holding Kai, Joseph was in the rear of the crowd, ignored and invisible as usual. But now, he spoke with animation, his hands fluttering. "A long time ago, I think people *did* do something wrong. To the air. The water. Not just here, but all over. And that's what caused all of this."

There was silence as people tried to digest his strange remarks. *How could anyone do something wrong to the air or water?* What the boy said made no sense whatsoever. They all turned to stare at Esther and Caleb.

"You knew," Rhea said suddenly.

"What?"

"About Prin. You two knew we had to leave."

Despite herself, Esther almost laughed. "We didn't know *this* would happen. We only said—"

"You were right," one girl said.

"We should have left a long time ago," another boy murmured.

Caleb realized something crucial: *They wanted to believe.* Unlike Esther, he was aware of the ever-shifting power dynamics in any group. The same people who had turned on them the night before were now frightened and uncertain. This was the moment to use their fear to everyone's advantage.

"We just tried to tell you this was no place to stay," he said.

Relief rippled over the faces of the crowd. A few whispered, "Yes."

"But if we leave Prin, you got to listen," he added. "And everybody's got to pitch in. All right?"

Meekly, they nodded again.

"There's a town nearby that might have supplies," Caleb continued. "Schroon Lake. It's just a few days away and I know I can get us there."

Standing in the back of the group, Rafe was watching. He too had been injured but not by the quake itself; he had fallen downstairs in the dark, bruising his hip and twisting his ankle. While his wounds were minor, he exaggerated them by leaning on a makeshift cane.

"Excuse me?" he said. "Excuse me, but . . ."

He paused until he had everyone's attention. He knew something the others didn't. And if he played it correctly, it would be his trump card.

Back when he used to visit the Source, Rafe would be kept waiting for hours by Levi's guards. It was, in retrospect, an insult, but Rafe had chosen not to see it that way. Instead, he had used the time to listen in on the guards' gossip. Mostly, they traded stories of far-off places and strange sights they had seen on their travels to procure goods. One tale in particular had caught his attention; and now, he thought, was a good time to share it.

"I can take us somewhere better than that," he said. "Someplace where you don't got to scrape by, on account there's food and water and for everyone. It's called Mundreel."

A few leaned in to hear better. Even Esther and Caleb didn't interrupt; they, too, seemed curious to hear what Rafe knew, or thought he knew.

"What do you mean?" someone asked.

"Where is it?" asked another.

"I got directions," Rafe said. "It's a clear route. We leave now, we can be there in a week."

This wasn't exactly true. What the boy *had* were a few crude notes he had scribbled hours after he had eavesdropped on the guards, a handful of mostly illegible words and diagrams. "Mundreel is bigger than a regular town. In fact, it's bigger than ten Prins set end on end. There's room enough for everyone." He had left the best for last. "And I hear people there live a long time, way past eighteen or nineteen."

As Rafe had hoped, the desperate survivors were warming to the idea. A few whispered to another, and a ripple of excitement passed through the group.

But Joseph spoke up once more. "I'm not sure that's true."

"What?" Rafe said. He was smiling unpleasantly.

"Mundreel may be real," Joseph continued, his voice earnest. "Or at least, used to be; I've seen it on my maps. But we don't know if it still exists . . . or even if it does, that it's any better off than here. Everything you're saying sounds like an old wives' tale." He paused, then added as explanation, "That means it's made-up."

Rafe looked with distaste at the boy who was challenging him—the *man*, if it were really true how old Joseph was. To him, Joseph was the town nut, even if he had read the most books. Who knew? Perhaps it was all that reading that had softened his mind in the first place. Still, he worried that the others might take him seriously.

"Well," Rafe said, "you admit the place exists. That's all that matters." Then he turned his back on Joseph, to end the discussion. But someone else spoke up.

"I've heard the same stories about Mundreel," Caleb said. "But never from anyone who actually been there. Or come back."

By now, Rafe's face was flushed with annoyance.

"So you're saying we should go just anywhere," he retorted. "I'm saying we go somewhere good." He turned to the others. "Because believe me, once you see Mundreel, you won't want to leave." He let this sink in. "I leave it up to you. You can listen to me. Or you can trust this one." He jerked a thumb once, at Joseph. Then Rafe pressed on his handmade cane and winced. "Let's take a vote."

From a quick show of hands, Mundreel was the clear favorite. And since he knew the most about their destination, Rafe was asked to be their leader.

Rafe suppressed a smile. He had once yearned to serve a powerful leader in Prin. In a place as fabulous as Mundreel, he might even *become* the powerful leader.

The first thing, of course, was to get there.

But he would deal with that later.

THREE

FIFTY-THREE RESIDENTS OF PRIN HAD SURVIVED, FEWER THAN HALF OF those who had lived there. For the dead whose bodies could be retrieved, there were hasty burials on the outskirts of town. The others had to be left where they were. Within hours, there were already more tremors that shook the earth, sending even more buildings crashing to the ground.

The first evening, people huddled together in one of the few structures that appeared intact, a bank on the main street. All night, they could hear the marble walls and ceiling creak and shift around them; and in the morning, everyone was covered in fine dust and grit that had sifted down. It was clearly too dangerous to remain in town much longer.

Yet there was work to do before they could take off. Sturdy vehicles had to be built that would still be light enough to be pulled by bicycle. Caleb volunteered for the job. He had a knack for making things, having once created a weapon that could fire multiple rocks in rapid succession. Now he wanted to use his talent for something positive: to get everyone away from Prin.

After he told the others what he needed, the townspeople spread throughout town and collected cloth, wire, and wood; nuts and screws and buckles; and tools like hammers and saws. Caleb also ordered that all intact bicycles be rounded up and others stripped for parts.

He put the townspeople to work constructing wagons, tall and wide enough to support four people, if necessary. They then attached a wheel on either side, threaded on a metal axle that could pivot and change direction. The carts were hooked to the backs of the bicycles with chains and aluminum shafts that provided both strength and flexibility.

Meanwhile, Caleb and Esther worked on a larger vehicle, one big enough to carry enough clean water for everyone. First, they hammered scrap lumber and two-by-fours into a sturdy base. Then, as Esther built the four sides as directed, Caleb created a crude chassis. Finally, he hooked two bicycles up front, which would provide enough power to pull the heavy load.

Within three days, Caleb and the people of Prin had created a bicycle caravan, all made from whatever they had managed to salvage. Although she was exhausted, Esther could not help looking at the vehicles with a mixture of awe and pride.

"They're beautiful," was all she could say.

"You helped," Caleb said; and Esther had to admit she had, though not as much as he pretended.

A sound now drew her attention. Asha had begged to take care of Kai while the construction went on, and Esther had been happy to oblige. But despite her good intentions, the girl with the child's mind was having trouble with the rambunctious boy, who was attempting to escape from her arms.

"He looks ready to go," Caleb said.

"Are you?" Esther said, taking his arm. Her tone was light, but her eyes were serious.

Caleb hesitated. All week, he had taken pains to remain positive, never once expressing anything but optimism and assurance. Now, talking in private to the one person he trusted, he looked uncertain for the first time.

"As ready as I'll ever be," he said. "You?"

"As long as you're there."

"Me, too."

They were about to kiss but were interrupted by a voice across the street.

"We about ready to go?" Rafe called. Esther could feel Caleb wince at the word "we"; Rafe had barely lifted a finger over the past three days. Still, her partner managed to keep his tone steady.

"Just about!" he called back. Then he turned to Esther. "I

got to help the others load their wagons. Where will you be?"

She thought for a moment. She still had to salvage what usable supplies and household goods she could find in what had been their home. "We need more water. But first, I'll make a last check of our place."

It wasn't easy.

The building was unrecognizable. Esther had to rely on all of her senses as she picked her way across the precarious wreckage, trying to extract anything of value without bringing the rest of the structure crashing down. It was like a deadly version of the game she remembered from her childhood, the one in which you had to pick a thin plastic stick out of a pile without disturbing the others. You had to move very slowly, and above all you had to concentrate.

Even so, Esther paused every few minutes to glance up at the sky.

Early that morning, she had built a strong fire on the highest surface she could find, a towering pile of rubble down the street that had once been a looted clothing store. Once the flames were hot enough, she had fed them with damp newspaper and a wet log, which caused black smoke to rise high into the sky.

This was how she and Skar communicated—or at least, how they used to communicate when they still saw each other nearly every day. Esther needed to see her friend one last time, to tell her of their plans, and to say good-bye. As she balanced on the remains of their home, she repeatedly checked the sky, gazing with growing frustration toward the horizon where the variant camp lay.

So far, there was nothing, and Esther was forced to return to the task at hand.

As agile and light as she was, she very nearly killed herself when she tried to work free a firebowl, and when she attempted to pull a stack of dusty rain ponchos from beneath a ceiling beam. The mountain she was standing on began to shift; she only managed to leap off, clutching the valuable raingear, before it collapsed with a roar and settled anew.

Her job was nearly done. Although it wasn't much, she had managed to extract a few essentials, white with plaster dust. Clothing. Cooking supplies. Food like salt and honey. A few knives. A precious firestarter, bright purple, small as a thumb, and halfway filled with fuel.

For the first time, she took a moment to study the wreckage of the building that used to be called STARBUCKS COFFEE.

It was a disorienting sensation.

Much of it had been reduced by the earthquake to an alien landscape of broken beams, brick, glass, and mounds of plaster. Yet although the roof had collapsed, there were entire sections of their old apartment that had been left nearly intact and were now exposed, incongruously, to the open air.

It gave Esther an odd feeling to see pieces of her life on display like that, under the yellow winter sky. A part of the living room wall was still decorated with a colorful poster for something called SKYY vodka. The kitchen table was half crushed by a wooden beam; yet it was set with a flowered tablecloth, and a bowl and spoon, as if the user had just stepped away. The bookshelf, her late sister's prize possession, tipped backward against a pile of bricks. While covered with broken glass and a heavy dusting of dirt and plaster, most of its contents were in place.

It took Esther a moment to identify what she was feeling, and when she did, it surprised her.

She was homesick.

Prin was the only world she had ever known, and many of her memories were not happy ones. She had fought with Sarah for years, only reconciling when her sister was ill. She had been Shunned by the town and sent away to die. Yet the thought that she would never see Prin again—as ruined and messed up as it was—made Esther tremble. She saw herself running down its streets, hiding in its fields, playing in its hot sun. There probably wasn't an inch of town she hadn't walked in, smelled, touched.

Now she found herself gazing at the books.

Caleb had told the townspeople that there was no room for frivolities or anything but the barest of necessities; and certainly, a book seemed the very definition of useless. Furthermore, neither she nor Caleb read much and, in truth, could barely spell.

Even so, Esther found herself clambering over the wreckage one last time, this time to grab a book at random from a shelf. The title of the one she chose, *The Wonderful Wizard of Oz*, meant nothing to her. Yet knowing it had once belonged to Sarah comforted her somehow and she slipped the slim volume into the back pocket of her jeans.

She turned to scramble her way onto the street. As she did, her heart leaped to see someone standing there, waiting.

It was Skar.

She sat motionless astride her black bicycle, still wearing the strange daubs of red clay on her neck and arms. Like all variants, she wore no dark glasses or head covering to protect her from the sun, so Esther could see her expression. Aloof, she was frowning with confusion.

"I came as soon as I was able," she said. Then she abruptly gestured at the wreckage. "Is this all because of the earthquake? Are you and your people all right?"

Esther balanced on a pile of rubble and jumped off, landing by her friend.

"It messed up the town real bad," she said. "So many were killed, maybe half. We're okay, though. How bad were you hit?"

Skar shrugged, as if the subject was of little interest. "Three of our people were lost. And several of our houses and much of our supplies. But it could have been much worse."

Skar paused. Then her reserve faltered as she noticed the wagons parked along the main street.

Other townspeople were moving in and out of their destroyed homes, carrying supplies which they handed to others, who then loaded them in waiting wagons. As Skar took it all in, her expression changed to one of worry, and that made her appear oddly childlike.

"What's going on?" she asked. For the moment, she

sounded like her old self again.

"We're leaving Prin today," Esther said. Then she swallowed, hard. Saying the words made them real in a way they hadn't been before. "There's nothing left for us here."

"But your signal. I thought you were only—"

"I know. I . . . I just wanted to say good-bye."

There was silence. And then Skar, distant and cold for so many weeks, recoiled. For an instant, her face crumpled as tears, the first Esther could ever remember seeing her shed, filled her eyes.

Then with a brusque movement, she recovered, rubbing her face dry with a forearm.

"Thank you for letting me know," she said. She spoke stiffly, although her voice caught.

Esther seized her by the elbow. "Come with us." She had no idea where the words came from; yet as soon as she spoke them, Esther realized they were a mistake.

Skar jerked her arm back, as if offended.

"I'm sorry," Esther stammered. "It's just . . . I'm really going to miss you. I can't believe I'm never going to see you again."

Skar's expression softened. Then she extended her hand, placing it lightly over Esther's.

"Me, too," she said.

Then she pushed aside the nylon pouch across her chest. Skar fiddled with something at the base of her neck. Then undoing it, she presented to her friend.

It was the braided-leather choker she always wore.

"I've had this since I was little," she said. "And perhaps it will help you remember me."

Esther took the necklace, still warm from Skar's touch, and closed her fingers around it. Then she slipped it into her pocket for safekeeping.

"Thank you," she said.

If Esther could have had her way, she and Skar would have spent their final afternoon roaming through the fields and talking, the way they had for so many years. But now, there was no longer any time; there was too much work to do. Skar helped Esther secure belongings in the back of their wagon. They lashed everything down with elastic cords, stretchy pieces of rope that were covered with braided nylon and ended in sturdy hooks tipped with white rubber. They packed with care, piling the items close together and then compressing them even further.

When they were finished, there was a final task: collecting more of the town's most precious resource. An hour later, the two girls were at the spring located beneath Joseph's former home, a hotel on the far side of town.

Esther, with her sneakers off and jeans rolled up to her knees, stood in the achingly cold water, filling one plastic gallon jug after another and handing them to Skar, who replaced their caps. Working together, the two had already loaded one wagon, child-size and made of red metal, and were nearly finished with the second. Both were attached to the girls' bicycles, which stood side by side.

The afternoon sun was strong, and Esther took a moment

to dip her hands into the icy spring and lift them to her lips to drink. Taking off her sunglasses, she undid her red hood and leaned forward, plunging her head under. The effect was exhilarating and when she emerged, water running down her face and neck, she let out a whoop of sheer pleasure. She shook her head like a dog, so the drops flew.

Skar laughed, too, and jokingly held up her hands to guard against the unexpected shower. Esther bent low and slapped her hand across the spring's surface, sending up an arc that splashed the variant girl.

"Hey!" shouted Skar.

Then she too waded in and began churning up a counterattack. Laughing and shouting at the cold, the two girls thrashed at the water, dousing each other and getting soaked in turn. It was an epic fight, one in which all of the day's weariness and tension, unspoken and unyielding, seemed to be swept away by the bracing water and their shared screams of laughter.

Finally, the two waded to dry land. Still panting, they sat together, attempting to wring out their sodden clothes. It was no good. Esther yanked handfuls of dead, sun-bleached grass from the ground beside her and tried without much success to wipe herself dry. Laughing, she turned to her friend to offer her some, as well. But what she saw made the words die on her lips.

There were dozens of bruises and welts.

Multicolored and vivid, they stood out on Skar's flesh, where the concealing clay had been washed away. One radiated from her upper chest like a spider's web of broken capillaries and blood vessels. A large handprint, tinged purple and yellow, circled her soft throat, and others dappled her arms like bracelets, the mark of individual fingers dark and distinct. A bruise across her shoulder seemed recent: It was an angry red, and its swollen welt glistened with fresh blood.

Esther let out a cry.

Skar, unaware of what her friend had seen, turned to her with a quizzical expression. When she saw the open shock on Esther's face, she gave a start, as her hands flew to cover her throat and arms.

"Skar," said Esther. She found she could barely speak. "What has he—"

"No," interrupted Skar. She sounded panicked. "This isn't what you think. I'm too clumsy and fell when I was hunting." But her face flushed at the obvious lie as she tried in vain to scrape up more mud with which to cover herself.

"Don't," said Esther.

She took the variant girl by the wrist. At her touch, gentle as it was, Skar winced, her face contorted in pain. As she let go, Esther realized with a sick feeling why her old friend had been avoiding her embrace all those times.

Skar gave up trying to cover herself. Instead, she drew her knees up to her chin and buried her face in her hands.

"Please don't look at me," she whispered. Her voice was muffled.

Esther crouched by Skar. "You can talk to me," she said.

Skar wouldn't take her hands from her face. "Only if you

look away," she said so quietly, Esther could barely hear the words.

Esther turned and stared across the spring to the ruins of the old hotel behind them. Then she listened as her friend began to speak.

It was not easy for Skar, being partnered. She had not known what her responsibilities were, for no one had ever explained them to her. Like all variants, Skar had been born with qualities of both sexes and chose her gender when she turned ten. A circle tattooed on her upper arm announced her decision. Yet she did not realize that being a girl would mean changing her behavior. For it soon became clear what was expected of her.

It started shortly after their partnering ceremony. Tarq had been gone all day, with no word of where he was or when he was returning. Skar, who had caught and cooked a rabbit for their dinner, ate half of it by herself and went to bed alone. But she was awoken when he pulled her out of bed, striking her across the back. She was not a good partner. She had not kept the food hot, had not waited for him to return, and had not cleaned their home sufficiently. Skar apologized; she had not known, and said she would try harder in the future.

But that was only the beginning, for it seemed there was nothing she could do properly. She could not hunt enough to fill the larder; she was too silly and undignified, like a little girl; she was not sufficiently respectful in his presence. As his partner, she was forbidden to socialize with others; this included her brother. She was not even allowed to mention Esther's name in his presence.

"So you see, it's all my fault," Skar said, her voice almost inaudible. "He gets impatient with me, but it is only because I am such a poor partner." She laughed, but there was no mirth in the sound. "I'm sure this is common with silly girls every-where."

The whole time, Esther had said nothing. Now she spoke, anger flashing in her dark eyes.

"It's not," she said. "Being partners doesn't mean only one person doing all the work and the other making all the rules. It means the two of you are there to help each other. As equals."

"But what if you make a mistake?"

"Then you apologize. But everyone makes mistakes."

Skar shook her head. "And Caleb has never punished you?"

Esther blinked. The idea of Caleb lifting a hand to hurt her was something she could not even imagine. "No," she said, "never. In fact, he'd never hurt anyone. At least, not anymore."

"Maybe you're lucky, then."

"It's not a question of luck. It's just not right, what he's doing to you. He's your *partner*."

She turned to face Skar and was struck by the utter hope-lessness in her friend's face.

"Yes," Skar replied in a low monotone. "We are partners. We made a vow." She held out her arm with its partnering scar, which wound its ornate way past the bruises and welts. "So you see, there is nothing I can do."

Esther took both of her hands in hers.

"Yes there is," she said. "You can come with us. They say in Mundreel there's plenty, enough for everybody. You can join us."

For a moment, Skar looked undecided. Then her brow

clouded and frowning, she shook her head once.

"No," she said. "I just have to try harder, that's all. If I do, Tarq will not hurt me again. I *know* he won't. He loves me."

"But—" Esther started to say before her friend cut her off.

"I shouldn't have told you," she said. "I knew you wouldn't understand." Then abruptly, she stood.

"Skar—" said Esther, scrambling to stop her. But Skar had already unfastened the wagon from her bicycle and had one foot on the pedal.

"Farewell, Esther," she said. Once again, she had resumed her mask, her face expressionless and detached. "Safe travels. And I hope you think of me sometime."

And with that, she took off down the road and disappeared.

By the time Esther finished bringing all the water, Caleb was hitching bicycles, two across, to their crude wagon. Nearby, Kai played by himself in the shade of an oak; a cloth harness kept him loosely tethered.

As she unloaded the water, Esther didn't have the heart to mention Skar. Instead, she handed the jugs up to Caleb in silence and he placed them in rows, counting under his breath. When they were finished, the two of them unfolded a heavy plastic tarp and dragged it over all of their belongings. The threat of an unexpected shower was constant, and they couldn't risk rainwater contaminating their supplies.

Caleb secured the tarp with elastic cords. Then the job was done.

Esther looked around. She saw Eli, Rhea, Rafe, Silas, and

others familiar to her, all getting ready to go. Yet someone was missing.

"Where's Joseph?" Esther asked. No one knew, and for a moment she felt a flicker of panic.

Then she heard the mewing of a cat.

She followed the sound until she reached the back of another wagon, covered by a drawn tarp. Behind it, her friend huddled amid a welter of clothing, books, and supplies. He carried a green nylon pet carrier which held the tabby he called Stumpy, the only one of his cats left after the earthquake. He was clutching a ticking desk clock and a tattered oversize book called *Rand McNally Road Atlas*.

"I hope this is all right," he said in humble tones. "That I'm here, I mean. I can't ride a bicycle. And being out in the open makes me feel . . ." His hands fluttered in agitation.

Esther just stared at him, feeling her usual blend of exasperation and affection. She knew that others were looking at Joseph, too, and not as charitably; they were probably wondering why he got special treatment. *Joseph could take care of Kai,* Esther thought; *perhaps it would all work out for the best.*

"I'll pull him," she announced, closing the subject. She had a quick word with the owner of the wagon, who was happy to trade places with her.

Astride his own vehicle at the head of the line, Caleb was waiting. Then he turned in his seat and glanced at Rafe, who nodded. He gave a piercing whistle that echoed down the abandoned streets of Prin.

And with that, the journey began.

* * *

The afternoon sun was shining brightly. It revealed what looked like a trail of ants, working its way down the thin, gray line that once had been the interstate highway. Only these weren't insects but a caravan of people.

Standing atop a crumbling mountainside home miles away, someone was watching them.

It was Skar. She held a pair of binoculars to her face, but she did so gingerly. Her nose was broken and her left eye swollen nearly shut, the skin a weird combination of dark purple, green, and yellow. Her fingers weren't working properly and to even hold the binoculars took great effort.

When she had returned from Prin that morning, Tarq had been waiting for her. She was surprised to see him, but she did not lie to him; it did not occur to her to do so. As she spoke, he listened, expressionless, hunched forward as he stared at the ground.

"So you just decided to visit Esther?" His voice was like his face, stony and without emotion. "Without asking me?"

Skar opened her hands in appeal. "She is my oldest friend, Tarq. And she is leaving for a place called Mundreel. I will never see her again."

She didn't even see his fist lash out.

The world exploded in a burst of light and shocking pain and the faraway sound of bones cracking. As she fell to the ground, Skar curled into a tight ball, her arms uselessly wrapped around her head. But it was no good; Tarq was already raining blows and kicks on her. It seemed to last an eternity, and even though she grew numb to the pain, throughout it all was her disbelief, repeating again and again like a voice in her head.

Why? Why was he doing this to her? What had she done wrong?

Finally, he stopped. Panting, he stumbled to their doorway, where he loomed for a moment, framed by sunlight.

"If you disobey me again," the voice from the silhouette said, "I will kill you."

Then he was gone.

Now, alone in her hiding place, Skar shivered. Her body hurt all over. She had trouble even drawing breath; navigating her way from the variant camp, slowly, on bicycle, had taken all of what little strength she had. Yet even greater was the shock of realization.

Esther was right.

It wasn't her fault.

Skar was filled with an emotion she had rarely felt before: anger. She had done nothing wrong, nothing that could possibly merit her partner's wrath. Understanding that simple truth made her decision easy.

The only thing that nagged at her were Tarq's last words. *If you disobey me again, I will kill you.*

Skar shuddered, and for a moment she hesitated.

Then, unexpectedly, a new and clear voice said something else in her ear, something that was so obvious, she was surprised she hadn't thought of it before.

He would have to find her first.

She would go to her friends, Esther and Caleb, and join them on their journey. Although she had no goods or water to bring with her, only the few items she had snatched up when she left her home, she was a good hunter and knew she could earn her keep.

It was torture to remount her bicycle, much less navigate through the dense and tangled forest. Yet once she reached the highway, Skar forced herself to ignore the pain and focused instead on riding as swiftly as she could. She didn't think Tarq was following her; in fact, she doubted he would even notice she was gone until evening.

They had been on the highway a few hours before Esther saw the figure.

It rode full bore down from the mountains toward the group of travelers. Many slowed or came to a halt, anticipating trouble. Yet Esther noticed there was something shaky about the intruder's control of the bike.

At last, at the bottom, it came to a stop, kicking up dust.

It was Skar.

Esther saw that Skar kept her distance. Even though she had dismounted, she stayed where she was, holding herself with dignity. Skar did not know, after all, if she would be welcomed; and Esther knew she was not one to beg.

"Esther," Skar said.

Seeing her friend, Esther was already smiling so hard her cheeks ached. But as she left her bike and rushed forward, she gave a low gasp and her hand flew to her mouth. She could see what Tarq had done to her.

Blushing, Skar made a move to hide her broken nose, the

dried blood, and fresh bruises. Then she seemed to think better of it and lifted her head high.

Esther approached her and took her by the hand.

"Welcome home," was all she said.

FOUR

THOUGH RAFE WAS THE OFFICIAL LEADER, CALEB RODE ALONGSIDE THE caravan, making sure that no one fell behind or was in need of help. He was on one of the dozen or so free bicycles, untethered to any vehicle.

Esther, on her wagon-mounted bicycle, was talking with Skar, who walked beside her. She had tried to insist that her friend ride with Joseph, and Skar had been just as adamant in refusing. Yet each step, Caleb knew, cost the variant girl; he was astonished and impressed by her toughness.

Caleb had wondered how the others would respond to having a variant travel with them. Once they took note of her bow

and arrow, most of the townspeople welcomed her, if grudg-
ingly; variants were famed as hunters. Even Rafe was open to
the idea.

"As long as she earns her keep," he said. "Maybe she can
even teach some of the others how to hunt."

As he approached Rafe now, Caleb saw that he was bicycling
with difficulty. Part of the problem was that he was attempting
to study something he had propped on his handlebars. Caleb
recognized the large, colored pages filled with lines as a book
of maps, something Rafe had likely stolen from Joseph.

Rafe had decked out his vehicle in grand style. He had
ignored Caleb's instructions to pack lightly and instead piled
his wagon high with everything he had been able to salvage:
food, clothes, furniture. He had a canopy over his bicycle, to
shield it from the sun. He even enlisted another boy to walk
behind and make sure the wagon didn't tip.

"Be careful it stays steady now!" Rafe yelled behind him.
"And watch for bumps!"

Caleb gazed at Rafe's luxuries. "Sure you got enough?" he
asked dryly.

Rafe considered the question. "I hope so!" he called.
"Maybe I missed a few things!"

"Want me to go and check if you left anything?"

"That's awful nice of you!" Rafe yelled. "But I really don't—"

But Caleb had already raced on.

He passed others, anonymous in their hooded robes and
sunglasses. They bore down on their pedals, their billowing
sheets belted at the legs so as not to get caught in the gears.

Many more trudged behind, some helping push the heavy carts. For the most part, no one spoke, although he could hear one voice, shrill and incessant, long before he caught sight of the speaker. It was Rhea. She was walking with Silas and talking nonstop.

Although she had spoken against him at the meeting, Caleb felt sorry for the older girl. Like many of the others, she had lost a loved one in the earthquake; but unlike them, she still wore her partnering cloth around her wrist. With life so short, mourning was a luxury no one could afford; to continue wearing the symbol of your relationship even a few days after your partner's death was considered self-indulgent. Yet having lost his first partner the year before, Caleb could sympathize. Rhea was chatting animatedly about herself to the younger boy, who didn't appear to be listening.

Caleb continued on, joining others. One of them seemed to be going slowly on purpose, wobbling from side to side in an effort to stay upright.

Eli was doing his best to accompany Asha, who walked beside him. The boy knew the rules of the caravan: Since there was only a limited number of bicycles, everyone had to take turns walking, free-riding, or pulling a wagon. Free-riding was the easiest and most pleasant form of travel, and frequent squabbles erupted when people thought that others had gone over their allotted time. Eli was worried that someone would take advantage of Asha, because she was too naïve to ask for her turn.

He was determined that this would not happen.

Eli couldn't deny that he thought Asha was pretty—round-faced and with a sweet expression—and her childlike quality made him feel protective. He also knew she'd lost her older brother in the quake and so had no one to look after her.

"I'm sorry for your loss," he said, gazing at the ground as he pedaled next to her. "Your brother, I mean."

"Oh, he ain't gone," Asha said, with certainty.

"No?"

"No. Someone just shook things up, then reached down and grabbed everybody. It's like that game, when you throw a little ball in the air and grab those pointy things? They'll all come down again, you'll see."

"You believe that?"

"I know it."

Eli couldn't help but smile. This idea, while ludicrous, still oddly comforted him.

By now, the sun was halfway down the afternoon sky, which meant it was time to find somewhere to stop for the night. Caleb assumed they would be taking the nearest exit; after all, only a fool would choose to camp on a major highway, especially with such a large group. Yet Rafe showed no sign he was thinking of pulling over.

They passed a sign for Schroon Lake, the destination Caleb had originally suggested. Perhaps recalling the name, Rafe arrived at his own decision.

"This way, for the night!" he shouted.

The group steered onto a narrow road that led off the highway. In the near distance, through the blackened branches of lifeless trees, they could see a huge, dry expanse that had once been a body of water. As they approached, Caleb noticed the rotting hulls of sailboats and other detritus resting on the cracked bottom.

He could also detect the distinct smell of charred wood and smoke.

The town itself was no more than a modest main street that had recently been gutted by fire. It was clear there was no place to stay and nothing to Glean. Any stores or businesses had burned to the ground, leaving little but scorched remains still drifting ash.

"*This* the place you wanted us to go?" Rafe asked Caleb, his tone contemptuous.

But Caleb didn't answer. He was focused on something else entirely.

Something lay by the side of the road. At first, it seemed to be a pile of filthy sheets, old robes someone had taken off and discarded. But it shifted, revealing a thin arm.

It was a person. And whoever it was was still alive.

"Watch it," warned Rafe. He was already moving on, covering his mouth with his sleeve. "You don't want to mess with anyone who got the sickness. You'll end up dead and getting the rest of us sick, too."

But Caleb was already off his bicycle and crossing to the stranger. He knelt by the person's side and spoke in quiet tones. Then he leaned in close. After a moment, he gave a start and pulled the hood away that covered the face.

He saw who it was and gasped.

The girl, fourteen or so, had hair the color of honey and

a face disfigured beyond belief. Her pale skin was lashed by ripples of flesh that cascaded from her brow to her cheeks and chin. One eye, the lid discolored and sealed shut, continually wept tears, and the other one, a disconcertingly bright blue, was staring and open.

"Michal," Caleb said. He could hardly breathe. It felt unreal to see his brother's former girlfriend again, and like this: miles from Prin, maimed almost beyond recognition, and left for dead by the side of the road.

"Caleb," she whispered. Her voice was tiny, like a dead leaf skittering down the sidewalk. "Help me."

"So that's who it is." A crowd of the curious had gathered around them, and a boy spoke up now. "Levi's girl."

"She don't look so pretty now, does she," said another, who spat on the ground.

"Levi's whore," Rhea said. She had pushed her way to the front of the crowd, her eyes glittering. "His slut." She seemed to relish the words.

Again, Caleb spoke to Michal, too softly for anyone else to hear. "Did Levi do this to you?"

The girl nodded once and said something Caleb couldn't hear. Then Rafe sauntered up, surveying the situation.

"What's going on?" he said.

It was only then that he noticed the girl at the center of the crowd and he squinted in vague recollection. Rafe had seen her at the Source, always in the background, but only once or twice, and certainly not since her face had been ruined. He recoiled.

"Somebody give me some water!" Caleb called.

As Esther fetched a bottle, the circle around Michal grew. People shoved and jostled to get a look, and a cruel, reckless gaiety filled the air. Silas pushed up his nose and pulled down his eyelids in a vicious parody, mincing and swaying his hips to the wild amusement of some. Others reached toward Michal, snatching at her robes and hair.

"We don't got anything for people like you!"

"You should have saved something to eat from the Source!"

Rhea reached out and pinched the new girl, hard, on the arm. "Ugly whore," she hissed. "You don't belong with decent folk."

Rafe was all for people enjoying themselves, but time was wasting and he was growing bored. "I'm sorry," he said to Caleb above the noise, "but looks like you done all you can. Leave the girl. We got to be on our way."

There was a rumble of outrage from the others; this had been their only fun since leaving Prin and it was just getting started. But Caleb cut it off.

"She's coming. She's one of us, and she's gonna travel with us."

Rafe opened his mouth to object, but Caleb continued. "If she doesn't come, we don't go another step. I made most of the wagons and I can take them apart."

Caleb waited until the crowd relented and broke up, with much muttering and reluctance. Then he picked Michal up in his arms and carried her to Esther's wagon. She was lighter than air, almost as light as Kai. There he laid her beside Joseph, who stared at her, a bit afraid.

Caleb gave Michal the water and some food and then closed

the tarp over her. He didn't explain but met Esther's eye and nodded once.

Rafe watched the crowd disperse before gazing after Caleb with poorly disguised resentment.

"All right," he said, "let's go!"

Esther dropped her pace so she could steal a peek at the new girl.

Michal now walked by herself, toward the back of the caravan, helping push the heavy water wagon. She spoke to nobody and kept her head down.

Yet although she had rewrapped her destroyed face in its protective sheet and again pulled her hood over her head, a piece of hair had escaped and now trailed down the side of her throat. It caught the rays of the setting sun, revealing itself to be a color Esther had never seen before: gleaming gold, with streaks of copper in it.

Michal used to live with Levi, Esther realized, *the boy who had the best of everything. So she must have once been beautiful.*

Esther felt a pang. She had no illusions about her own attractiveness; although she was too thin and dark with flyaway hair and eyes that were too big, Caleb liked the way she looked. Still, she had no idea what kind of connection her partner had had to this girl. What did it mean that he had risked the entire caravan to defend her?

As she mulled over her thoughts, Esther became aware of a bad smell that grew until it became an overpowering chemical stench. Ahead of her, the caravan slowed and then stopped.

Even from where she was, Esther could see what was wrong. In the distance, an oily mass spread across the highway, gleaming black and impassable. It reached deep into the woods on either side, as big as several fields put together. Here and there, lumps bulged from the otherwise smooth surface: animals that had been caught in the poisonous mess, and perhaps unlucky travelers, as well.

Esther heard a rustling sound. Perched on his bicycle, Rafe was turning Joseph's maps one way, then around again. He seemed agitated.

"I know where we are," he kept saying. "Don't anyone panic, now."

Caleb managed to convince Rafe to turn the caravan around; the sun was dropping in the sky and finding shelter was more important than figuring out a detour. They backtracked to the exit, then continued past it until they reached another town, less than a mile away. The center of the village was tiny—not much more than a handful of stores clustered around a four-way intersection—and showed the aftereffects of the earthquake. Yet it would do as a place to spend the night.

Most of the townspeople, including Rafe, headed into one of the few buildings still standing, called RITE AID. There, several curled up on the trash-strewn floor to sleep. Outside, Silas took the tools that let him break into buildings and wandered off to see what he could find; Skar, too, disappeared into the nearby woods with her bow and remaining arrows. Joseph released Stumpy from her carrier and Kai sat in the dust, watching the cat stalk and pounce on grasshoppers.

Esther and Caleb took two of the free bicycles. They continued down the road past the ruins of houses until they found what Caleb had spied on the horizon: a dented sign that loomed overhead on a giant metal pole. It read STOP & SHOP. Beneath it was a brick building, its large window frames edged with shards of broken glass and the entrance gaping open where swinging doors once hung.

Inside, dust motes danced in the air. Trash was strewn everywhere—not only long-discarded food cartons and packages but also an old mattress, sodden newspapers, the remains of a fire, dead leaves.

Caleb and Esther worked their way down aisles of filthy shelves, going quickly to take advantage of the failing light. They avoided the piles of cans that bulged, leaking the foul, black liquid that used to be things called baked beans, tuna fish, soup. They bypassed several shelves of once-colorful cardboard cartons, which they knew held only the rotted dust of ancient cereal, mixed with insect casings, rat droppings, and mold.

But on one high shelf, empty except for spilled flour, Esther came across a windfall: a white and blue box.

"Hey," she called. "Look what I found."

By the time Caleb showed up, Esther had already torn it open. Inside were two neat layers of small yellow cakes, ten in all, each individually sealed in clear plastic. He took one out, tried to squeeze it, and sniffed it. So did she.

"Pretty hard," she commented; "but seems like they're okay."

They were called Twinkies. True, the yellow cakes were stiff as dried mud and filled with white stuff that was just as unyield-ing; but they were sweet and relatively edible. *At least*, Esther thought, *they wouldn't kill you*. She closed the lid and placed the box with care in her backpack.

"And look what I found," Caleb said. Fumbling in his pack, he revealed two small jars. They were dusty and covered with grit; but when he brushed them off, she saw that the glass and lids were intact and that they were filled with amber liquid. GOLDEN BLOSSOM, the label read.

When he wrenched one lid open, it gave a satisfying pop. He stuck one finger in and pulled it out.

"Here," he said.

Esther parted her lips and tasted. The honey was cool and sweet, tickling her throat in a delicious way as she swallowed; she ran her tongue over his finger even after it was gone. When she glanced up at Caleb, he was smiling. His face was streaked with dirt, and he wiped a cobweb from his brow.

"I also found some sugar and a bag of beans," he said, "so I think we'll be okay for a few days."

"Even with the one extra person?"

Esther bit her lip. She hadn't meant to say anything, but she couldn't help it; the question had just popped out. In the grow-ing darkness, she could hear Caleb exhale.

"You want to talk about it?"

"I do."

Esther knew it hurt Caleb to think about his late brother. Yet she was filled with not only an intense curiosity about the new girl but also something she had never experienced before:

jealousy. She needed to know about this stranger, the one with the beautiful golden hair, and so she stood in the dim light of the store, waiting. And after a few moments, Caleb spoke.

"Michal helped me," he said. "She saved my life when Levi tried to have me killed. Hid me in her room and took care of me."

Esther thought of the scars she knew so well: the one on his chest and the matching one between his shoulders, where the arrow had pierced him through. "Then she helped me find Kai." Caleb took a deep breath. "I figure Levi found out what happened. That's why he did what he done to her. With something that burns. To punish her in a way that would hurt the most."

Michal's melted features flashed in front of Esther's eyes and she shuddered.

"I guess I feel responsible." Caleb rubbed his face with a sleeve. When he spoke again, his voice was so soft, Esther had to lean forward to catch his words. "So it's the least I can do for all she did."

When he had started to speak, Esther had been full of questions about Michal and how pretty she had been. Now that she had heard what actually happened, she was filled with shame, as well as a deep feeling of gratitude toward the stranger. She took Caleb's hand.

"If Mundreel is as good as Rafe says it is," Caleb said, "feeding another won't be so hard." He had been gazing at the ground, then glanced up at her with a smile. "Maybe we can even try to give Kai a little brother or sister."

Esther's smile broadened as she squeezed his hand. Then they were in each other's arms; it was as if they could not hold each other close enough.

"Come," she said after a moment. Her face was flushed and her eyes sparkled. "The others will be wondering where we are."

They left the STOP & SHOP hand in hand. Caleb helped Esther over a pile of shattered glass, and together they went to their bicycles.

They were unaware that across the street, someone was watching them from the deepening shade of a tree.

It was Asha.

She often liked to spy on Caleb and Esther. The best times were when they were far from the others and did not know that anyone was watching. If Asha was very careful, she caught a rare glimpse of them that nobody else saw, not even their best friends, the old man Joseph and the variant girl, Skar.

Asha liked to see the two hug and kiss, even if that kind of thing made her face turn red and she would turn away until they were finished. Yet it was moments like this, when they spoke quietly and laughed between them at some private joke, that she liked the best.

Although Asha had never had a partner, it was something she dreamed about. "When I grow up," she would often say to herself, unaware that at close to sixteen, she was more than grown up and well past the age of partnering. Still, in her fantasies, she always envisioned herself in a relationship like the one shared by Esther and Caleb.

Mostly, Asha wanted a baby of her own. She always hoped Esther would let her care for Kai; but Esther seemed to prefer Joseph instead. This made no sense to Asha, since he wasn't even good at taking care of little ones. *Not as good as she was*, that she was certain.

Now she decided that she too would go off and explore the small town they were in. Pulling up her sleeve, she made a show of examining her wristwatch, a purple Swatch with a daisy pattern. It was something she had seen Joseph do many times, winding and adjusting the three watches he wore on his arm. Asha wasn't sure what it meant, but it made her feel grown-up nevertheless. She decided that like Esther and Caleb, she too might be able to find food somewhere and bring it to the others. If she did, people were sure to look at her with approval. Maybe even Eli—who was always patient with her and would never dream of playing tricks—would say how smart she was, how capable.

The thought made her glow and giggle, as if he had really said it.

Asha avoided the first few buildings on the street. They had collapsed against one another, and while they were still standing, barely, she didn't much like the look of them. Humming to herself, she continued down the street, walking with one foot on the curb and one in the gutter. Behind her, she could tell the townspeople had begun cooking a meager supper; there was already the scent of wood burning and the faraway clatter of metal spoons and firebowls.

The building she chose lay a distance from the road, at the

end of a small, curved driveway. It was a good-size brick structure, with long windows and a strange fixture on its roof, a long, white beam that tapered to a point high overhead. The setting sun revealed a sign in the midst of the overgrown grass; beneath the cracked glass front were crooked white letters spelling out words Asha didn't understand.

Inside, Asha found a high-ceilinged room set with orderly rows of wooden benches. By now, it was so dark, it was almost impossible to see. Vaguely, Asha was aware it was probably not a good idea to keep going. Yet she continued to inch toward the front of the room, where a round window was crisscrossed with two white planks, one long and one short, that formed a sort of T. In front of it, a separate stall of benches faced long metal pipes on the wall that gleamed dully in the waning light. Asha put her hands in front of her as if trying to feel her way through the velvety evening air.

She was not prepared for the stairs that suddenly appeared beneath her feet.

Screaming and windmilling her arms, Asha pitched forward. As she fell, she grabbed onto a flimsy wooden banister that snapped off in her hand. At the same moment, her left foot broke through a step and kicked free. With a groan of ancient wood, the entire structure collapsed beneath her in an explosion of dust and splinters.

In pitch-blackness, Asha found herself half sitting on the pile of rubble. Uncertainly, she pulled her foot out from underneath her and attempted to stand. She could feel a hot stickiness on her leg and her ankle felt funny. But standing on tiptoe, she could sense a gaping void where the staircase once stood. Above her head, her waving hands brushed the splintered end of a faraway board. Beyond it, she could imagine the open doorway, which at that moment seemed as far away as the moon.

Asha didn't know how long she shouted. After a while, her throat was ragged and still no one came. Finally, she gave up. In the dark, she sat on the lumber and hugged her knees, whimpering to herself as she rocked back and forth. As she wept, she could taste the salt of her tears, and it reminded her of supper, of companionship and comfort.

Then there was a sound from above.

It was the murmur of voices, male voices. Hoping against hope, Asha quickly got to her feet.

"Eli?" she called in a harsh croak.

The voices grew louder. Without warning, a lit torch suddenly thrust down toward her, nearly setting her hair on fire. With a squeal, Asha attempted to bat the nasty thing away; the flaming rag tied to the end of a stick reeked of gasoline. When she looked up at its source, the doorway at the top of what had been the stairs, Asha was blinded by the light. Squinting, she held up an arm to block it.

"Well, look what we got here," said an unfamiliar voice.

Another person—a boy? a girl?—snickered.

Asha, still covering her eyes, waved her other hand. "Help," she said. "I fell down."

The torch withdrew; the room grew dark again, and the girl felt a stab of dismay. Were her rescuers abandoning her? Then something hit her across the face.

"Hey!" she exclaimed.

It didn't hurt. Whatever it was bumped against her face again, and this time, she grabbed it. She was holding a piece of rope that dangled from above. The glowing light found her once more, as if to provide guidance.

"Grab hold," said the stranger's voice. "We put a noose at the end so you can put your foot in it. Ride up that way."

Awkwardly, Asha did as she was told. She stuck her right foot, sneaker and all, into the loop at the end. Then she gripped the scratchy rope with both hands. When the cord tightened and began to lift her, she let out a small scream. She twirled in the glow of the torch, her white robes billowing as she ascended to the doorway.

Hands reached to pull her to solid ground. Giddy with excitement, she stumbled, nearly knocking over her saviors.

"Thank you," she said again and again. She could not see their faces, but her relief was immense. "Thank you, thank you."

She sensed her rescuers were guiding her through the large room. Outside, a winter moon gave off enough illumination for her to see a little better.

There were three boys who looked to be her age or a little older.

One of them was large, hulking and immobile. He held the torch, which he kept close to her face. After a while, she wished he wouldn't; the heat and glare of it were starting to bother her eyes. As if he had heard her, he lowered it so it moved slowly over the rest of her body. A second boy, shorter and nervous in his movements, began to whisper and giggle to himself.

Asha decided she didn't like either of them very much.

But the one who had spoken to her was different.

"Care for some candy?"

He proffered a small package and shook a few pieces into her hand. She couldn't stuff them into her mouth quickly enough, and as she crunched on the hard sweetness, he chuckled, and the sound was friendly.

"Ain't you a long ways from home?"

"No," she said. "I mean . . . we're going to Mundreel. That's where there's lots to eat and we can live a long time. That's our new home." Swallowing and wiping her mouth, Asha grinned foolishly in the bright light. It was so hard to explain herself sometimes.

"We?"

"The people from Prin," she said, speaking slowly, the way she had been told to do whenever she became too excited. Then she gave up altogether and just gestured down the road. "Over there. Want to come with me?"

The one with the candy turned to the others and said something Asha couldn't hear. The smaller one giggled again and whispered in response. The big one said nothing, but Asha didn't care. She had been given some candy and was heading back to the others. She was happy.

"That sounds," said her new friend, "like a real good idea."

FIVE

ELI WAS THE FIRST TO NOTICE THAT ASHA WAS NOT ALONE.

He had been looking for her, using a torch to check around the wagons. He was worried that she had wandered off into the evening and become lost in the unfamiliar surroundings. When he spied the girl on the dark street, his relief was so great it took him a few moments to register that she was accompanied by three strangers. Like her, they were clad in dirty robes that gave off a faint glow in the gloom. She was sucking on a piece of candy as she walked, nearly skipped toward the camp.

"Hey," he said, approaching.

"Hi," Asha said, her face brightening, biting the sweet now with a piercing crack.

By the light of his flame, he could see the candy had dyed her mouth and tongue bright orange. "Where have you—"

"I was getting stuff, by myself. But things got real scary, and these guys saved me."

She gestured toward the three behind her, and Eli lifted his torch higher to see.

They were old: perhaps sixteen or seventeen. The one in front seemed to be the leader. He was medium height, solidly built, with a broken nose and a wolfish grin that he flashed at Eli. Another was slight, with dark hair pasted flat across his brow; for no reason, he giggled and whispered to himself as he chewed a tattered thumbnail. The last towered over the others. Hulking and silent, he was bigger than anyone in camp. Although his face was in deep shadow, Eli could see his expression was witless and crude.

"Who's this?" the first one asked Asha. His tone was friendly, but his smile grew even more aggressive. He hadn't taken his eyes off Eli.

"This is Eli," Asha said. "Why don't you say hello to them, Eli? You never know. You might need their help one day."

"We're all out of candy, Eli," the first one drawled. "Sorry."

Eli felt his shoulders tensing up at the joke. "I'll get by."

"Yeah, sure you will. I was just playing with you. I'm Lewt."

He extended a hand. After a moment, Eli clasped it. He wasn't sure, but he thought Lewt held the handshake a moment too long, squeezing before he let go.

"This here's Tahlik," Lewt said, indicating the giggling boy, who chewed his nail harder after the introduction. "And this big fella's Quell." The giant blinked in acknowledgment.

"They ain't the sharpest tools," Lewt said, as if in confidence. "But you can't travel alone in this world, can you, Eli?"

"Suppose not."

"You know not. Look at all the support *you* got." He gave an expansive hand wave to the campsite that lay in the distance. By the light of a large bonfire, townspeople could be seen moving about, preparing dinner. "Though you might keep a better eye on pretty here, to see she doesn't wander away."

At this, Asha giggled, and again, Eli felt a wave of tension.

"We been looking after her fine," he said. "And her name's Asha."

"Sure you have. And that's a nice name. I was just playing with you, Eli. You know, between us, maybe I'm a little envious. Maybe I'd like to be part of a big band like you got here, myself. People taking care of each other like you do."

"Is that right?"

"Sure. We get a little lonely on the road, Tahlik and Quell and me, truth be told."

Eli just looked at the other boy and said nothing.

"Girly says you're all going to a place called Mundreel. Where they give away food, and everybody lives to be thirty or something." He chuckled at the absurdity, and after a moment, his two friends joined in. "That must be a long ways, ain't it?"

Annoyed, Eli shot a glance at Asha. It wasn't a secret where they were headed; still, he didn't like that these strangers knew.

He shrugged without answering.

Lewt continued to stare at Eli with a shrewd eye, sizing him up and assessing his place in the scheme of things. Then he glanced away, as if he had come to a conclusion.

"Who's the boss around here, Eli?"

Something told Eli not to speak the full truth. "The boss? No one special."

"Every place got a boss. *Somebody's* got to tell the others what to do. Right, fellas?"

Although Eli didn't think this was funny, Tahlik giggled even louder, nodding his head. Even Quell, the big one, seemed to smile as he stepped closer to Lewt.

Someone else was laughing at this remark. It was Asha, dancing around by herself.

"That's funny! Don't you think that's funny, Eli? Why don't you stop being silly and tell him Rafe's in charge? He's the boss, you know that."

Eli felt his face flush. But Lewt was already ignoring him, looking past him as if he no longer existed.

"So where's Rafe?"

Before Eli could respond, someone did it for him.

"Right here." Rafe had wandered up behind them, squinting in the light of a torch. "What's the problem?"

Eli began to explain, then decided against it. *Let Rafe deal with them*, he thought. "Come on," he said to Asha. "Let's get you cleaned up."

"But what about my—"

Without looking, Lewt cut her off. "We'll see you later, pretty."

As Eli led Asha away, Lewt grasped Rafe's limp paw and shook it.

"Nice to know you," said Rafe. He was hungry for dinner and already losing interest in the newcomers. "Just passing through?"

"In a way."

"Well," Rafe said as he turned to go. "Good luck to you."

Lewt stopped him. "In fact, we wouldn't mind some food and water to get us on our way. If it ain't no trouble."

Rafe stopped and thought about it. In fact, there was precious little of either food or water and there was none to spare. Still, he liked the respectful way the stranger addressed him; it made him feel magnanimous. "I guess we could donate something."

Lewt smiled. "That's mighty kind," he said. "In fact, while you're being so generous, you think we might tag along for a bit? That fella thought it'd be okay."

Rafe was puzzled. "Eli said that? That's strange. He—"

"Everything all right?"

It was Caleb who spoke now. He had been watching with Esther from a distance and had already taken stock of the strangers. The big one and the giggling boy who refused to meet your eye seemed harmless enough. But the one in front was now staring at him with an air of confrontation. Then the boy glanced at Esther, his eyes sweeping up and down her body. He seemed to take special note of the tattered partnering cloth around her wrist. Or was it a trick of the light? Caleb couldn't be sure.

When the newcomer turned to Caleb, he seemed polite enough. "I'm Lewt. And this here's my boys."

As the two shook hands, Rafe was inwardly seething. He didn't like the way Caleb inserted himself into the conversation. It made Rafe look weak, as if he weren't the real leader. *Didn't Caleb think he could handle a perfectly ordinary situation by himself?* Rafe hitched up his jeans in a display of decisiveness.

"Sorry, but you can't join us," he told Lewt in a brusque voice. "And I'm afraid we can't give you any of our supplies. I wish you luck on your travels."

Caleb nodded; then he and Esther started back to the camp. Rafe was following when Lewt caught up with him.

"Wait," he said to Rafe in a low voice. "We might be of use to you."

"Oh, yeah?" Rafe said. All he wanted now was supper. "How's that?"

"Well, Quell here's real strong. Boy like that comes in handy when something needs lifting. And Tahlik knows how to fix tires pretty good in case any of your vehicles need mending."

Rafe gave him a pinched smile. "Thanks, but we already got folks who can do that." Before he could leave, Lewt spoke one last time.

"Then how about you go with us, where we're going?" he said. "Seems there should be room for us all, if it's what they say it is."

"Yeah?" Rafe said. "And where's that?"

"Mundreel."

Rafe stopped and stared at the other boy. He glanced at

Caleb, who had already disappeared into the darkness. Then he swiveled away, excited, confused, and self-conscious. He shifted his torch to his other hand and wiped the copious sweat that had somehow sprung up on his face.

Lewt drew closer. "You heard of it, I can tell."

"Matter of fact, it's where *we're* headed," Rafe said. He felt faint.

The other boy smiled his peculiarly wolflike grin. "Well, looks like we come along at the right time then. Right, boys?" This last was addressed to Quell and Tahlik, who giggled once more. "We know how to get there. We just need some help with provisions and backup, case there's trouble. We could travel together. After all, there's strength in numbers. Ain't that what they say?"

Rafe avoided Lewt's piercing gaze and looked down at the dirt.

He alone knew that his own directions were worse than shaky. And no matter how hard he studied them, Rafe couldn't make any sense whatsoever out of Joseph's maps. As a result, he had only the vaguest sense of where they were headed.

"Okay," he said, impulsively.

"Great." Lewt slapped his companions on the back. "You won't regret it. We'll just go get our stuff." Smiling, the three boys turned and disappeared into the night.

Alone, Rafe breathed a sigh of relief. Then Caleb stepped once more from the darkness.

"What'd you do that for?" His voice was stony. "We don't know them. And we got enough people to care for."

"You got that girl to come," Rafe retorted. "The useless one, with the messed-up face. At least the mutant can hunt." He turned to go, but Caleb grabbed his arm.

"That's not an answer."

"Then I'm in charge," Rafe said, freeing himself. "*That's* the answer."

Rafe walked away. He knew Caleb was staring after him with anger, but, as he reminded himself, it was loser's anger. Rafe had won this little fight of theirs and there was nothing, really, Caleb could do to change it.

Rafe could hear the strangers laughing in the distance.

That night, the three newcomers stayed by themselves on the outskirts of the bonfire. They spoke to no one as they ate their meager rations. Later, as the townspeople scattered through the village's desolate buildings looking for a secure place to sleep, they instead chose to stay in the open, under the cloudless night sky.

When Rafe awoke in the morning, he discovered that the book of maps he had taken from Joseph had disappeared from his wagon. But at breakfast, he saw Lewt poring over it, nodding his head as if it made sense to him and clapping it shut when Rafe approached.

"Yeah," Lewt said, "it's what I thought. It's the same as our directions." He then suggested the caravan continue on the side road in order to avoid the oil spill. After several wrong turns and many hours, the caravan finally returned to the desolate interstate.

The three strangers rode their own bicycles, which were dusty, rickety, and defaced by obscene carvings. Each carried an overstuffed backpack or shoulder bag. Lewt's was a battered black duffel half as tall as he was, with the words OKLAHOMA STATE COWBOYS on the side. Like the others, he kept it with him at all times.

Most of the time, Tahlik and Quell rode up front, next to Rafe. They said little to nothing, pedaling in silence. Lewt, on the other hand, was more sociable and kept dropping back to chat with the girls in the caravan.

Many of them were receptive to his playful tone and rough good looks. He often bicycled next to Rhea, bending close to say things that made her giggle. Asha would ride near him, too, trying to draw his attention. Later that afternoon, when the townspeople encountered a break in the road and had to carry everything over by hand, he went out of his way to help the girls, talking to them the whole time. The only females he ignored were Skar and Michal, barely glancing at either of them. As for Esther, she did her best to avoid him.

Throughout, Caleb kept watch over Lewt. Once or twice, he attempted to make eye contact, which Lewt avoided. In fact, he noticed that the boy had nothing to do with any of the males, even after the caravan stopped for the night.

Since there had been no exits for miles, Rafe ordered everyone to pull their wagons under the shelter of an overpass and set up camp on the concrete shoulders that tilted upward at a steep angle. Yet after dinner, Lewt and his companions once again moved off by themselves, setting up their own camp near an abandoned truck farther down the road.

Esther had set up their sleeping bags against one of the massive pillars that held up the overpass. It wasn't much, but it afforded her family at least a modicum of privacy.

Around her were the rest of the townspeople, buried in piles of quilts and blankets. Only an occasional snore or muffled exclamation broke the silence. To her right, Kai had finally nodded off. But she could tell that next to her, Caleb lay wide awake.

Esther couldn't sleep, either. She flopped over for the hundredth time, her hip bones pressing against the hard road. Then she shifted to be nearer to Caleb. She strained to see his features in the dark, then ran one finger, light as a feather, along his profile. When she pressed forward to kiss his neck, he turned to her.

"Maybe this will help," he whispered with a smile.

Esther moved into his arms. It was risky, she knew, with so many people close by. Yet it had been so long, neither could control themselves any longer. It became a challenge, an oddly exciting one, not to be detected by the others.

When it was over, they lay drenched in sweat, their fingers intertwined.

"I love you," Esther whispered.

"I love you, too." But Esther could tell he was thinking of something else.

"What is it?" But she knew: It was the strangers. She didn't trust them, either.

After a moment, Caleb sat up and pulled on his jeans. "I'll be right back."

Walking with care, Caleb picked his way down the steep

ramp filled with slumbering bodies and then along the highway. The three strangers were huddled close together around a small campfire, too engrossed in whatever they were doing to look up. But when Caleb stepped on a shard of broken plastic, Lewt grabbed a lit branch and swung it upward to cast light down the road.

When he saw it was Caleb, he hesitated, then smiled.

"What can we do for you?" His voice sounded too casual. "Abel, was that the name?" There was something around Lewt's mouth, which he wiped off on his sleeve. Behind him, Caleb noticed the other boys trying to cover something on the ground.

"Caleb."

"Right . . . you're the one with Esther. What can we do for you?"

"I want to know what you're up to."

"We're sleeping. What's it look like?"

Tahlik snickered and even Quell gave a bearlike rumble, which seemed to indicate amusement. Caleb kept his voice steady.

"Where'd you get it?" he asked.

"Get what?"

"What you're eating. You can't smell it from down the road, but I can now."

Lewt stared at Caleb, the bonfire throwing flickering shadows across his face. Then he shrugged and dropped the branch back into the fire. The flames blazed up, revealing platters of cooked beans and flatbread.

"So you caught us," Lewt said. "Congratulations."

"When did you steal it? Just now, when everybody was asleep?"

Lewt chuckled, then shook his head, still smiling. "Now that hurts my feelings," he drawled. "We didn't steal this. Did we, boys?" The other two murmured a negative. "It may surprise you to hear it, but some folks are happy to share. Like the pretty gal whose mind ain't right? We saved her life, so she wanted to give us extra. And Rhea—turns out her partner died in an earthquake, poor thing, so she's a little lonely. Other gals felt the same way." He licked his lips, which glistened with saliva. "Why, you might even say, they feel like they *owed* us."

Caleb's heart had begun to pound. His old impulse was returning, that dangerous, violent part of himself he had sworn off for good; it was starting to fill his veins and pulse through his body like cold fire. His fingers twitched at his side, reaching for the weapon he no longer carried.

With a shudder, Caleb closed his eyes and took a deep breath. Slowly, he forced his hand to relax.

"This is the last night," he said.

"Why? You going somewhere?" Lewt's tone was insolent and the others laughed.

Caleb met his eyes. "The last night it happens."

Lewt smiled, yet seemed unnerved. He spread his hands, indicating the array of food, and this time, he sounded sincere.

"I got a better idea. Why don't you just help yourself?" he said in a soft voice. "Not just tonight. Any time we get some, you get some, too. Who would ever know?"

Caleb said nothing, and under his unblinking gaze, Lewt's smile faltered and then died. "All right," he muttered as he glanced away. "You made your point."

Esther was waiting by the time Caleb returned. "Everything okay?" she whispered.

He nodded and kissed her on the forehead as he slipped beneath their shared blanket.

"Try to sleep," he said.

In the darkness, Esther curled close to him, draping one arm across his chest as if in protection. Within moments, the soft and even sound of her breathing filled the air.

But Caleb was unable to sleep, for every time he closed his eyes, all he could see was Lewt's leering face. Instead, he stared up at the night sky and counted stars until, one by one, they were scrubbed out by the light of a new day.

The next morning was even more suffocating than usual. Esther could feel the heat of the road beneath her sneakers, and far away, waves of air danced on the horizon like a field of tall grass.

She trudged behind her wagon and paused to run her fingers through her spiky hair, trying to catch a breeze. She and Skar were taking turns on the bicycle that pulled the wagon; one would walk behind, pushing it when needed.

In front of them was Rafe's opulent wagon. It moved slowly; the load was clearly too much for the boy pedaling its bicycle, who struggled to keep it moving. As she and Skar drew alongside, Esther wondered why no one was helping push it from behind. She glanced inside and was startled to see Lewt.

He was leaning back, propped up on his elbows, the book of maps in front of him. When they passed, it seemed Joseph noticed him, too. He opened the tarp and leaned out to speak to him.

"Excuse me," he called. "Are you sure we're heading the right way?"

Lewt, who had been dozing off, cocked an eye open. "Sorry?"

"It seems we're heading west." Joseph's voice quavered; it cost him to talk to the stranger like this. "But if I could just look at my maps, I'm sure I could—"

"Hush," Esther said.

"No, let him talk." Lewt spoke deliberately. "I just wanted to see if your maps match with our directions. And they do."

"That's fine," Joseph said. He seemed frightened by the boy's attention. "Never mind." Then he disappeared behind the tarp.

Lewt settled again into the shade of his vehicle. "You a good friend to that boy, pretty. *Esther*, I mean," he said hastily when he saw the flash of anger in her eyes. "You wanted to save him embarrassment. Or worse. That speaks good of you." He paused, then lowered his voice. "I bet you a good friend to your partner, too."

His tone was suggestive. Esther ignored it and kept her eyes ahead, although her cheeks flushed. He continued speaking, keeping his voice soft and low so no one else could hear.

"I could use a friend like you. All three of us could. I think maybe you got enough friendship in you to go around."

Again, Esther said nothing but threw her weight behind the wagon, pushing it onward. "Hey . . . everything okay?" Skar called from the front.

"I'm fine," Esther replied, her throat tight. To her relief, they had passed Rafe's wagon by now and within moments pulled even farther ahead. Yet she imagined she could feel Lewt's gaze, boring into her from behind.

Esther managed to avoid Lewt for the rest of the day. By the time the sun began to drop in the sky, she saw that he was on his bicycle and riding in front of the caravan with Rafe. Without drawing attention to herself, she fell back so she was well out of his view.

"Getting late," commented Rafe. He had bicycled a great deal that day and had the sore legs to prove it. The caravan was approaching an exit and he raised his arm, ready to pull everyone over for the night. But Lewt shook his head.

"We're near that shortcut I mentioned," he said. "Why don't we get a start on it before we break? It's a lot more protected than we are here."

Rafe hesitated, then agreed. By now, he had no idea where they were; there was no choice but to trust Lewt.

Time, he knew, was of the essence. Lewt and his boys, especially Quell, ate a shocking amount. They winked at the food restrictions and helped themselves to seconds, especially when Caleb wasn't around. Rafe was aware of this, yet felt helpless to enforce the rules; he needed Lewt's directions too much. As a result, even with strict rationing for the rest of them, their stores of food and water were dangerously low and getting lower.

Taking any shortcut that would trim a day or two off their journey would be well worth it, Rafe decided. So he dropped his hand and let the caravan continue. It wasn't until the sun brushed the horizon that they finally reached the exit Lewt spoke of.

"That way," Lewt said, indicating an off-ramp.

The caravan swung its way up the ramp and around a wide circle, where it joined with a smaller road. By now, Joseph had peeked his head from the tarp again.

"Where are we headed?" he asked.

"They say it's a shortcut," Esther replied. She too was wary.

The caravan now found itself on a narrow, two-lane road that cut its way through a darkening forest. No one spoke; everyone was too exhausted, and it was a difficult path to navigate, badly damaged by earthquake and deeply pitted and split. Still, they continued.

Skar caught up with Esther. "Why aren't we stopping for the night?" she asked in a low voice. Esther shook her head. She didn't know, either. But up ahead, Lewt was waving everyone on, pointing them toward a turn in the road.

"There's a place to rest up ahead," he called. His voice was faint but it carried well in the windless dusk. "We just about there."

Esther saw that the road they turned onto was no more than a street, narrow and heavily wooded on both sides. Next to her, Skar stumbled on a fallen branch and Esther grabbed her by the arm to keep her from falling. Lewt ordered them to take one turn, then another.

Eventually, they all came to a stop. They couldn't help it;

there was simply no way to proceed.

They faced an immovable barrier, a wall of a fallen bridge, which blocked any forward motion. On either side, they were hemmed in by the forest and its dense undergrowth. The travelers were crushed together, wagons overlapping, bicycles pushed into others. There was general confusion as people milled around, looking to Lewt for an explanation. But he had disappeared from his position at the head of the caravan. Esther looked for Caleb but couldn't find him in the squall of others, in the growing darkness.

"Look," someone said, pointing.

Several townspeople turned. They saw something too bizarre to comprehend.

Lewt, Tahlik, and Quell stood at the back of the group, straddling their bicycles at the open mouth of the road. The smallest held a loaded and cocked hunting slingshot at eye level. The largest carried a retractable steel club, which he tapped against an open palm. And Lewt gripped the strangest object of all, an item made of wood and steel, with a long, narrow muzzle.

"If you do what we say, no one gets hurt," Lewt said. His attempts at charm were over; his voice was cold and business-like. "Pass up any weapons you got."

The crowd murmured as, one by one, they began to understand what was happening. They had walked willingly into a literal enclosure, boxed in on all sides; there was no way to escape.

Asha turned to Eli. "What's going on?" she asked in a

plaintive voice. "What're my friends doing?"

"Never mind," he said, his voice dead.

Tahlik had lit a torch, which he held high. Now he moved among the townspeople, collecting items that he handed off to Quell. More than a few resisted. One of them, a sixteen-year-old boy, exchanged sharp words with Tahlik and shoved him. As Tahlik staggered backward, Quell stepped forward with surprising speed and hit the boy, hard, on the skull. As he sank to his knees, two others jumped on the giant and took hold of his arms, as another attempted to seize his club.

In one swift movement, Lewt raised the weapon to his eye and fired. The explosion stunned everyone, who reeled backward in terror. Esther could hear Kai start to wail from the wagon where he lay; and as an unfamiliar acrid smell filled the air, someone else screamed. The boy who had tried to take Quell's weapon lay on his side, his legs jerking. The gaping wound in his chest pulsated black as his life bled out of him.

"Now do as you're told!" Lewt yelled. "I ain't playing!"

After that, everyone handed over their weapons: slingshots, knives, clubs. Skar was the last to relinquish her bow and arrow. Yet even as Quell yanked them from her hands, she spat on the ground at his feet.

"Now hand over whatever food and water you got, too," Lewt said. Silas was already slipping a bottle out of the water wagon and attempting to conceal it in his robes. But without turning around, Lewt seemed to understand what was happening.

"If you don't put that back," he said, "you ain't gonna have a mouth to drink it with."

Silas froze. Then he returned what he had lifted. Around him, the townspeople were already unloading their supplies, passing along the remaining water hand over hand, as well as bags of beans, salt, coffee, and sugar. As they placed everything into a single wagon, Quell moved along the line, supervising. Tahlik and Lewt stayed a few feet away, keeping an eye on the others with their weapons cocked.

"Please . . . don't leave us with nothing!" Rhea's voice rose shrill above the silence. But no one answered her plea.

After a final check of the remaining wagons, Lewt seemed satisfied that there was nothing left to take. Turning to Quell, he handed him his rifle.

"Keep an eye on them," Lewt said. Then he nodded to Caleb, Rafe, and Eli. "You three. Drive this and two extra bicycles to the main road and wait for us. And if you try anything, you'll regret it."

None of them moved until Quell pointed his weapon at them. Rafe was trembling, his eyes filled with tears. With an unreadable expression, Caleb walked to the bicycle attached to the wagon, the heaviest and most difficult to power. After a single glance at Esther, he maneuvered the vehicle until it had turned around. Then he took off down the dark road. Eli and Rafe chose two other bicycles, and they, too, were soon gone.

Lewt flashed his wolfish grin. He then addressed his partners. "I'll meet you up at the road in five minutes. I got some business to take care of."

Lewt lit a torch and lifted it high. In the flickering light, the people of Prin looked like a sea of drawn faces, gaping and

pop-eyed with fear. He searched through them until he found
the one he wanted.

Esther.

When he saw her, his smile widened.

"You," he said. "Come with me."

SIX

ESTHER RECOILED.

Next to her, Skar drew a sharp breath and touched her arm. Esther understood her silent question as if she had spoken it aloud: *Should we fight back?* But she saw Quell pivot the weapon their way and had a terrible presentiment of what would happen if they did. She only had time to shake her head, once. Then Lewt grabbed her wrist and pulled her forward.

He was surprisingly strong and his grip was like a vise. He dragged her into the forest, not waiting for her as she stumbled over tree roots and through piles of dead leaves. They walked this way for several minutes, his lit torch throwing shadows deep into the woods. Soon they were alone, totally surrounded by lifeless trees. There, Lewt released her so quickly that she tripped and fell to one knee.

"You'll leave with us," he said.

At first, Esther thought she had misheard. "What?"

"Don't make me force you. There ain't nothing for you here and you know it. You ain't weak and stupid like them other girls. I can tell just by looking at you."

"I don't care what you think of me. I'm not coming with you." Dazed, she got to her feet, rubbing her wrist where he had hurt her. "Now I got a baby that needs looking after."

But before she could take one step, he grabbed her by the wrist again and yanked her around, hard. "We can take it with us. There's gonna be plenty for us all in Mundreel. But you can only get there with me. Your boy Caleb's all talk. I ain't."

There was something to his voice that Esther couldn't understand, something she hadn't detected before. Lewt spoke with a peculiar earnestness; *he was*, she realized, *being as sincere as he knew how.* And as this confusing thought dawned on her, he pushed his face forward to kiss her.

"There's something about you," he said.

She jerked away in time, his stubbled chin scraping her cheek; with a wave of disgust, she caught a whiff of a body that stank of sweat and breath that reeked of decay. Now, a strange wounded expression crossed his face. Angered, he yanked her back, this time grabbing her by the hair. He stabbed the end of his torch into the ground to hold it and pulled her close.

"I don't mind fight in a girl," he whispered, "as long as she don't mean it."

Esther reached down and grabbed his thumb. She pulled it backward as hard as she could, digging her nails into his palm. Lewt screamed and let go with a curse. He stood there for a second, wincing and rubbing his hand. Then he started toward her again, furious this time.

Esther turned to run, but caught her foot on a tree root. And as she fell, before she had even hit the ground, she could feel Lewt on top of her, clawing at her clothing.

After Caleb brought the wagon to the highway, he had to wait for the others. When Rafe showed up, he refused to make eye contact; Caleb knew the boy was still stunned and abashed by the betrayal. But Eli jumped off his bicycle, stumbling in his haste.

"As I was leaving—" he began. He was wheezing with exertion. "He's got Esther. I think he was taking her to the woods."

In a flash, Caleb understood why Lewt had sent him away. He remembered how the boy had looked at all females, Esther in particular, and he cursed himself for not suspecting this. Without a word, he seized the discarded bicycle, even as Eli tried to grab his arm.

"They got weapons. Are you sure you—"

"Yes."

"Let me help."

"I don't need it." Caleb broke away and took off.

Caleb was one against three, and unarmed. If he had stopped

to think, he would have admitted he needed all the backup he could get. But he was beyond reason.

Caleb rode fast back to the road. Well before he approached Quell, Tahlik, and the others, he leaped off his bicycle and headed into the woods on foot. He ran blind, his arms held up to prevent branches from whipping him in the face. Yet he didn't have far to go before he saw the flickering of a torch in the distance.

In a circle of light, Caleb saw Esther on the ground, struggling beneath Lewt. He was torn by a surge of emotions more powerful than any storm.

Caleb had seen what terrible things violence could do not only to its victims, but the perpetrator as well. Yet he had not felt this kind of murderous hatred since his first partner, Miri, had been killed and his son kidnapped. If he had had his weapon, he would have reached for it now.

"Let her go," he said.

Lewt started at the sound of Caleb's voice. He struggled to his feet, yanking Esther up with him, and turned to face Caleb with a smile.

"Why? She wants to come with me. She just playing."

"I said, let her go."

Lewt reached under his robes and into a back pocket. His hand emerged holding a small knife with a jagged blade. With a single move, he sliced off the red partnering tie from Esther's wrist. She gasped as it fluttered to the ground.

"She ain't yours no more," said Lewt. "She free for the taking." When it became clear that Caleb wasn't going to do anything, his smile widened. "Okay then," he drawled. "Guess I might as well help myself."

He brought the knife to the bottom of Esther's sweatshirt. He made to slice it up the middle. At the first glimpse of Esther's pale stomach, Lewt stopped cutting.

The knife had vanished from his hand, knocked out of his grip by Caleb's foot.

Lewt looked up, surprised, just as Caleb jammed a knee into his groin. The boy doubled over, grunting in agony. When he raised his head, Caleb drove his elbow into Lewt's mouth, and the woods echoed with the crack of breaking teeth.

Lewt fell forward, his hands to his bloody mouth. Caleb let him lie there only an instant before pulling him up by the tattered collar of his shirt. He was acting blindly, obeying the instinct he had tried in vain to bury. Now it was bursting up from someplace deep, unearthed by rage.

He couldn't deny it: the feeling was exhilarating. He couldn't have stopped if he had wanted to.

Lewt was nearly unconscious, his mouth oozing blood. With seemingly superhuman strength, Caleb hoisted him with one hand. With the other, he bent to retrieve the knife. He brought the blade to Lewt's throat and pressed it hard against the lump that bobbed there as the boy swallowed.

"Please," Lewt said, spitting a few drops of blood onto Caleb's face. Instead of begging, he tried to bargain. "You can come with us, too."

At this, Caleb felt contempt mix with his fury. Lewt had not only learned nothing, he was offering one more bribe—the kind of deal he himself would welcome. That meant he still believed Caleb was like him—and the thought of it made Caleb want to destroy him.

"Wait," Esther shouted, but her voice sounded faint, as if underwater.

Then Caleb noticed someone else was in the clearing with them.

A figure was standing just past Lewt. Although it was thrown into deep shadows by the flickering torch, Caleb would have recognized him anywhere.

It was his dead brother.

It was Levi, whose rage, cruelty, and greed had come so close to destroying Caleb and everyone he loved. Levi now stared at Caleb, his familiar cold smile playing at the corners of his mouth.

"Finish him," Levi said simply.

Then his brother's ghost vanished into the night.

Caleb tightened his grasp on the knife. It would be so simple to press it into the pale, soft flesh and slash sideways. And it would feel so right.

Yet he stopped. And as he did, he felt his anger subside.

He had done what needed to be done: He had saved Esther. He would not become like Levi; he would not drown in his own hatred ever again. He released Lewt, who dropped to his knees. Then he tossed aside the blade as if it burned his flesh.

"Get away from here," Caleb whispered. "All three of you. And leave what you stole."

Still at a crouch, Lewt nodded.

Caleb turned away. He was so tired, his limbs felt like lead, and there was a strange roaring sound in the distance, something approaching that he couldn't quite place. Yet he felt free. And he had won. He turned to Esther with a smile, but for some reason, she was staring at something behind him.

Her face was white with shock. She was trying to say something, but the roaring sound had grown so loud, he couldn't make out the words.

"Watch out!" she screamed.

It was too late.

Caleb felt time expand to infinity as the object struck him, as the white-hot blade entered his back and separated muscle from bone. His legs turned to liquid, to quicksilver. He took another step, then fell face forward, onto the dirt.

By now, the roaring sound was overwhelming. Beyond it, he was distantly aware of someone kneeling above him, someone who seemed to be saying his name.

It was Esther. Esther, whom he loved. Esther with her dark, spiky hair. Esther of the sudden giggle, the stubborn nature, the generous heart. She was gripping the knife now, pulling it out, but it all seemed so far away, miles and miles. The sound was so loud now, it was like a tornado.

And that's when Caleb realized what it was.

It was the sound of blood. It was the sound of his heart. It was the sound of his life slipping away, forever.

"Caleb," Esther whispered.

Then she was screaming it.

* * *

Eli saw someone emerge from the woods.

Lewt was pushing the discarded bicycle. He moved slowly, as if every movement hurt him. By the loaded wagon, Tahlik and Quell stood on guard, the strange weapon pointed in Eli's face.

Eli noticed that Lewt was injured, his face bloody. He also noticed that he was alone.

"Where's Caleb?" Eli shouted.

Lewt looked at him, dazed, his eyes hooded and filled with hatred. "Where he belongs," he said. Then he turned to his boys. "Let's get out of here."

Eli stepped forward, but Lewt slapped him hard across the face, nearly knocking him down. His tone was a warning, almost compassionate. "You'll get worse if you don't watch it." Quell raised his rifle and a moment later, the boy felt the butt of it slam into his back, sending him to the ground in a spasm of pain.

Rafe was already stepping over him to reach Lewt, his voice eager.

"Take me with you," he begged.

Lewt laughed, although the sound had no mirth in it. "Why? You ain't got no idea where you going. You never did."

"Because—" Rafe flailed for an answer. "Because you ain't in no shape to ride. You stay in the wagon and I'll drive you. The others got to pedal on their own."

Lewt considered it and was surprised to find it made sense.

"I can do other things, too," Rafe went on in a rush. He didn't intend to die with the others. "I can cook, I can clean.

Whatever you want me to do."

"All right," Lewt growled. "On one condition."

"Anything."

"You don't talk unless I talk to you first."

"Okay," Rafe said. "Yes. Of course."

"Now let's go."

"Ain't you bringing the girl?" Tahlik asked.

Lewt paused. "She ain't worth the trouble," he spat.

The four boys—Lewt, Quell, Tahlik, and Rafe—climbed onto their vehicles. Quell kept the weapon pointed at Eli even as they left, taking everything with them.

After a while, there were no sounds except for their wheels bumping on stone and gravel.

Eli thought that, in the distance, he could hear a girl scream.

PART TWO

PART TWO

SEVEN

By MOONLIGHT, SKAR STOOD BY THE SIDE OF THE ROAD, TESTING THE
low-hanging branches of an oak tree. She did her best to focus
on what she was doing and not pay attention to the chaos that
was raging around her.

At first, the townspeople had trouble understanding what
had happened. Then the shock of the news spread among them
like fire through a dry field, leaving panic and confusion in its
wake. Yet it was only after Lewt and his boys disappeared with
Rafe that the full extent of their predicament sank in.

The outlaws had taken nearly everything of worth: not
only their best wagon and bicycles, but also their food, water,

weapons, and tools. Now torches flickered and cast deep shadows into the night as people ransacked the remaining vehicles in a blind and desperate panic, clawing for anything of value. Fistfights erupted as enraged accusations filled the air. Someone set fire to one of the wagons, and the night was suffused with heat, acrid smoke, and pulsating orange light. Pieces of soot as big as leaves wafted across the sky as a child wailed, unattended, over the sound of popping embers and smashing glass.

Like everyone, Skar was badly shaken by the murder. She had liked and admired Caleb, who was a good and brave person, someone who had always treated her fairly and with respect. She would miss him. She also had a premonition of how devastating his death would be for Esther, who had insisted on burying him herself. At the moment, Skar didn't even know where her friend was. Yet that was a relief: Esther was out of harm's way, far from the madness that had gripped the people of Prin.

In the meantime, the variant girl had something else on her mind that was even more pressing.

For the first time since she could walk, Skar found herself without a weapon or tool of any sort. Quell had taken her bow and arrow, and she had nothing to replace it with, no throwing stick or club, not even a paltry kitchen knife. While senseless battles raged around her and people fought over broken firebowls and morsels of food, she alone realized that staying alive meant finding or making something with which she could hunt and protect herself.

At the moment, it was more important than even food or water.

Skar broke off a branch that seemed the sturdiest and examined it. Then she tested its jagged end, pressing it into her palm to see if it might be sharp enough to be used as a spear. But even as she wondered how she might be able to hone it further, the point bent and then snapped. Skar, who was accustomed to carbon-core arrows sheathed in metal and hunting knives with steel blades, tossed it aside in disgust.

Wood was clearly useless. Until she could find a real weapon, she would have to rig a standby out of something man-made and sturdy: perhaps a piece of aluminum, fiberglass, even plastic.

But at the moment, she did not dare approach the wagons.

By now, the townspeople had torn apart some of the vehicles in their search for goods. Splintered boards were tossed onto the fire, twisted bicycle gears and broken shafts lay scattered in the road, and still the boys and girls of Prin fought over what wasn't there. When a half-empty bottle of water was discovered beneath a tarp, the boy who found it was pummeled almost to death by three others. In the commotion, no one noticed when someone trampled on the plastic container, cracking it open and spilling its contents. There was a raw desperation in the air that could only be spent through violence and anarchy.

Skar couldn't help but feel both sickened and uneasy. Her own people had often faced hardship and deprivation; but they had never resorted to lawlessness and pointless fighting among themselves. *It was like watching wild dogs tear themselves apart,* she thought, *so crazed by the smell of their own blood that they thought the other was the enemy.* For the first time, she wondered if she had been wise in fleeing the variant camp.

Only then did she notice that something had fallen in the dust by her feet. She bent to pick it up. It was a broken bicycle wheel, its rim badly bent. Several of the metal spokes had sprung free from the hub, but they were relatively straight and, as Skar discovered, sharp-tipped. She wondered if they could somehow be turned into slender spears or even arrows. As she turned the object over in her hands, mulling its possibilities, she became aware of the silence around her.

She looked up and saw that three boys were standing still nearby, staring at her. Their robes were torn and muddy, and their eyes glittered in faces that were bleeding and blackened with soot and sweat. One of them held a flaming torch, which he jabbed in her direction.

"What's that you got?" said the largest one. His voice was hoarse from shouting.

Wary, Skar showed him the broken wheel. "It's nothing. It's worthless. I thought I could use it to make—"

Another boy grabbed the object from her hands.

"Worthless?" he jeered, mimicking her. Two others had joined the group, and the five now circled her, moving in close. "Who says this is worthless?"

"You trying to steal, mutant?"

"Yeah, mutant. What else you got there?"

"You hiding anything under that dress?"

Skar was confused. These were the same people she had traveled with and lived among for many days; she had toiled and eaten and slept alongside them. She had even helped feed them, sharing what she had been able to hunt. Still, she was not surprised. Ever since she joined the people of Prin, she had always sensed that should the situation ever deteriorate, this might happen. When it came to living among the norms, it seemed she had always been on borrowed time.

The largest boy reached to grab her by the tunic, but Skar was able to duck away. She saw a gap in the crowd and made to dart through it; she was not much of a fighter, but if she could break clear, she knew she could outrun anyone alive. But Skar didn't notice the one behind her who lashed out a foot, tripping her. As she pitched forward, she felt for the first time a flash of genuine fear. She twisted onto her back, one arm up to defend herself. But before anyone could move toward her, they were interrupted by a clear, loud voice.

"Leave her alone!"

Skar looked up, and so did the others. To her shock, she saw that the loner, Michal, stood there, veiled as always, with just a piece of her golden hair snaking from the side of her hood. Although she seemed tiny compared to the others, she stood straight and defiant, her fists clenched by her sides.

For a moment, the boys hesitated. Then one of them laughed. It was an ugly and brutish sound, and the noise seemed to ripple around the ring.

"Look who's talking to us."

"It's the whore, sticking up for the freak."

As Skar got to her feet, one of the boys shoved Michal into her, hard, as if to knock them both down; and again there was mocking laughter. But the girl regained her footing and Skar moved next to her. Before, Skar had barely spoken a word to Michal; now, she could only marvel at her bravery and shoot her a look of gratitude.

Around them, Skar sensed a shift in the dynamics. Although every muscle in her body was tensed and ready to flee, she understood there was now an unspoken game of dare going on. If either girl flinched or made a single move, if they panicked or attempted to run, the entire pack would descend on them like wolves.

Skar knew she stood a good chance of getting away, at least deep enough into the dark woods that they could not follow her. But from a glance, she guessed that Michal was no runner; she wouldn't stand a chance. So Skar kept still, holding her ground with Michal as the others stared at them.

Several long seconds passed. Then the largest boy laughed again, although this time it was different. It was a dismissive sound, one of disgust, and as he made an abrupt gesture and turned to go, the mood was broken.

"Ain't worth the effort," the boy was saying to the others. "Let's just go."

A look of confusion passed among the boys. "Go? Go where?" one of them asked.

"Back," the first boy said. "To Prin."

Skar was so relieved, it took her a few moments to wonder if she had heard correctly. The idea made no sense. If the towns-people didn't have enough supplies to last them the night, how could they survive the long journey home? And even if by some miracle they made it back, what did they hope to find there?

Yet to her disbelief, the other townspeople embraced the suggestion. Within a few minutes, a vote was held, and most of those who remained raised their hands, agreeing to head home to Prin. They would leave at once.

Skar noted those who kept their hands down. There were Michal and herself, as well as Joseph, Asha, and, of course, the baby, Kai. To her surprise, Rhea chose to stay. "I got no one to go back to," the girl said, her voice bitter. The one called Silas opted to remain as well, his face drawn and pale. Esther had still not returned, but Skar knew that she would never agree to such a suicidal plan.

As for Eli, he attempted to talk sense to those who were leaving, even as they were reattaching the remaining wagons to their bicycle shafts.

"At least wait until morning," he kept saying.

But no one listened to him; a few even shoved him aside. It was as if Lewt and his murderous crew still haunted the dark woods surrounding them: Returning to the open road with all of its dangers was clearly less frightening than spending the night there. Before long, all of the townspeople had either remounted their vehicles or had begun trudging up the steep road, helping to push the wagons. They took what little of value had been left, with only four bicycles in bad repair and worthless trash for those who remained.

Eli followed them to the main road and could only watch as they rode away into the darkness. Then he shook his head in disgust.

He was still reeling from Caleb's murder. *If only he had insisted on helping,* Eli thought now, *or ignored Caleb and just gone with him, he could have prevented it.* From the beginning, Lewt had sized him up and known not to take him seriously. Perhaps he sensed that Eli had always been weak. Maybe he had been that way since birth. Eli looked down and kicked the dirt, hard.

"What happened?" asked a voice close by.

It was Asha, her face pale in the moonlight, who stood beside him, twisting her hands together. Clearly, she had witnessed everything: the townspeople fighting among themselves and then taking off. Yet it made no sense to her, and her brow was furrowed in bewilderment and concern.

Eli felt a flare of exasperation. "What do you *think* happened?"

"I don't know." She glanced at the ones who were left, the small and pathetic band of people lit by the dying fire, and her features crumpled. "I don't *know.*"

Eli hesitated, then relented. He put his arm around Asha's shoulder and was startled when she clung to him, gripping his robes and burrowing her face in his chest like a child, a baby.

But of course, that was what she was, really.

Asha was helpless. She needed someone to take care of her, to cherish and protect her as if she were a newborn bird that had fallen from its nest. With a start, Eli realized he could be that person, Asha's protector.

Her hero, even.

"Don't be afraid," he said into her hair. "I'll take care of you."

As he held her, his shame began to lift. He would have to rise to the occasion, he knew: He had no choice.

"You will?"

"I promise."

Dawn broke.

A lone figure in a red hoodie lay curled on its side in a small clearing, motionless on a patch of fresh dirt. The earth was marked with thousands of claw marks.

As the previous evening had deepened into night and a sliver of moon rose high overhead before disappearing, a single set of hands had raked across the hard ground, over and over again. For hours, they dug deep into the packed red soil that lay underneath. Afterward, they scraped the mountain of loose soil and rocks into place, handful by handful. Then they pressed everything down hard to prevent the ground from sinking when it began to settle.

Throughout, Esther's eyes remained blank and unseeing. Her vision was directed inward, focused on images that kept playing in her mind over and over again.

Caleb, turning to her. Behind him, Lewt scrambling to snatch up the blade from where it had fallen, the metal glinting as it sliced through the air. Caleb's face as he staggered, then fell.

Throughout the long night, Esther had not cried or uttered a sound. Nor had she taken a rest, despite the fact that most of her nails had been torn away and her dirt-caked hands were now raw and sticky with her own blood. If she could have done so, Esther would have kept digging for days; she would not have stopped until she had worn away not just her fingers but her hands and arms and body, not ceasing until she herself was somehow erased and at one with the earth and what lay beneath it.

She had not let anyone approach, once Eli had carried and lain the body by her. She alone had prepared it for burial. With stony face, she had closed Caleb's eyes and smoothed his features, combed his hair with her fingers. Because she had no water, she took off her hoodie and wiped him with that, not caring that it grew black and crusted with his blood. Afterward, she slipped the stained garment back over her head. Finally, she dug his grave and buried him in it.

Now, even as the first rays of sunlight warmed her back, she turned her face to the soil, breathing in its overpowering scent. It would not have meant anything if the entire world were to vanish. Her mind was still reeling to grasp the impossible:

Caleb was dead.

Esther would never see her beloved partner again, never hear his voice, or feel the comforting warmth of his body when she awoke in the middle of the night, confused and afraid.

And she would never be able to ask for his forgiveness.

Esther thought of all the times she had argued with him, when she refused to give in or apologize out of either pride or stubbornness, and guilt and anguish pierced her heart.

With her usual recklessness, Esther had assumed Caleb would always be there for her, just as she would always be there for him. She had taken his love for granted, as if it were an eternal thing, as constant and unremarkable as the air she breathed. Now, she understood how foolish she had been, not to remember that life was nothing more than a thread that could be snipped by a momentary glint of metal. The two of them had shared only a few precious months; and she had wasted so much of it feeling hurt, picking fights, and bickering over trifles.

If she had known, Esther would have lived her life so differently.

But of course, now it was too late.

Joseph made his way through the dense underbrush with difficulty.

Neither he nor his cat, Stumpy, had ever been in the woods before. Yet while she seemed to find it fascinating, sniffing at rotted tree stumps and mushrooms, he was filled with crippling anxiety.

Still, he continued. Because of Esther.

After Caleb had been killed and the bad ones had fled, he had gone to his friend and tried to comfort her because she seemed so sad. But Esther had rebuffed his overtures, as well as those of Skar and the others. Joseph wasn't good at reading emotions. Still, he knew what it felt like to want to be left alone and so, respecting her feelings, he withdrew. But now, it was well into the next morning, and Esther was nowhere to be found.

It was agreed that Joseph, Skar, and Eli should spread out and check through the forest for any sight of her. Yet there was no trace of Esther anywhere, either by the grave or in the surrounding area.

Ahead of him, the trees seemed to thin to some sort of clearing, and from that direction Joseph could detect a faint but steady thrumming sound. Stumpy had been exploring and now her tail lifted in interest as she trotted toward it. Also curious, Joseph followed her as the noise grew louder. He emerged on the bank of a river and cowered in panic even as his cat threaded her way down to the rushing waters.

"Stumpy!" he called. "Get away from there."

He knew animals were immune to the waterborne disease and that she could drink without problem. Still, he didn't like the possibility of his cat getting her paws wet; she often slept on his chest. And if she fell in, he had no idea how he'd be able to retrieve her. He was so busy trying to coax the animal from the steep banks that at first he didn't notice what she was looking at.

A girl was standing still on a large, flat rock in the middle of the stream. Her eyes were shut and her face lifted to the sun. On both sides, the deadly waters rushed and gurgled past, splashing so close to her feet that Joseph flinched.

"Esther!"

Confused, Joseph noticed the smaller rocks she had most likely stepped on to get to where she was, but none of it made any sense to him.

"Don't move!" he called. "It's very dangerous where you are!"

At that, Esther opened her eyes. Then as Joseph's confusion and panic mounted, she lifted her arms from her sides and bent her knees.

It looked like she was going to jump into the water. But that was impossible.

At the moment his mind struggled to make sense of what he saw, Joseph noticed something equally bizarre going on a few yards away, on the opposite bank. Out of the brown and gray of the January landscape stepped Skar. She moved in a way that reminded Joseph of a cat, with deadly intensity and focus.

Before Joseph could speak, everything seemed to happen at once.

Esther sprang toward the water at the same instant Skar launched herself from the shore, tackling her. They landed, hard, on the flat rock. Esther was fighting, trying to claw her friend in the face as she struggled to break free. But the variant girl was stronger and was soon able to subdue Esther, twisting one of her arms behind her back and jerking it upward between her shoulders.

Skar seemed to be saying something to Esther, something that Joseph couldn't hear. Then, without loosening her grip, Skar yanked her friend to her feet. She forced Esther to walk ahead of her on the smaller rocks that led to dry land. Once they reached the shore, she released Esther's arm, but still kept secure hold of her wrist.

Throughout, Joseph watched in astonishment.

Although he was confused, he understood that somehow Esther had been in danger and that Skar had saved her. Yet there was still no explanation for why Esther had been standing in the middle of the river in the first place. No one would put herself at such risk on purpose, would she? *Not unless*, Joseph realized with sudden clarity, *she was sick or confused.*

They would have to watch over her, he thought, *until she got better.* It was an odd and uncomfortable idea, for he knew he had always depended on her. He could not help hoping she would get better soon.

And as he was mulling over these disturbing thoughts, he heard something odd from the other side.

For the first time since Caleb had been killed, Esther was crying.

Alone, Skar made her way back through the woods.

She had spent much time tending to Esther. The first thing she did was send Joseph to fetch a clean cloth, which she used to wipe and bandage her hands. Then, after making certain Esther did nothing else to hurt herself, Skar merely allowed her to cry, cradling her in her lap and stroking her head until her friend fell asleep.

Skar knew that tears indicated that healing had begun; still, she didn't underestimate the depth of Esther's anguish. Crying was no guarantee that her friend would not try to kill herself again. But at least for now, Esther was asleep, and Skar knew she was needed at the makeshift camp to attempt to find food and water for herself and the others. After much trial and error, she had cobbled together a crude weapon: a throwing stick that could launch one of the bicycle spokes she had sharpened. So she left Esther alone with Joseph, who fluttered about, wringing his hands with anxiety and concern.

Skar was approaching the camp when a movement in the underbrush made her freeze. She relaxed when she saw it was a person in white, kneeling behind a tree, apart from the others.

It was Michal, her head bowed as she knelt over a pile of discarded clothes. As Skar drew near, Michal glanced up, startled.

"Oh," she said. "You scared me."

Dappled sunlight filtered through the trees, illuminating the girl's bare face. Skar had caught her as she was attempting to clean herself, rubbing her hair with a sweater; it was the first time Skar had seen her without her heavy veil. An instant later, Michal seemed to realize this, too. Blushing, she seized the long white cloth that lay next to her and began winding it around her once more.

"Don't," said Skar.

With reluctance, Michal stopped, her head bowed. Skar knelt in front of her. Then she reached out and took her by the chin. The two girls stayed like that a moment. As if making up her mind, Michal tilted her head back with an air of defiance, revealing her face.

She had eyes that were a startling cornflower blue, but one of them was red-rimmed and staring, the lower lid dragged down and perpetually weeping. Her face was a smooth oval marred by great gouges of melted flesh. Her nose was no more than a misshapen lump, and one side of her mouth drooped open, the red gums glistening past the mutilated lips. Only her hair, honey-colored and soft, seemed untouched.

For most of her fourteen years, Michal had been used to being gawked at because of her beauty. She took it for granted, considering herself lucky; for although she had no control over her looks, they were what had made Levi choose her, allowing her to live in unheard-of wealth and comfort. Since the attack, however, she had learned what it felt like to be stared at with horror, disgust, and derision.

Yet the person who knelt before her now had no such judgment or cruelty in her gaze, only thoughtfulness and kindness.

Although they had barely spoken, Michal had liked the variant girl with the mysterious lavender eyes from the start. On the first day, Skar had shared her own food and water with Michal when she saw there wasn't enough to go around. So when Michal saw her surrounded by those thugs the night before, it hadn't crossed her mind not to come to her defense. Now she felt herself relax at the touch of Skar's hand, as gentle as a bird's wing on her chin.

"Each scar tells a story," Skar was saying. "But they are not you. They are only images drawn on your surface."

Michal was jarred out of her thoughts. "That's crazy," she said under her breath. But Skar continued.

"That is why we variants embrace them. Because scars mark the important events of our lives."

With her finger, Skar traced the circle carved on her upper arm. "You see? This was the event of my tenth birthday. The day I chose to be a girl."

Michal said nothing but could not keep from listening. She indicated a series of scrolls that encircled Skar's ankle. "So what's that for?"

"It was the day I first walked."

"And this?" It was a rabbit, above her right elbow.

"The occasion I killed my first animal."

Michal nodded, but her mood once again darkened.

"Not all scars are positive," Skar added. "Sometimes, others write them on us without our consent."

Michal's jaw tightened. "What would you know about that?"

Without a word, Skar bent forward, lifting her tunic so Michal could see her naked back. When she did, the girl gave an involuntary gasp. After a moment, Skar pulled her garment down again and sat up.

"I thought—" Michal tried to speak, then stopped. She swallowed hard. "Who did that to you?"

"My partner."

"And did you ever—"

"No," said Skar. "I have never shown it to anyone before. Not even Esther. Only you."

"It's humiliating. Isn't it?" Michal looked away and when she spoke, it was in a whisper. "When I see my face, I feel so ashamed." But Skar was shaking her head.

"It is not your shame," she said, her voice hard. "It is the shame of the ones who did it to us."

"But my face." Michal's hands fluttered across her features. "He . . . he shouldn't have done that to my face."

Skar's expression was still serious, but her tone softened.

"Maybe the worst injuries are not the ones we can see," she said. "If they heal, they are nothing. Just another story written on the skin. But I think the worst damage is in here." She pointed to her chest. "I was frightened this would kill me. But it did not, and with luck I will become stronger. Perhaps." She bit her lip. "I only hope Esther can survive what she has gone through."

In the distance, the faint wail of a baby made both girls look up.

"Kai," said Michal. "Asha said she'd watch him, but she don't know anything about babies."

But Skar was still thinking about Esther. "Perhaps we can help speed the process," she said.

That night, Eli was the first to notice her.

He and the others had gathered around a small fire, when he saw something stir in the woods. Moments later, Esther appeared, looking pale and drawn, her eyes swollen. A watchful Joseph followed close behind.

Whispers traveled around the fire, but Skar shook her head. Without a word, she made room next to her and Esther sat down.

For a while, there was no sound except for the popping of the fire. At last, Eli caught Skar's glance and raised an eyebrow. It was a question. She frowned, then gave a slight shrug in acquiescence.

"Esther," Eli said. "I don't know how much of this you know. But most everyone's gone. Rafe, he went away with—" Eli stopped himself in midsentence, then finished clumsily. "Anyhow, he's gone. And the others decided to head back to Prin. Whatever was left, they took with them. It's just us, now."

Esther didn't look at him and he was struck by how still she was. It seemed like she wasn't even breathing and her eyes, unblinking and dull, were like lumps of charred wood in her white face.

It's like she died, too, thought Eli.

"We aim to keep going to Mundreel," he continued after

a moment. "Ain't no choice . . . if we stay, we all gonna die soon enough. We should of set off this morning, only—" Eli stopped again, then continued in a gentler voice. "Anyways, that's no matter. We aim to set off at sunup. And we need to know if you are with us or not."

A violent shudder passed through Esther. It was the only sign of life she had shown. Eli thought she was about to speak, but after a moment, her face grew blank once again.

Eli was so focused on Esther, he only now noticed that Skar had slipped away from the circle. She came back, carrying something in her arms.

It was Kai, who stirred in his blanket. Eli wondered why Skar had awakened the child and brought him to such a meeting. Puzzled, he watched as the variant girl walked to the other side of the circle, where Asha sat.

"Here," Skar said in a clear voice. "He wants his mama." Then she pulled the blanket away and handed the child to Asha. The girl, startled yet delighted, took him in her eager arms.

A chunk of wood broke off from a burning log, illuminating Kai. Shocked by being awoken and having his warm coverlet removed, the boy flailed his arms and legs as Asha struggled to comfort him. She tried to rock him the way she had seen Esther do. But her touch was clumsy and Kai began to wail and then shriek, his face turning red and rosy, the round cheeks streaked with tears.

Eli was not the only one who was confused. "What are you playing at?" Rhea's voice was shrill with indignation. "That ain't his mother." Annoyed as well, Eli was about to tell Skar to take the boy away, when someone else spoke.

"Give him to me."

It was Esther. She stood, swaying yet alert, and addressed Asha. "He's mine."

Now Asha stood as well, her lower lip jutting out as she held the infant away. It was clear she didn't want to give him up; petulant tears filled her eyes as she glanced in appeal to Eli. Confused, he nodded toward Esther.

"Give him to her," was all he said.

With obvious reluctance, Asha handed the boy over. Esther had already retrieved the blanket from Skar and was fashioning it into a sling. From where he sat, Eli could see Kai's face, and for a moment he was struck by the baby's resemblance to his late father.

In a flash, Eli understood.

Esther was already cradling the child and murmuring his name. Struck by Skar's cleverness, Eli glanced at her to express his thanks, but the variant girl had already risen to her feet.

"I'll go check on the bicycles," was all she said. Then she disappeared into the night.

EIGHT

BY MIDMORNING OF THE FOLLOWING DAY, THE DEPLETED GROUP OF NINE was trying to make up for lost time.

Yet progress was slow, much slower than it had been when they had traveled as a larger group. There were now only four bicycles between them. They had managed to cobble together two wagons from various parts, with Joseph, his cat, and Kai riding in one. All of the vehicles were in poor shape and the caravan was forced to stop again and again for repairs.

Eli insisted on leading, so he rode at the front. Before they set out that morning, he had conferred with Joseph in private about which direction they should take.

"I'm afraid I don't know," the older boy had said after a long pause.

"What do you mean?" Eli was confused.

"The bad ones," Joseph started, then stopped. "They took everything. My books, my maps. I don't even know where we are."

Eli had nodded, although his mind was whirling. *If Joseph had no idea where to go, who would?*

"Well," he managed to say, "can you at least point us in the right direction?"

Joseph considered the question for some time. Then he reached down and drew an X in the dirt at their feet.

"Look," he said, "this is us. The sun rises in the east and sets in the west. North is this way. That's where we have to head." He drew a line and glanced at Eli, apologetic. "I'm afraid that's all I know."

Eli found it impossible to follow the major highway for more than a few miles. Frequent obstructions made it impassable at times, forcing them to take exits that led to other roads, roads that sometimes led in wholly new directions. After a few hours, Eli wasn't sure that they hadn't gone in a complete circle.

There were other problems he didn't know how to solve, either.

No one had had anything to eat or drink in nearly two days. Skar's improvised throwing stick was a poor substitute for her finely wrought bow made of fiberglass and wood, and she despaired of ever mastering it to the point where she could catch any game. By now, everyone held clean pebbles in their mouths, sucking them to create the illusion of moisture. But thirst was beginning to affect them all.

The youngest and smallest—Asha, Silas—fell farther and farther behind. Kai had been crying incessantly from within his wagon; even more frightening was when at last he grew silent.

Eli did not share his greatest fear: that Lewt and his gang might be lying in wait for them. He couldn't help scanning the horizon and every bend in the road with dread.

He felt a massive sense of relief when a lone sign finally appeared on the horizon, resting high on a metal pole above the trees: EXXON. It would be a place to stop, he figured, and was perhaps even an indication that a town lay nearby.

"Over there," Eli called, raising a hand.

From the rear of the caravan, Esther saw the others take the exit and she followed. By the time they pulled into the gas station, she was so faint she had to steady herself against the handlebars and her legs trembled with exhaustion. She turned to check on Kai, so quiet in the wagon behind her. Despite the suffocating heat, his skin was clammy and cold; and Esther felt a stab of fear deep in her gut.

All day, she had tried to hold her tongue, even when Eli made decisions that she sensed were rash. She knew he was trying his best and the last thing she wanted was to undermine his authority; their morale, as poor as it was, was literally the only thing they had left. Yet as he floundered from one bad decision to another, she sensed they were on the verge of losing their most vulnerable members.

Without water, Kai would surely die. And one by one,

they would all succumb as well.

By now, the others had dismounted and moved into the shattered remains of the gas station. There she assumed they would Glean the convenience store and attached garage, searching for water and food. Silas and Rhea were already carrying out implements they had found—a coil of rope, various tools, a good-size knife, and other items—and loading them into the wagon. *But without something to drink*, Esther realized, *it was all pointless.*

"Why don't you rest?" Off her bicycle, Skar crouched low, easing her legs and back.

"No," Esther said, "I'm going to see if there's anything nearby." She tapped on the wagon, and Joseph emerged, drawn and pale. A listless Kai lay in his arms. "Keep an eye on him until I get back."

Before Skar could say anything more, Esther had already remounted and taken off.

She refused to think about Caleb.

His murder had killed something inside her; and she had sealed all thoughts of him deep within, a howling void of loss and fury she swore she would never again confront. Instead, she chose to focus on survival: that of her son and of her friends. They were all she had left.

The empty cart rattled behind her on the overgrown country highway that curved and bent in the dimming light. Then she saw something promising: a shack that hadn't been destroyed, set back from the street.

Sure enough, Esther found what she had been looking for:

a street in which the storefronts and small buildings appeared occupied. As Esther slowed, she even saw a few bicycles parked in various front yards.

She soon came to a small store, one that had faded words painted on a cracked window: POLANSKI'S DELI. Outside, a girl with a tangle of dark, curly hair, perhaps six or seven, sat on the lowest step. She had been drinking soda from a large plastic bottle but stopped to stare. A stranger on the bicycle was in front of her, her lips cracked and her expression desperate. But the child was already scrambling up the stairs, terrified.

"Please." Esther's throat was so dry, the word was little more than a croak. "I just need—"

An older girl burst from the building, brandishing what looked like a table leg. She had the same dark-brown cloud of hair; she and the little one were clearly sisters. As she advanced, with fear and defiance in her eyes, her sibling ran behind her and clung to her robes.

When she saw it was only a thin girl, exhausted and covered with dust, the older one hesitated. The three stood like that, in a silent tableau. Then at last she spoke.

"We was attacked," she said, and didn't elaborate.

Had it been Lewt and his boys? Esther wondered but said nothing.

"So what you want?" said the older sister. Although she had lowered her weapon, she still gripped it by her side and her expression was suspicious.

"Something to eat or to drink," Esther said, "anything you could spare. You see, we—"

"We ain't got nothing," the older girl snapped.

Esther turned to go, then realized she could not. "Please," she said. "It's for a baby. My little boy."

The older one said nothing, but the little girl emerged from behind her sister's robes. Her eyes were wide. "You got a baby?"

Esther nodded.

The sisters shared a glance, and the older one gave a slight shrug. At that, the young one stepped forward and handed Esther her bottle. The soda was warm, flat, and tasted like plastic; yet it was delicious. Forcing herself not to take too much, Esther swallowed a few long sips. Then with difficulty, she handed the bottle back.

"Is there," Esther said, "nothing else you could spare? We are nine of us."

Again, the sisters glanced at each other and the older one nodded. The little one disappeared into the store. Moments later, she returned, barely able to support two large soda bottles and several packets of food, which she carried pressed to her chin: dried peas, cough drops, coffee. Esther held each item for a moment as if to savor it before placing it in the wagon. Then she looked up at the girls.

"Saying thanks isn't enough," she said. "But thanks."

The younger one shrugged it off. "Where you from?"

"A place called Prin. We had to leave on account of the earthquake." The siblings nodded in obvious sympathy and Esther felt a flicker of hope. "How are you folks set around here? You got enough for more to stay?"

The older one shook her head. "Me and her, we were just getting by before. Now, everyone around here plans on moving on. Soon."

"Where you headed?" asked the younger one.

"Mundreel. Ever heard of it?"

The little girl shook her head, but the older one spoke up. "Some people from around here went there once, I think. It was a while ago."

"You ever get word from them?"

The girl shrugged. "They musta liked it. Because they never come back."

"Got any idea which way they went?"

The older girl shook her head. "Sorry."

Esther knew she had to get back to Kai and the others; it was several miles on a hilly road. "Well," she said. "I better go."

As she remounted her bicycle, the bigger girl spoke up. "I reckon you could ask Aras."

"Who?"

"Aras. He used to be a guide. Or so he say."

Esther debated whether to stay or go; she didn't think another half hour's wait would do any harm. And the idea of a guide sounded promising.

"Where can I find him?" she said.

Esther stood in front of a large, strange rectangle of a building, windowless and with only one floor. A sign spanned an area above the large entrance, with a few random letters embedded there that made no sense. There was a rounded, glassed-in cage adjacent to the front door and next to it was a torn poster with the unpronounceable word MATINEE.

Esther entered the building. The daylight that spilled in the doorway revealed a medium-size room dominated by a steel-topped counter, with two curtained doors on the far wall leading to greater darkness. Broken glass scattered across a stained carpet crunched underfoot as she picked her way across.

"Hello?" There was no answer.

But she did notice the smell. It was an acrid aroma, sweet and heavy, that mixed smoke with vegetation; it made her recoil. Still, she was able to follow the scent as it deepened across the room, through one of the doors, past a thick curtain made of a plush and dusty fabric.

"Hello?"

Esther could tell from the sound that she had moved into a vast space with a high ceiling. She was forced to walk with her hands held in front of her, feeling her way in the dark. As she moved forward, she bumped into what turned out to be a row of attached folding seats, upholstered, with heavy metal backs. There were many such rows, broken and torn, yet arranged in an even pattern that filled the room. As her eyes adjusted, she saw that a veritable sea of trash swamped the place. Soon she could make out a far wall, which gleamed faintly silver; it appeared to be made of some shiny material that was torn and stained.

The smell was coming from the front row.

Faintly lit by the glow of the wall, a shadowy figure sat,

almost lay, its long legs propped up on the edge of the small stage that ran across the front of the room. There was a bright orange dot in the darkness. It moved slightly, and Esther realized it was the lit tip of an object the person held to its lips, sucking in audibly before expelling smoke with the awful smell.

"Excuse me?" Esther called.

The response wasn't human.

Great bursts of barking broke out. Some kind of wild animal erupted from the darkness. It came bounding up the aisle toward her; Esther could hear the rapid scrabbling of its nails on the floor and the click of its teeth, could practically feel its hot breath on her face. There was nowhere to run, and in desperation, she threw her arms up to protect herself as best she could.

And then it stopped.

With a sudden twang and the clanking of metal chain, the dog gave a sharp yip as it was yanked backward, having reached the end of its tether.

"Pilot," the person murmured from the front row. "That's enough. Shut up now."

The dog obeyed, quieting down instantly. Then the figure rose from its seat and turned to face Esther.

"Here," he said. Something flew through the dark air, and somehow Esther managed to catch it. It was a firestarter. She clicked it, and by the light of its small flame, she could finally see.

A boy had risen from his seat to face her, using one hand to hold on to the edge of the stage. In the flickering light, Esther saw that he was bone thin, not much taller than she was, with brown skin and matted dark hair that fell past his shoulders in thick locks. Even though he had been sitting in close to pitch-blackness, his small oval glasses were dark.

With a stick used as a cane, he made his way with difficulty into the aisle. Smoke wafted from a small paper cylinder, which he held in his teeth.

"What can I do for you?"

"I'm looking for Aras, the guide," Esther replied. Her heart was still pounding from her close encounter with the dog, which now lay in the aisle, panting, its dark eyes fixed on her.

"You are?" he said, sounding perplexed. "What for?"

"I need to ask him something."

As the boy came closer, Esther noticed that he used the backs of seats, leaning on them. When he reached the dog, he bent down and undid its chain. Then he held the animal's collar and allowed it to lead him the rest of the way.

With a start, Esther realized that the boy was blind.

When he reached her, the smoke smell was overwhelming. "Well," he said. "You found him."

Esther was stunned. "Oh!" was all she could manage to say.

"What you want?" he asked, ignoring the obvious shock in her voice. He seemed to be sixteen or so. "Need help getting someplace?"

She decided to be blunt. "Mundreel. You ever been?"

He didn't say anything for a moment. Then, "I been there," he said, as if remembering something long ago. "Well, right outside, anyway. I left some people there, I think. Of course, it

was a while ago, but . . . I don't think it's moved, or anything."
He chuckled.

Aras had a vague way about him that Esther found both
confusing and annoying. Furthermore, she was nearly choking
from the smell of the thing he was smoking, which he never
removed from his mouth.

"Hey," she blurted out. "Could you get rid of that?"

"What?" Aras asked, dumbly. "This?"

"Yeah. I can't breathe."

The boy shrugged. Then he dropped and rubbed it out
with a foot in a dusty boot. "It's just natural," he muttered.
"From the earth itself."

"Look," said Esther. By now, her voice was grating with irri-
tation. "I got to go. Thanks anyway." She turned to leave.

"So what are you gonna give me?"

Esther stopped halfway up the aisle. "What?"

"To get you there. I'll take food and water. But I'm willing
to take whatever you got, if I like it enough." He laughed again.

"I'm not asking you," Esther said, almost laughing, too, at
his presumption.

"You ain't gonna get there yourself. I mean, you might get
there. But dead." His brow furrowed, as he considered if what
he'd said made sense. He seemed to decide that it did. "You
already way off the main road. There'll be plenty more detours
and the roads are shot." Still, Esther said nothing, and the boy
seemed to lose patience. "Look, I don't got to do it. I don't got
to make trouble for myself. I got a good life here." And with
that, Aras started back down the aisle.

Then he stopped and turned.

"Hey." He gestured, snapping his fingers, and Esther realized he was talking about his firestarter. She almost tossed it at him when she remembered he couldn't see. After she retraced her steps and handed it over, however, Esther hesitated.

Although she hated to admit it, everything he said was true. It was clear they could not make it to Mundreel without a guide.

Aras was the only hope she had.

"Look," she said. "I can't give you anything."

Aras nodded. He already seemed distracted as he reached down for his dog and patted its muzzle.

"But if you get us there," Esther continued, "you can share whatever we find. That's the best I can do."

Aras brushed his long hair back, one side and then the other, appearing to think. Then he lifted his face and in the dark, she could have sworn that he saw her, in one way or another.

"Maybe," he said, as if doing her a favor. "Maybe I just will."

Esther realized that Aras had no bicycle of his own and so when the two emerged on the sidewalk, she had an idea.

"You can go in the wagon," she said. "Or if you want, I can bike standing up and you can sit behind me and hold on." It was the way she and Skar often gave each other rides when there was only one vehicle between them. But the moment she said it, she realized her mistake.

Aras bridled. "I ain't helpless," he snapped.

Esther grew flustered. "I didn't say that. But it's a long way back, and I thought maybe—"

"Forget it," he said. "I'd rather walk."

With that, Aras slung his battered nylon backpack over his shoulder and pulled a length of chain from his pocket. "Hey Pilot," he called, and the wolflike animal nuzzled his hands and allowed the makeshift leash to be attached to his collar. Then Aras straightened up.

"You just go on ahead," he said to Esther. His tone was patronizing. "Pilot can pick up your trail."

Esther bicycled at a fraction of her usual speed, weaving back and forth across the highway and glancing over her shoulder to see how the boy and his dog were doing. It wasn't encouraging. The two ambled along the road and into the woods that surrounded them, and even backtracked once or twice. Since Aras said nothing, it took Esther a while to realize he was actually communicating to his animal through a complex series of soft tongue clicks and whistles.

Throughout, the boy continued to smoke his bad-smelling papers. When he finished one, he would signal Pilot to halt, fumble in his pack for a small tin box, and roll up some more dried plants into a fresh package before lighting it. Each time, this operation seemed to take forever.

Esther and Aras didn't exchange a single word. When he finally spoke, what he said surprised her.

"We almost there."

In fact, they were. Esther was so focused on Aras's progress, she hadn't noticed that the gas station was visible in the distance, on the side of the highway near the exit. A skilled tracker like Skar relied on her eyes above all. Aras was blind: *Did he have some special ability?* As if he had heard her thoughts, the boy bristled.

"It ain't magic," he snapped. "It's called listening." And a minute later, Esther, too, could hear the faraway thread of voices.

It had taken her perhaps five times as long to return, and by now the sun was low in the afternoon sky. The others flocked around her, so frantic for whatever she had brought that at first they paid no attention to the boy and animal who stood at a distance. Esther could not give out the bottles and packages fast enough; people seized them from her hands, ripped them open, and began eating and drinking on the spot. Only Joseph, who took a sip for himself, made sure to give a long drink to Kai.

Aras crouched by his dog and rubbed its ears. "They better slow down," he remarked to no one in particular. "They gonna get sick."

Again, Esther was unnerved by how much the boy seemed to know without seeing. Then she realized that anyone could hear the ravenous noises that filled the air.

"Tell them," Aras insisted.

Esther hesitated, then spoke up. "Hey," she said. "Slow down." But no one paid attention.

"I bet half that stuff ain't even cooked," Aras said. He had straightened up and now his voice rang out, arrogant and overbearing. "You eat too much, you gonna kill yourself. Or end up wishing you was dead, anyhow."

In the silence that followed, the others turned to gaze at Esther's companion. They took in Aras's bony, disheveled appearance, his long hair, the reeking smoking paper still dangling from his mouth, and the wolflike animal that crouched by his feet with yellow fangs bared, panting. Then one by one, they turned to Esther.

"Who's this?" Silas asked.

"We can't take anyone else," Eli said at the same time. "We don't got enough as it is."

With everyone staring at her, Esther took a long swallow down a dry throat. She avoided eye contact, choosing instead to look at the ground. She especially dreaded Eli's reaction.

"This," she said, "is our new guide." She paused, then cleared her throat. "Aras here is going to help get us to Mundreel."

Esther winced, bracing for the uproar that she knew would follow. Instead, there was a silence that was even more damning.

She looked up and saw the others studying Aras with open disbelief, distaste, and hostility. First Michal and then Joseph flinched; they had just picked up the terrible smell coming from not only Aras's smoking paper, but his hair and clothes. And Silas and Rhea were smiling at each other, giggling and whispering.

Esther had no choice but to take full responsibility for her decision. Instinctively, she turned to the one she could always count on for support: Skar.

Yet her friend was gazing at her with a mixture of concern and compassion that rattled Esther far more than the other reactions. When Skar spoke, it was as if she were talking to Asha or someone else not quite right in the head.

"Esther," she whispered, "I know you've been upset since . . . what happened. Are you sure this was the best idea to—"

Since she wasn't sure at all, Esther responded with decisiveness. "Yes, I'm sure," she said. "I wouldn't have asked Aras if I—"

Eli cut her off. "You should have asked *me*."

Esther sighed. She knew that she had insulted Eli by going behind his back and usurping his new authority. With difficulty, she began, "As I said, he's just here to help, Eli, he's not—" but she never finished her thought.

"Your guide can't even *see*!" Eli shouted.

At this, Rhea and Silas burst into laughter.

Throughout, Aras had said nothing. But as if sensing the group's hostility, the dog growled and then exploded into loud barking as he strained against his chain.

Everyone jumped, none more so than Joseph. Stumpy bushed up her fur and seemed to grow three times her usual size, hissing and spitting. Joseph scooped her up and together they fled to the safety of their wagon, where he pulled the tarp shut behind them.

Unless she was able to think of something, Esther realized with a sinking heart, her plan would be over before it began.

"Listen," she said, addressing the group. "Aras has been to Mundreel. He can get us there. He—"

But she was interrupted by the sound of more barking. Goaded by Rhea, Silas was taunting the dog, poking a branch at its snapping mouth and slapping the leaves across its muzzle. As he and the girl laughed, the animal's yelps grew to a deafening frenzy of screams and growls.

"Stop it, Silas," Esther said, annoyed, over the noise.

"Let him have his fun." Even though Aras understood what was happening, he seemed unperturbed.

Silas, emboldened by Rhea's shrill laughter, stepped even closer. Wielding his branch like a sword, he whipped the animal across the eyes; and when it recoiled with a yip, he hit the dog, hard, across the ribs.

Esther could hear the crack from where she stood, and she moved to yank the boy away. But before she could, she saw Aras drop his end of the leash. The animal coiled down like a spring and, with a roar, lunged forward. He flew at the boy and, ignoring the stick, sank his teeth deep into Silas's thin arm.

It all happened so quickly, Esther couldn't even react. Above the sound of growling, there was a shrill, high-pitched whistle which took her a moment to realize was coming from Silas's open mouth as he tried to wrestle free. But the dog refused to let go and began to worry the limb, shaking its head from side to side and dragging the small boy to his knees.

"Pilot," Aras's calm voice pierced the commotion.

The dog seemed to hesitate. Then, with a final toss of its massive head, it let go and returned to its master's side, panting, its tongue lolling out. Aras once more picked up the chain and wrapped it around his wrist. Silas was left crumpled on the ground, sobbing, bright red staining the dingy white of his robes. Rhea ran to his side, shooting Aras a terrified look.

"Don't hurt animals," Aras said, his voice even. "They our kin, you know."

Silas deserved to be punished for his cruelty, Esther thought; *still, he had nearly had his arm torn off.* Glaring at Aras, she pushed past him, about to rip a strip of fabric from her sweatshirt.

"Wait up," said Aras.

"What?" Esther was in no mood to talk. "He's bleeding. I got to tie up his arm."

"You gotta clean it first. Don't you know anything?"

Esther bridled, but managed to keep her temper. "We don't got any clean water."

"You don't need clean," he replied. "Dirty is good, too."

Baffled, Esther and the others could only stare at him. But Asha was already speaking up, her face flushed with eagerness at being the one with the answer.

"Over there," she said, pointing. *"There's* some water!"

She was indicating a small, abandoned truck parked to one side. It had been destroyed long ago: its windows were smashed to spiderwebs of broken glass, its fittings had been mostly torn off and tossed aside, and one of its doors gaped open.

The hood was badly dented and held a rusty pool of water, left over from the recent rain.

Even looking at it caused a murmur of apprehension to ripple through the crowd.

"Good," said Aras. "Somebody fetch a bowl. A firebowl. And some kind of cup or bottle, too."

There was again a silence, during which the only sound was

Silas snuffling. Aras cocked his head and then shrugged.

"It's up to you," he said. "Don't matter to me if your friend dies."

Esther saw Eli's face darken and his fists clench. But just as she was about to hold him back, Joseph poked his head from his wagon. He held out a dented firebowl that had seen better days, as well as a chipped mug that had the words FIRST NATIONAL BANK on it.

"Here," Joseph said. He handed them to Esther and ducked back inside.

"And a piece of clothing," Aras said. "A shirt or something would be good."

Esther was as confused as everyone else. Nevertheless, she went into the other wagon and rummaged in it until she found a T-shirt. It was still clean and in good condition, with months of use left. Still, if she was to convince the others to trust Aras, she had to commit to his plan, whether she understood it or not.

She only hoped Aras knew what he was doing.

"Okay," he said. "Now we need a fire."

"You better hurry up," Esther said to him, under her breath, as she bent to gather kindling. "That boy's bleeding bad."

Aras grunted. "Here," he said. He dug his firestarter out of his pocket. "Use this. Only don't waste any. I need it."

Skar alone volunteered to help. She looked dubious, too. Together, they built a good-size pile from twigs and trash they found littering the small woods that surrounded the garage. Then Esther used the firestarter to get it blazing.

Throughout, Aras crouched to one side. His dog lay in the dust on its back; its owner tickled its spotted stomach, and the animal, which moments ago had almost killed a boy, now writhed with a kind of innocent pleasure.

"You done yet?" Aras called.

"Just about," replied Esther.

The boy got to his feet and Esther handed the firebowl and mug to him. He checked them by touch before giving them back.

"Okay," he said. "Take this and scoop as much water as you can into the bowl."

Everyone murmured and Eli glanced up sharply.

"Don't do it." His voice was harsh. "He's crazy."

But Esther shook her head. Then she approached the destroyed truck, its hood brimming over with the deadly liquid.

Holding the cup by its handle and using the utmost care, Esther lowered it into the pool. It grated across the corroded hood as she scooped up a small amount of water. It was mostly clear, although there were orange flakes of rust in it, a few dead insects, and a dried leaf. Forcing herself to move slowly, she poured it into the firebowl on the ground next to her, taking care not to spill any. She did this again and again until there was no water left in the hood.

"Okay," she said. "Done."

Behind her, she could sense the others give a collective breath of relief. But it wasn't over.

"Now bring it to the fire," said Aras. "Take your time."

Again, the warning was snide.

Carrying the water was even more of a challenge. When Esther picked it up, the firebowl, nearly full, sloshed its contents and some of it splashed onto the ground at her feet. She froze; and in the silence, she could hear Rhea exclaim. Only after she made certain that none of it had touched her did she dare to continue. She finally settled the metal container on some stacked bricks that held it over the leaping flames.

"Now what?" she asked.

"We wait," replied Aras.

Boiling water was nothing new; it was how Esther and her friends prepared much of their food. But they used only the safe kind of water that either came from the spring or in sealed bottles from the Source.

It was terrifying to think what would happen if you heated the other sort of water, the sort that could kill you. As steam began to rise from the firebowl, everyone shrank back, and more than one of them covered their mouths and noses.

But eventually, curiosity won out. Within minutes, everyone had edged forward and now peered over Aras's and Esther's shoulders to watch the water churn and bubble. Even Joseph could be seen observing from his wagon. No one paid any attention to Silas, who sat alone, nursing his injured arm and whimpering in pain.

Aras snapped his fingers at Esther.

"That's long enough," he said. "Take it off and let it sit."

Again working with great care, Esther used an old towel to lift the firebowl off the flames. She set it on the ground, where it sent out white tendrils of vapor.

At Aras's instruction, Michal presented the cup, now draped with the clean shirt. Esther lifted the firebowl and poured its contents onto the folded fabric. The cloth acted as a strainer; as the steaming water seeped through, it left a fine residue of grit and rust. Within seconds, the cup was nearly full.

"Now," Aras said, "get the boy who teased my dog."

Startled, Esther glanced up. She caught Eli's reaction; he shook his head *no* once, with emphasis. As for Silas, he was backing up, terror in his eyes as he clutched his injured arm to his chest.

"I ain't coming near that stuff!" he shouted, his voice shrill. "You trying to kill me!"

Aras sighed. Then he fumbled for the cup, steam rising from it.

And he brought it to his lips.

Everyone gasped. Michal made a move to knock the cup from his hand, but Esther held her back.

"Wait," Esther said.

Aras blew on the cup and then drank. After he had finished a few gulps, he lifted his head, a faint smile on his face.

Was he mad? Esther's eyes flickered toward Skar, then Joseph, but they were looking to her for guidance. Although her impulses had failed her many times in the past, she had no choice but to trust them today.

After what seemed an eternity, she nodded.

"Do what he says." It was Eli who spoke, although it was

with difficulty. He had seen Esther's response and that was enough for him.

When Silas didn't move, the older boy picked him up and carried him, even though he fought and kicked. Then Eli held the whimpering Silas down as Esther used the hot water to bathe his arm.

In moments, the wound, though still deep, was clean.

"*Now*," Aras said, "tie up his damn arm."

NINE

As Esther tipped a bowl over her head, moonlight made the hot water gleam silver as it ran down her shoulders and her naked back.

It was a delicious feeling and the first time she had bathed since leaving Prin. Back home, cleaning oneself was something one did rarely, if ever, with a washcloth and a scant cup or so of precious bottled water. But tonight, after she had dipped out another firebowl's worth from a nearby stream and repeated the process Aras taught them, Esther found she could allow herself the impossible luxury of a hot shower.

She was not alone. In the dark woods around her, she could

hear the others bathing themselves, too, scrubbing clothing, and washing off the accumulated dust of the road. The idea that water—the poison that fell from the sky, filled lakes and streams, and collected on the morning grass like a deadly veil—could be made harmless was almost too miraculous to be believed. The revelation brought a sense of boundless plentitude and with it, a rare festive mood to the caravan. People called to one another through the trees and shouts of laughter rang in the night air.

Yet while one of their biggest problems had been solved, another was not.

Esther was starving.

She had eaten only a few mouthfuls of the food she had brought back; she wanted to make sure everyone else had had enough, and now there was nothing left. She could barely recall the last meal she had eaten nearly three days earlier: a meager bowl of rabbit stew and some flatbread. And although she had drunk deeply, trying to fill herself with water, it didn't begin to dull the painful emptiness that gnawed at her gut.

Then she heard a jangle of chain.

Two eyes gleamed in the moonlight: It was the dog Pilot. Holding on to his collar was Aras.

"Who's that?" he called.

Blushing, Esther tried to hide her nakedness. Then she remembered the guide couldn't see her and after a moment, let her arms drop.

"It's me," she said.

"You weren't at dinner," he said.

"I wasn't hungry."

Aras snorted at the obvious lie.

"Yeah," he said, "maybe not. But maybe you better come with me. I got something to show you."

Esther dried herself off as best she could and put her damp yet clean clothes back on. Then she trailed behind as the dog led its owner deeper into the forest, skirting trees, an empty metal barrel, a destroyed sofa. Esther found herself keeping her eyes on the white of Aras's robes, which gave off the faintest glow in the moonlight; the darkness had rendered her nearly sightless, as well.

As he walked, Aras kept one hand in front of him, touching trees, brushing their rough surfaces, and making his own calculations. Occasionally, he made the strange clicking sounds he used to communicate with his dog; the animal responded to each one, turning or slowing down. Aras finally stopped under one tree. Kneeling, he felt around on the ground. Then he stood.

He extended his open palm. Esther had trouble making out what he was offering her until she felt it. It was a small round object, something she had encountered many times before, littering the ground underneath trees in Prin: greenish brown, with a tiny point at one end and a leathery cap.

She looked at him, baffled. "What do you want me to do with it?"

"Eat it," he said.

Esther laughed.

Other than the occasional rabbit or squirrel, food wasn't something you found outside. Eating something that fell off a tree or grew in the dirt would be like swallowing a rock or piece of plastic: It was impossible, nonsensical, and probably deadly. Food, real food, was something that came sealed in packages, bags, jars.

But Aras seemed serious, and Esther was again reminded of her empty stomach. She tried to examine the small object in the moonlight. Then she decided to trust him.

She gave it an experimental nibble. "It's too hard," she said.

Aras snorted. "It's an acorn," he said; "a nut." It seemed he was about to add the word "idiot" but thought better of it. "You got to break the shell first. Use your side teeth or you'll hurt yourself."

Esther did; and there was a resounding crack. She removed the pieces and found that there was a small kernel inside. Hesitantly, she popped it into her mouth and chewed. A moment later, she spat it out and glared at him.

"That your idea of a joke?" she snapped.

Aras smiled. "It's bitter, but you can boil the taste away. Ain't much, but if you pick a bunch, it's something. They keep a long time. I shouldn't have to tell you."

Feeling around on the forest floor, he scooped up a few more and handed them to her. After a moment, Esther joined him and began storing them in her pockets. The bad taste was still on her tongue, but she was so hungry, she didn't care.

At that moment, something flittered past her in the darkness and landed on the back of Aras's hand. Without hesitation, the boy grabbed it and examined it, running his fingers over its tiny body.

Esther recognized it. It was a greenish insect with long legs, the kind that lived in tall grass and jumped high. Aras twisted off its tiny head and limbs and flicked them aside. Then he held it out.

"Go ahead," he said.

A wave of nausea swept over her. To put an acorn in her mouth was one thing; but insects were disgusting and filthy things, skittering creatures of death. Esther had seen flies feed off fresh carcasses, both animal and human; and after they were done, she knew that beetles and worms crawled through the bones, picking them clean.

As if sensing her reaction, Aras smirked. Then he put the thing into his month and deliberately bit it in two.

"Not bad," he said.

He offered the other half; after a moment, even as her stomach rebelled at the thought, she raised the bug to her lips, squeezing her eyes shut as she did. With one swift movement, she popped it into her mouth and chewed, crunching loudly.

To her amazement, it didn't taste bad. *Better than the acorn, that was for sure.*

Even more surprising, the tiny mouthful made her hungry for more.

Esther dropped to her knees and began scrabbling through the darkness. She lunged in vain at the tiny shapes that flitted past, slapping at them in clumsy desperation. Yet it was impossible to see her hand in front of her face, much less an insect, and she was much too impatient, and hungry, to wait for them to come to her. After a few minutes, she realized it was an impossible task.

Aras had already headed to the campsite. By the time Esther, chastened, caught up with him, he was crouched in front of the dying campfire, scratching Pilot behind the ears and smoking another paper.

"You catch anything?" he asked. His voice was lightly mocking.

"No," she admitted. "Although I bet it's easier in the daylight."

He grunted. "Well," he said, "there are other ways to eat." Feeling around on the ground, he located his heavy duffel bag. Then he unzipped it, pulling something out.

"Here," he said. It was an unstrung bow made of gleaming wood that sparkled in the fading campfire light; and at that moment, it was the most glorious thing Esther had ever seen. "Carbon tips, extra catgut. But I only got a few arrows left. You know anyone here who can shoot?"

Esther thought of Skar and smiled.

"I think I do," she said.

The sun was already well into the morning sky, and Aras was still asleep.

Everyone else had been up for hours. They had poured boiled water into bottles, repacked their belongings, and checked their bicycles for repairs. Esther had recruited Skar and Michal to help her collect acorns. Although the girls seemed doubtful at first when she explained it to them, they went along. Using a backpack, the three gathered hundreds of the nuts, which they dumped into one of the wagons.

Now, they all waited outside the gas station for their new guide, one whose knowledge—if not personality—they had begun to appreciate.

Keeping an eye on Pilot who lay next to his owner, Esther picked her way across the cluttered floor of the gas station and approached the sleeping boy. Without his sunglasses, he looked oddly young and defenseless; and for the first time, she saw the prominent white scars that ran across his forehead and eyes.

Esther nudged him with her foot, and his eyelids flickered.

Then in a single movement, he lashed out a hand, grabbing his glasses and putting them on. Hidden once more, he jumped to his feet and grabbed hold of his dog's collar.

"Let's go," he said, as if it were his idea.

As they headed toward the caravan, Esther was about to offer him a ride, but thought better of it.

"I'll be in front, pulling one of the wagons," she said. "Eli's got the other one. We got only two free-bicycles, and it's Rhea's and Silas's turn. Joseph and Kai ride with me. Everyone else walks until we switch off."

Aras kept his head down, listening. Then he spoke. "Show me where the sun's at. How high is it?"

Feeling awkward, Esther turned Aras and took his free arm, raising it so it pointed at the sun. He thought for a moment, chewing his lip, then pulled something from his pocket. Esther feared it would be another smoking paper, but the guide surprised her.

It was a small, round object made of metal; it looked like a wristwatch, but lacked a strap and a clear plastic cover. Instead of numbers, it had four letters printed on its face; and at the center, a thin needle spun and wavered. Aras skimmed the surface with his fingers before he spoke.

"North by northwest. Which means that way."

Esther noticed that Joseph was leaning from his wagon, listening. When she caught his eye, he nodded in agreement.

Overhead, the dirty-yellow sky was bright and cloudless, but a breeze made it bearable. Esther pedaled in front but slowly enough to allow Aras and his dog to keep up. She learned that staying close to the guide was essential.

At Aras's request, Esther told him about their progress, the condition of the road ahead, and the weather. She identified upcoming exits, laboriously sounding out the numbers posted on the small signs along the low railing, and reading the town names and mileage markers, as well.

Often, there were obstacles. Most of them could be steered around—abandoned trucks jackknifed across asphalt stained black with oil, their trailers gaping open and interiors plundered. One time, it was a monstrous pile of crushed and twisted steel. The structure was so huge, it filled the road and flattened the trees on either side. On examining it, Joseph decided it was an "airplane," a vehicle he claimed could fly across the sky. He was so excited by this fanciful discovery, Esther had a hard time convincing him to go. He only agreed when she allowed him to take a souvenir, a shredded canvas strap with a buckle attached that he found underneath a twisted metal sheet.

As they traveled farther north, the hurdles became more

frequent—and more serious. Entire sections of forest had been uprooted, toppling dozens of trees across the road. At other places, earthquakes had ruptured the surface, breaking it into plates that sheared off in different directions, revealing gravel and red clay beneath. Each time, Esther would call a stop and, after consulting with Aras, had everyone unload the wagons and carry everything across, item by item.

But they had to stop when they reached a narrow mountain pass. Some tremor from the earth had triggered a landslide from both sides, forming a massive pileup of dead trees, boulders, and loose slag that filled the road. In the wreckage, Esther could make out the remains of crushed cars, trucks, and what looked like an entire house.

"It's bad," she said as they approached.

Next to her, Aras clicked his tongue, and his dog halted. "Can we get across?"

Skar had already approached the roadblock and was testing the footing. When she was no more than a few steps up, she had to leap to the ground. Loose gravel and dirt collapsed around her, setting off another small landslide. "It's too unsteady," she called.

Aras lit a fresh smoking paper. "Well," he said. "Guess we got to go back and cut around. Quarter mile or so."

They turned and retraced their steps. When they had gone far enough, Aras had everyone dismount, unload the wagons, and detach them from the bicycles. They then hoisted everything over the low metal railing by the side of the road and headed into the overgrown forest.

Dappled sunlight filtered through the trees. A dense bed of decaying leaves did little to cushion the ground, which was rocky and treacherous. After one jarring bump, Esther decided to save her tires and got off to walk. She led the way, the others in single file behind her. The only sound was the jangle of Pilot's chain.

"Start heading that way." After several minutes, Aras had stopped to relight his smoking paper and now spoke through clenched teeth. "See if we around the roadblock yet." Esther was about to do as he said when she noticed something through the trees.

"Wait up," she said. "Something's ahead."

She and the others found themselves on the edge of a small field, badly overgrown. Looming in the distance were the skeletal remains of a sprawling building, its large windows smashed. Near them were a rusted swing set, as well as a miniature house made of plastic, still colorful after so many years, large enough to fit several children. This place was similar to those she had seen many times in Prin.

"What is it?" Aras asked behind her. "Anything good?"

"Don't think so," Esther replied. "But we might as well check."

The two of them waded through grass that was hip deep, followed by the others. Other than the clanking of Pilot's leash, the only sounds were the rustle of leaves and the snapping of twigs beneath their feet. Behind her, Esther could hear Silas whisper something, and then Rhea give a shrill laugh in reply.

"I dare you!" Silas said.

"Hush, now." Esther was annoyed. If anyone were hiding inside, it would be foolish to advertise their presence.

Then she saw what had drawn their attention. In the distance lay a large, rectangular patch of dead yellow leaves, surrounded on all four sides by a white strip of cracked concrete. In the midst of what felt like a jungle of overgrown grass, the precision of the shape and brightness of its color were striking.

Esther described it to Aras as best she could. "Be careful," was all he said.

"About what?"

"Just tell them to be careful," said Aras. "That's all."

Behind them, Rhea had remounted her free-bicycle. Now, wobbling on the soft ground, she rode straight at the blanket of leaves.

"Hey," Esther called. "Don't get too close!"

Either Rhea couldn't hear or was pretending not to. "Watch me!" she yelled to Silas, who cheered her on. Esther watched in disbelief as the girl sped right toward the leafy rectangle.

As soon as Rhea landed on it, it became clear that it was not solid. The bicycle tipped forward, dumping the girl directly into the golden mess. As she screamed with laughter, floundering and wallowing in the decaying vegetation, they all heard another noise.

It was the sound of something tearing. Rhea had landed in the middle of an ancient rubber tarp, and it was ripping beneath her.

"Don't move!" shouted Esther.

But it was too late.

Rhea was already sinking through the spreading breaks in the flimsy cover. Her foolish smile vanished and her face went deathly pale.

The others were frozen, staring. Esther had already dropped her bicycle, but before she could make a move, Aras grabbed her arm.

"Stop," he said.

Rhea was floundering on the tattered surface, her robes ballooning around her. Dazed, she flapped her arms, struggling to climb out, but her movements only seemed to drive her in deeper.

Then with a final shredding sound, she tore through completely. There was a loud splash and for a moment, she disappeared from view.

"Help me!"

When Rhea resurfaced, her sunglasses had fallen off and her hair was plastered across her face. There was apparently water hidden beneath the tarp, ancient rainwater that had leached underneath the rubber, filling the deep depression in the ground. Rhea was frantically thrashing her arms and legs like a bird Esther had once seen in its death throes. Water sprayed through the air and the others shied away.

Esther again moved toward her, but Aras's grip on her arm was like a steel cuff. Behind her, she could sense Eli, Skar, and the others staring with shock.

"Don't no one get near!" Aras shouted. But as Rhea's panicked gaze flickered across the others, it found what it was looking for.

"Esther . . . help me!"

Esther flinched and, again, tried to break free.

"Help me!" Paddling like a dog, Rhea was only visible from the neck up: a human head that looked more like a naked skull bobbing up and down in a sea of dead leaves and torn rubber. Her voice was ingratiating, fawning, and Esther wanted to put her hands to her ears. "I know you can do it. I know you can." She spit out the water seeping into her mouth.

"Esther! Your sister and I were so close. For Sarah's sake, Esther. Save me!"

It was a lie: Rhea had been nothing but cruel to Sarah, tormenting her for years. But Esther could bear it no longer. She yanked free of Aras and ran to the wagon for a rope. Fashioning one end into a noose, she tossed it toward Rhea, where it landed on the surface of wet leaves and torn tarp. Buried to the neck, the girl struggled to reach it.

But at a command, Pilot was already lunging at Esther, dragging Aras with him. Flailing his free arm, the guide grabbed her shoulder. Again, Esther broke free.

"We can still get her out," she said.

"Don't you get it?" he shouted. "She already dead!"

Esther knew he was right; yet she shook off the memory of how the disease had eaten away her sister, day by day. "We can take care of her," she replied stubbornly. "I can take care of her."

"We taking time for nothing," said Aras in a rough voice. "And even if you get her out, we got little enough to eat as it is."

Appalled, Esther was about to reply when she was jerked to the edge of the pit. Rhea had grabbed hold of the noose and was pulling with all her strength. Eli made a move to help her, but Aras was there first. Locating her with his free hand, he elbowed Esther to the side, jabbing her once, hard, in the stomach.

Esther fell to the ground, the rope flying from her hands. It slithered like a snake into the leafy mess, where it sank, beyond reach.

It was only now that Rhea seemed to understand what had happened to her. A wave of panic crossed her face. Then she began to shriek, still clawing at the shredded rubber floating around her, slapping the water with her palms.

Esther crouched on the ground, wheezing painfully, when she felt something wet nudge her arm. It was Pilot, with Aras behind him.

"Let's go," he said over the screams. "Ain't nothing left to do."

Skar pulled Esther to her feet. Then one by one, everyone turned around and began drifting from the backyard. No one said anything; and no one looked at Silas, white-faced with shock, who trailed far behind the others. Only Asha, trembling, kept her hands pressed against her ears.

Soon the house was well behind them. The sound of shrieking grew fainter and fainter.

And then it stopped.

TEN

As the caravan made its way down the two-lane highway, no one spoke. The only sound was the clank of bicycle gears and the incessant creak of the makeshift wagons as they shifted in their traces.

Esther sensed a change in the way the others viewed Aras. Even though he had once won their trust, now they avoided him. Only Skar appeared untroubled; while somber, she seemed serene as she calmed a shaken Michal. But Silas, who had been closest to Rhea from the start, hung back, whispering to Joseph and Asha.

As for Eli, he was clearly furious. "He's got to go," he hissed to Esther when he caught up to her. Yet she refused to be pulled into an argument and bicycled ahead.

Esther knew that Aras's decision had been the right one. It was not only more sensible to let Rhea die quickly, but kinder, as well. Or did she just feel that way because she had never liked Rhea? With an uneasy feeling, Esther realized she didn't know for certain and wasn't sure if she ever would.

By now, the muscles in her legs burned so badly that each downward movement of the pedal took enormous effort. Still, she kept to the front of the caravan, setting a steady pace so the others could keep up.

Everyone except Joseph and Kai still had to take turns on the remaining bicycles; but because of the steep grade, this had become a chore rather than a welcome break. To Esther's surprise, Aras turned out to be a strong cyclist, as long as he was tethered to a wagon, riding at a slow pace and on a straight road. In fact, he was able to follow so well, she found herself forgetting he was blind. It came as a surprise when, after several hours, Esther stopped without warning and he collided into the back of her wagon.

"Watch it," he said. His voice was muffled around the smoking paper he still had clenched in his teeth. Pilot, who had been trotting a pace or so behind, stopped as well. "What happened?"

"Not sure," she said over her shoulder.

A hundred yards back, the road had expanded to four lanes as they left the protective shade of the forest. Esther knew that even with sunglasses, the brightness of the midday sky could play tricks on one's eyes. Still, it couldn't explain what she was staring at now. It seemed incomprehensible.

The road ahead of them had vanished.

Behind them, everyone else had stopped; they had seen it, too. Esther dismounted and walked down the road on stiff and aching legs, as the others waited. When she got closer, she saw that it wasn't a mirage.

The two-lane road ended abruptly, as did the land around it. Esther found herself on the edge of a steep cliff that seemed sheared from the mountainside they were on. She had to be careful not to stand too close to the crumbling edge as she gazed down; the earth under her feet was heavily cracked and seemed ready to give way.

Far below, the ruins of a bridge that had once spanned the now-dry riverbed lay scattered on the pitted ground. From where she stood, she could make out giant slabs of concrete still painted with fading yellow lines, steel cables that lay tangled in thick coils, massive girders that were twisted and bent like a child's toys. Together, they formed a broken path across to the other side, a quarter mile or so away, where the road picked up again.

Aras stood at her side, his dog panting by his feet. He cocked his head, seeming to feel the sun on his face.

"Hey," he said. "What is it?"

"There was a bridge," she replied. "Now it's gone."

He nodded. Then he bent down and brushed the ground with his free hand. He found what he was looking for and stood up. It was a large, gray rock the size of his fist. He threw it off the cliff. Esther watched it arc into the sky before dropping. A few seconds later, there was a distant clack as it hit the ground.

Aras grunted. "That a long ways down," he said.

But Esther wasn't listening. She was already investigating the side of the destroyed road, her feet scrambling over the remains of the bridge standing in the dusty shoulder.

"Where'd you go?" Aras called. He sounded irritated. By the time she returned, he was leaning against the hood of a car left on the side of the road. "I don't like when you walk off like that."

She bit back the retort that sprang to her lips. "I wanted to see if there's any way down."

He took a long drag, and when he spoke, it was in a strangled voice. "There ain't."

Esther didn't want to admit it, but he was right. It seemed that an earthquake had caused an entire section of the mountain to drop away, carving up the road as cleanly as if it had been sliced by a knife. The exposed cross section of earth was dry and crumbling, with tree roots that stuck out and dangled over thin air. It was impossible for anyone to make her way down, much less an entire party.

Aras took her silence as confirmation. "This must of happened last year or two . . . first time I heard of it, anyways. We got to go back and try another road. Too bad, though. Long detour." He stood up, and his dog got to its feet as well, its collar jangling.

But Esther didn't move.

"Ain't you coming?" he asked. He turned to her, his dark glasses flashing in the sun.

"It seems crazy to make a detour," Esther said at last. "That's going to add days." She didn't mention another fear: that the others, repelled and frightened by Aras's callousness, might rebel altogether and refuse to follow.

He laughed. "What you suggesting? We fly?"

"No," she said. "But there's got to be something else." After a second, she added, "We could lower ourselves down."

Aras grew silent. Esther assumed he was getting ready to dismiss the idea and braced herself for more of his scorn. Then to her shock, he nodded.

"That ain't the worst idea," he said.

By now, Eli had approached, his brow creased with concern. "Can we get across?" he asked. But Aras ignored him and was already pushing past, his dog nosing its way to the supply wagon.

Esther saw Eli shoot the guide a look of pure hatred and spoke up hurriedly.

"Come," she said. "I need your help."

As she had hoped, Eli brightened at the suggestion. Together, they walked to the precipice. "We're going to have to get down there," Esther said.

Eli glanced up sharply. "Whose idea is this? You or him?"

Esther hesitated for only a second. "Mine."

The boy nodded. Then he too peered over the edge of the cliff, gauging the distance.

"We need someplace secure," Esther said. "Somewhere that won't give under our weight."

Eli gazed at the ground, crumbling and cracked beneath their feet. When Aras returned, he was carrying a large coil of bright blue, braided-nylon rope. Eli addressed him.

"Maybe we should try over here," he said. "The pavement seems pretty strong, and we—"

But Aras cut him off. "That stupid," he said. "You can't just throw a rope over and let people down."

Eli bristled, but before he could say anything, Esther touched his arm. "He's right," she said. "If the rope drags along the edge, it'll wear down."

As Eli bit his lip, Esther turned to Aras. She had already examined the trees that edged the cliff on the side of the road, towering oaks and pines that grew so high, it was hard to see where they ended. "Maybe if we found a strong enough branch," she said. "We could throw the rope over that, so it hangs clear of the edge. That way, we could—"

"No," Aras said, interrupting once again. "Same problem. The rope will wear down over the wood. And it's still too heavy."

Eli's face darkened. "Listen," he said in a rough voice. He stepped toward Aras, his fists clenching by his sides. "You don't know what you're talking about. And I don't like how you talk to people. Why don't you—"

"Wait," Aras said.

It was as if he hadn't been listening. He and his dog headed back to the supply wagon, where he groped around. When he returned, he was holding a large metal spool that held a short length of brown rubber cord.

"That's not long enough," Eli started to say, but Aras ignored him; he was already pulling off the rubber cord and discarding it.

"Give me the rope," he ordered, and Esther handed it to

him. As Aras spoke, he demonstrated.

"We got to lower stuff without snapping the rope. So what we should do is take this"—he held up the spool—"and hang it away from the edge. We thread the rope over it and tie it to the thing we're going to lower. And we do it that way."

Esther was concentrating, trying to understand. Then she nodded. "Yeah," she said. "That makes sense."

"So where can we hang this?"

To her surprise, Esther realized Aras was addressing her. She took the object from him—threading her hand through its narrow core so it rested on her arm like an oversize bracelet— as well as a kitchen knife. She had identified a massive oak that was far enough from the cliff to be secure, but close enough so that its branches extended well over the drop. Now she stood before it as she looped the coil of nylon rope over her shoulder, as well.

"No," said Eli, "it's too dangerous. Let me."

Esther shook her head, even as Aras snapped at him, "You weigh too much." By now, Skar had joined them. She also met Esther's eyes in a silent question.

"It's okay," said Esther. "It's my idea. I'll do it."

She gazed up at the tree. It rose straight up and the lowest branches were more than twenty feet above her head. Yet Skar had taught her how to climb even the smoothest-seeming wall, and this was rough and pitted with knotholes.

Esther began to pull herself up on the rough bark. She gripped the tiny bumps and cracks of the tree's surface with her fingers and the battered tips of her sneakers, pausing every few feet to reassess her position and plan her next handhold. Even so, she moved upward with surprising speed and soon made it to the heaviest branch. Then, still holding the metal spool and length of nylon rope, she lay on her stomach and inched along its length, until she was far over the precipice.

Working with meticulous care, Esther cut off a section of cable and strung the core on it. She then attached it to the branch, passing the cord around the thick limb again and again to make it as secure as possible. Then she knotted it tightly.

Esther tried not to look down. She didn't want to be distracted by what lay below; she couldn't risk dropping anything. Yet when she glanced away for a moment, the world seemed to spin around her. Esther shut her eyes and counted to ten, clinging to the rough branch until she regained her composure. Then she opened her eyes, steeling herself to focus on the task at hand.

Finally, the metal spool hung in place. Esther leaned forward, hugging the branch, and tested it; it rolled without a hitch. She took the coil of rope off her shoulder, threaded one thick end around the pulley, and secured it around her waist. Feeding out line as she went, she edged her way back along the limb and down the trunk. At last, she was able to jump to the ground, where Aras was waiting.

"Did you tie it tight?" he asked. "Because if you didn't—"

This time, it was Esther's turn to cut him off. "Of course."

Aras started experimenting with the rope, feeling how the pulley rolled and testing its strength as he pulled on it. "Seems about right," was all he said.

"What should we send down first?" asked Eli, but Aras shook his head.

"It got to be *somebody*," he said. "Someone got to make sure everything else steers clear of the wall."

Esther noticed that Aras didn't say what was on everyone's minds: that they had to send someone so they could see if the pulley system worked or even held up. If it didn't, whoever it was would plunge to a certain death.

Skar reached for the rope but Esther was already there, taking hold of it and knotting a small loop in one end. "I'll go."

Eli started to object, but Aras pulled him aside.

"If she want to go, let her," he said. "You best off staying here so you can help me bring down the others, anyway."

"It's easy for you to tell someone else to go," Eli retorted. "Since you can't."

"I said," Esther repeated, "I'll go."

This quieted the two boys. As they took hold of the other end of rope, Esther stuck her foot into the loop. She wrapped one arm around the braided nylon, holding on to it with her free hand. Then she stood on the edge of the cliff.

The air was thick with humidity. Far overhead, black dots circled in the air. She recognized them as scavengers, birds that lived off the dead. *Did they know something she didn't?* She shook off the thought, smiling at her own superstitions.

And with that, she stepped into the void.

As Esther dropped and swung, she could feel her weight yanking on the rope and straining the pulley attached to its branch high overhead. So far, it seemed to be holding.

She kept her eyes open, and as she dropped back, Esther extended both a hand and her free foot to absorb the impact when she collided with the dusty cliff face. As she bounced off, she began to spin, faster and faster, as the rope straightened. She had not expected this and feared that she would lose her grip. Any more acceleration, and she would be thrown to the rocks below.

Then as her friends paid out the line a few inches at a time, the revolutions grew slower and slower. Soon, she was heading straight down. The ground came rushing up to meet her and dizzy yet safe, she stepped onto it with her free foot.

"Made it!" she called up.

The next to try was Skar. She had brought another long length of rope; she tied one end to the cord supporting her and dropped the other end. This Esther used to stabilize her friend from below, steering her away from the cliff wall. After Skar made it down, the nylon cord with its guideline was pulled back up. Then Asha, Michal, Silas, Joseph, and Kai followed, the last wailing from inside a wooden crate. After everyone was safely on the ground, Eli and Aras lowered the four bicycles and two wagons, one at a time, to those who waited below.

Eli came next. He was the heaviest, and Esther wondered how Aras alone could handle the task of lowering him. But again, their guide surprised her with his strength. Eli made it safely; the pulley had held up well.

Esther was gazing upward, waiting for Aras, who was securing his dog in the wooden crate that had held Kai. They had agreed that after he sent the dog down, he would lower himself last of all. But a touch on her arm made Esther look back.

Skar was pointing at the horizon.

"We have to hurry," she said.

At first, Esther didn't know what she meant. Then she realized that a heavy wind was blowing. The sun had disappeared and, in its place, turbulent clouds filled the sky. The stiff wind swept unchecked across the dry and exposed riverbed, blowing grit that stung the skin and blinded the eye. As Esther watched, distant lightning flickered along the horizon.

A rainstorm was approaching. And the nine of them were outside and exposed, without tarps or protection of any kind.

Above, Aras was calling, but his words were almost impossible to hear.

"No time! I'm coming down with Pilot!"

As he spoke, there was a distant boom of thunder. The others hesitated and Esther could sense their mixed feelings. Part of them wanted to save themselves and leave the guide to his fate. Yet they couldn't quite abandon him.

Esther glanced at Skar, who nodded.

Skar led the others toward a section of the destroyed bridge that was still standing. It wasn't much, but it had a roof of sorts and was surrounded by piles of broken concrete that would afford some protection from the driving rain.

Then Esther turned her attention to the guide.

The crate was swaying crazily in the wind. From it, Esther could hear the dog barking. Aras had straddled the wooden box and was holding tight to the rope, letting it out as quickly as he could. His long, matted locks were lashed by the wind. Even from where she stood, she could see the muscles in his neck and shoulders strain from the effort.

Esther did all she could to stabilize them with the guideline. It was almost impossible to do; buffeted by the lashing wind, the heavy wooden box swung and spun, and the force of it nearly yanked her off her feet. Yet if she let go, it would collide with the cliff face, where it would shatter in midair.

Esther glanced over her shoulder, and when she did, her heart contracted in panic. Dark storm clouds had massed in the sky, extending toward the horizon. Heavy rain was already visible in the distance.

Above the roar of the approaching storm, Esther could hear Aras's voice.

"I'm all right! Go to the others!"

But Esther ignored him and continued to steer the crate, using the guideline. She refused to look behind her; instead, she shut her eyes to better focus on what she had to do.

Then someone grabbed her by the shoulder. It was Aras, holding his dog by its collar.

"Let's go!" he screamed at her over the wind.

Together, they bent low and ran for the shelter. Esther went first, pulling Aras by the hand; he stumbled over the broken ground but still managed to keep up. Ahead of them, Esther could see the group watching from deep inside the overhang.

As Esther and Aras fell into the shelter, the dog at their heels, the sky seemed to crack open behind them. With a roar of thunder that echoed across the valley, lightning blazed across the blackened sky, illuminating the landscape as brightly as a comet. Then torrential rain began to fall.

Hands were already dragging them deeper into the protective cave. There, Michal was ready with a dry sweatshirt while Skar checked the two for any traces of rain. But both Esther and Aras had escaped unscathed.

In the recesses of the makeshift shelter, a warm glow revealed the others who had gathered around a small fire. Eli was already tending a pan, filled with dirty water. Once it boiled, he scooped up a mugful, which he strained through a folded-up towel. He passed the drink up front to her.

"Here," he said. "You need this."

Esther smiled her thanks, but after a moment, gave the cup first to Aras, pressing it against his fingers. He hesitated, then accepted it. That was when she realized that not only was he trembling from exertion, his hands and arms were torn and bloodied from handling the rope.

Aras blew on the steaming liquid before taking a long sip.

"Thanks," he said, "for sticking around."

He was already fumbling a fresh smoking paper from his pocket. He lit it, then held it out.

"You want some?" It was the first time Esther had ever seen him offer anything to anyone.

"No," she replied.

He hesitated. Then abruptly, he flicked the object outside. It hit the ground, throwing sparks before the rain extinguished it with a sizzling sound.

"Thank you," said Esther in a soft voice.

* * *

The torrent continued for several hours. Afterward, even after the sun emerged, everyone stayed in the shelter, waiting for the water to either seep into the earth or disappear into the warming air. Most of the party took advantage of the break by curling on the ground and sleeping.

A few remained awake.

Skar used the time to explore the length of the overhang, taking with her the fine new bow and arrows Esther had given her from Aras. When she returned after an hour, she carried a dead crow. It wasn't much and she knew its flesh would be stringy and acrid; still, fresh meat would be a welcome surprise and she set to work plucking and cleaning it.

Although Esther was exhausted, she also chose to stay awake, checking the bicycles and wagons while keeping an eye on the sky. The scavenging birds she had seen circling earlier had returned after the storm. Clearly, a large animal had perished out there, perhaps a wild pig or even a deer. She calculated how long it would be until it was safe to venture outdoors. If they were lucky, they might be able to steal whatever dead thing was on the riverbed and take it for themselves.

Skar had the same thought.

"I'll go with you," she whispered. The two girls set off.

The ground was baked to a cracked white clay and so dry, most of the rainwater had run off altogether or collected in shallow pools. Even so, the girls took care heading across the desolate landscape, avoiding the deep cracks in the earth that still glistened with moisture.

Ahead of them, they could see that the seething mass of birds had piled atop their food, fighting and squawking. The sound of their cries echoed across the valley. As they ate, the sun shone on their shifting black feathers, creating an oily sheen. Smaller scavengers also hopped along the outskirts, squabbling over bits of meat that fell to the side.

When they were close enough, Esther and Skar both began to shout and clap their hands. Startled, the birds rose in the air as one, a feathered mob with a single mind. Then as the girls ran forward, their cloud broke apart and each bird took off alone, screaming its fury.

Smiling, Esther got to the dead thing first, already reaching for her knife. But when she saw what it was, she gave a cry.

It was a human body.

Still clothed in tattered robes, jeans, and sneakers, it lay facedown, one arm extended in front of it as if in appeal.

When Skar joined her a moment later, Esther had one hand pressed to her mouth and her face was white. For while the birds had done terrible damage to the body, the worst wound had clearly been inflicted by another person. The back of the person's head had been blown away.

Esther hesitated, then turned to Skar, who nodded. Her expression was grim.

Esther reached with a foot and taking great care, prodded the shoulder, which was sodden with rainwater. In one quick movement, she turned the corpse over, so that its face was revealed.

It was a boy. And although time and animals, not to mention

exposure to the sun and rain, had done their cruel work on what used to be its face, there was no mistaking who it was.

Rafe.

Attached to the front of his robe was a tattered piece of paper, damp around the edges. It was a frayed remnant of map, with clumsy, block letters scrawled across it that were just legible. Esther needed several moments to decipher it.

He wunt git to Mundreel neethr.

Skar and Esther had to improvise a burial. The ground was too hard to dig and they had no tools; the two girls ended up collecting rocks to cover him with, so more animals couldn't get to him. As she worked, Esther's heart was cold as she thought of all that Rafe had done and brought upon her.

Still, he had been human, like her.

"Let's keep this between ourselves," Esther said, as they headed back.

Skar nodded. Neither girl spoke what was on her mind: *Lewt and the others had killed him. But where were they? Why had they left the message? Even now, were they lying in wait for them?*

"What will we do if they . . ." Skar began, then trailed off.

At first, Esther didn't answer. Then she said the only thing she could think of. "We'll find out when we get there."

ELEVEN

THREE DAYS LATER, JOSEPH POKED HIS HEAD FROM HIS WAGON AND squinted at a road sign.

"Look."

From her bicycle in front of him, Esther tried to read the sign, but the letters swam in front of her eyes in a senseless jumble.

"I think it's another language." Her friend sounded excited, although Esther didn't know what his words meant. Seeing her confusion, he added, "I think we're almost there."

She could only hope so.

While the caravan had managed to rejoin the major highway

and get back on track, a trance seemed to have settled over the group.

It wasn't due to hunger. The pointed nuts with the leathery caps were plentiful; and after they were boiled until the water ran clear and then ground into a thick paste, they were even good to eat. Skar, too, was able to catch an occasional rabbit or squirrel to add to the pot, sharpening and reusing her remaining arrows as best she could. And while the drinking water they boiled was often cloudy and musty, there was enough of it as well.

Yet the travelers faced a new crisis: Everyone was dazed by exposure.

After so many days on the road, the incessant glare of the sun and the air itself threatened to erase any vestige of civilization they had once known. As Caleb predicted, they had begun to feel like animals.

Esther realized how badly she missed sleeping in a familiar bed, in a home that was hers. Even a solid roof and sturdy walls would mean so much to all of them; she hoped that the next building they reached would be intact, if only for the night.

They took the next exit and followed the smaller road another mile.

There they saw it.

A strange-looking rectangular structure stood by itself on the edge of an asphalt lot, a dusty pickup truck still parked in front. Looking like one of the ancient train cars that sat on rusted tracks leading outside of Prin, the little edifice, one-roomed and almost too small to be called a building, had windows on all sides, as well as two short steps leading up to a door in the side. Though most of the paint had long since peeled away, a bit of green remained.

When she poked her head in, Esther realized it was a restaurant, though different from others she had Gleaned. There was a long, dusty counter that ran down the length of the room, with round-topped stools in front. No more than an arm's reach away was a row of booths, each made of two cracked-leather couches facing a narrow table. The black and white tiles on the floor were mostly intact; the windows were unbroken and even the ceiling had no holes that she could see. All in all, it was a good place to spend the night, to rest and regroup, if only for a while.

Skar and Michal decided to remain outside and look for game while there was still light. The others filed in, grateful for the shelter. Eli was already gathering twigs and rubbish to start a fire in their one remaining firebowl, as Silas headed to a booth in the back. He curled up and promptly went to sleep. Asha and Joseph did a quick Glean behind the counter, but found only a few inedibles: oversize bottles of what smelled like cleaning liquid, large plastic bags full of an unfamiliar powder, a broom. A small kitchen behind swinging doors seemed more promising, and they disappeared within to continue their search.

In her own booth, Esther tried to soothe a restless Kai. First, she held him in her lap, bouncing him up and down. Then she took his soft hands and clapped them together. But the boy jerked in her arms, fussing and struggling, so at last she set him on the ground.

Kai had been crawling for months, and in the past few weeks had learned to pull himself to a standing position. Now, he jerked free of Esther's guiding hands. He tottered forward, concentrating hard, and took four stumbling steps before sitting down hard.

When she saw Kai's astonished expression, Esther burst out laughing.

"You did it!" She crouched by his side and hugged him tight. *It seemed like a miracle.*

But Kai was already trying to wriggle away. He wanted to try again; but it had been a long day and he was clearly tired, yawning even as he struggled to be set down. Esther knew that a baby could grow too tired even to fall asleep. She rummaged in her bag for something to distract and calm him with, some toy or piece of clothing.

Her hand struck something hard.

It was the book that Esther had taken as a reminder of her sister: *The Wonderful Wizard of Oz*. Over the past few weeks, Joseph had gotten into the habit of reading from it each night to help the boy fall asleep. Esther had listened, as well. Although at first she had to stop and ask Joseph many questions, she soon became absorbed by the strange tale of the girl named Dorothy and her quest to find the elusive Wizard. A piece of paper marked where Joseph had last read; they were almost at the end.

Now Kai grabbed at the book, familiar with the ritual and impatient for it to start. With a pang, Esther wished she could read well enough to complete the story. She was about to look for something else when she sensed a person standing opposite her.

It was Joseph, apparently no use in the kitchen. "Shall I finish it?" he asked.

Relieved, Esther smiled and slid over on the bench, making room. "Sure."

Joseph settled next to her, folding up his long legs in the restricted space as he found the book marker. And then he began to read.

The girl named Dorothy and her three friends, on their way to see Glinda, were being menaced by frightening creatures with no arms and terrible, flat heads that they used to attack. Esther didn't notice that Kai grew heavy and still in her arms; she was wholly engrossed by the strange and exciting tale. Before she knew it, he was on the final page.

"'From the Land of Oz,' said Dorothy gravely. 'And here is Toto, too. And oh, Aunt Em! I'm so glad to be at home again!'"

Joseph closed the book. In the sudden silence, he tiptoed away and Esther became aware of the sleeping child in her lap. As she lifted him onto the table, she found herself moved by the ending of the tale. She could not explain why. Then she sensed something behind her and heard the familiar jingle of a dog's collar.

Aras was sitting in the booth at her back, Pilot resting his head on the boy's feet.

"Were you listening?" she asked. After a moment, he nodded.

"Is it true, that story?"

At first, Esther thought he was joking. Sarah had often read to her when she was little, fanciful stories of talking animals, trolls, goblins, and fairies. But Aras seemed sincere. "I think," she offered, "that it was made-up."

"What you mean? Ain't it in a book?"

"Not everything in books is true."

Aras seemed to bristle. "Well, if it ain't true, then what's the point?"

Esther thought this over. Then she spoke, choosing her words with care.

"I think it means . . . that maybe you shouldn't trust in a wizard who doesn't even have any power. 'Cause the power's with you, all along. And that home is people. The ones you love."

Aras stayed still, looking in the direction of Esther's voice, petting Pilot's head. Then Esther heard the creak of leather and the jangle of Pilot's chain as the boy stood up and walked away.

Esther sat alone, staring at the baby. Then she curled into the booth like a child herself. She meant to rest her eyes for only a few moments. Yet soon she was deeply asleep.

In her dreams was a highway paved with golden bricks, one that led to a magical city ruled by a benevolent leader.

Another person in the restaurant was wide awake.

Asha sat alone on a soft, cracked seat that dripped stuffing. Unlike Aras, she had paid no attention to the strange story. Instead, she played with the tattered remains of blinds that covered the window and stared openly at Esther and Kai.

She had watched as the baby nestled in Esther's arms, as his hands reached up and explored her mouth or got lost in her hair. Although Esther kept her attention on her strange friend, Joseph, she never stopped soothing the child, stroking his cheek, bouncing him gently. Without even knowing she was doing it, Asha copied her exact movements in the air.

Soon, Kai was nearly asleep and Esther lowered him into her lap. Asha did the same thing. She held her thin arms by the elbows in her lap, creating a cradle. Then she began to rock it.

"Shh," she whispered, "shh," for her baby was crying.

Across the room, Eli had watched Asha watching Esther. Now he came over and sat across from her.

"What's your baby's name?" he whispered.

Asha looked up, surprised she had been seen. Yet she wasn't embarrassed.

"Asha," she said, after a moment's hesitation. Then she frowned. "No, that's not right. That's *my* name." She glanced around, and her eye fell on a dusty object stuck to the wall above the table. It had a broken glass panel and a push-button alphabet in the middle.

"What's that say?" She pointed at its name.

Eli squinted at the squiggly script, sounding out the letters under his breath. "Crosley," he said at last.

"Crosley," she repeated. "That's my baby's name." Then she resumed her rocking.

Eli smiled. He had noticed Asha's interest in Esther before. But he had not understood how far it went, until now.

Asha imitated Esther not simply because she wanted to be

the other girl. She did it because she wanted to be older—as old, in fact, as she really was.

And what could be more grown-up than having a child?

"Shh, Crosley," Asha said to her baby. "Shh."

Asha seemed natural as a mother. Yet no matter how much she yearned to have a real child of her own, whether she could handle it was another question.

She could not do it alone.

Eli didn't know what his future held. His life, already short, was ever more precarious. But he was only fifteen; perhaps he would live another three or four years. For as much as he disliked Aras, Eli had to admit the guide was far more competent than he ever would have imagined.

Maybe he could get them to Mundreel, after all.

And yet, Eli couldn't help glancing at Esther. In the flickering light cast by the firebowl, her face glowed, and for the thousandth time, his heart ached. For Eli had always loved her, ever since childhood. He had protected and helped her when the town turned against her; he had even asked her to be his partner. But she had turned him down, choosing Caleb instead. And now that Caleb was dead, she seemed to have space in her heart only for his child.

Esther would never let Eli into her life, no matter how badly he wished it. It was clear to him, now. He had to live in the real world, today. If Esther would never be his partner, someone else might. Someone right across from him.

"Maybe," he said, "you need a little help with the baby."

Asha looked at him, as Eli extended his arms, palms up.

"Here," he said. "Maybe I can get him to stop crying."

Asha thought for a second. Then, very carefully, she passed the imaginary child to Eli.

"There you go," he said, nuzzling it and holding it close. "There you go."

Outside, the sky was an unearthly pink as the giant orange sun hung close to the horizon. Michal and Skar were hunting, as they did together nearly every evening now.

Of course, Skar was the only one hunting. Michal tagged along for reasons she couldn't name. With each passing day, she found herself opening up to the variant girl as she had to no one else. And she loved to watch Skar as she looked for prey. Skar, so small and friendly and vulnerable-looking, moved with the same grace and intensity as Joseph's cat. The tall grass barely rippled as she advanced through it, her bow drawn.

Now Skar cocked her head and froze. Behind her, Michal stopped in midstep and held her breath.

Skar paused, motionless. Then in one movement, she brought the loaded bow to her shoulder and released. Michal had no idea what she was aiming at; but ahead, there was a high squeal and a flurry in the grass. Then all was still.

Skar relaxed. Then she turned to Michal with a smile.

"You bring me luck," she said.

Michal smiled back. The hood of her robe was down, as it always was when the two were alone, and the soft breeze of the evening felt good. Being with Skar was the only time she felt she did not have to hide. It was the only time she felt safe.

Skar had walked to her prey and was skinning the rabbit, as her friend watched.

"Teach me to hunt," Michal said.

"What?" Skar turned. "Why?"

"Because," she blurted out, "I want to know everything you know."

Skar smiled a little, then shrugged. "I don't know if I can. They started teaching me when I was just a baby."

In fact, Skar had taught Esther how to shoot, much as she had taught her many other variant skills over the years. But teaching Esther had been easy, because her feelings for her were simple. Skar would always love Esther, who was her best friend. Yet Esther had never once made Skar feel breathless and fluttery in the pit of her stomach.

The way Michal did.

"Okay," Skar said. "Come here."

As Michal advanced to her side, Skar was aware of total silence in the woods, except for the far-off cry of birds. She wiped the blood from her fingers before she placed her curved bow into the girl's outstretched hands.

"Don't be afraid," Skar said. "You won't break it."

The weapon was smooth and rounded, shaped from a single length of wood, with catgut strung between the two notched ends. Michal still hesitated, so Skar moved the other girl's hand until it gripped the center.

"Feel okay?"

"Yes," Michal answered.

"Now put three fingers around the string," Skar said. "One

finger curled, the other two holding each other. Hugging."

"Do it for me."

Skar hesitated. Then she moved behind Michal and placed her hand on top of hers.

By now, Skar's cheek was an inch away from Michal's. Michal could not remember the last time she had been so close to another human since she'd been maimed.

"Now pull it back," Skar said.

Together, the girls drew the string until it could go no farther. They stood like that for an endless moment; and then Michal let her face rest very gently against Skar's cheek. Michal wasn't sure why she did it, and for a moment dreaded Skar's response. But while it lasted, she closed her eyes and luxuriated in the smooth, soft warmth of someone else's flesh.

"I'm sorry," she said in a small voice, her eyes still closed. "I can't help it. It feels so good."

There was a pause. Then as if nothing unusual had happened, Skar reached her other arm and helped Michal steady the bow. Michal was now enfolded in the other girl's arms; she could feel the heat of her body pressed against her back and the small muscles clenched against her. The sensation was one of strength and softness at the same time, a strange and dizzying mix. And she could now smell Skar, a scent that was sweet yet spicy, a bit of both boy and girl.

"Okay," Skar said. Her voice shook a little. "Now let go."

They did, together, and the empty string snapped forward with a twang.

"That was good," Skar said. "For your first time."

The violent motion had separated them, and Michal staggered a bit. She felt self-conscious and averted her gaze. Yet when she glanced back, she saw that Skar was looking at her, with a serious, questioning expression.

"I love you." The words came out before Michal knew what she was saying and she blushed.

"Me, too," whispered Skar.

Michal had never felt this way in her life—not with Levi, certainly, with whom she felt at best an employee, at worst a slave. His skin had been pasty white and grotesquely soft; yet his physical attentions had been rough, even cruel. She had endured his touch, never desired it. But this was the opposite of how she felt with Skar.

As for Skar, she was shocked by the depth of her feelings for Michal. Unlike the other girl, Skar had known love. She loved her brother and Esther; she had even loved Tarq, at least at first. But what she felt for the girl who stood before her, the one with the rare soul beneath the damaged face, was beyond all that. It was something new.

"I want us to be partnered," Skar said.

Michal started and her face flushed.

It wasn't that the idea of being with a girl shocked her. After all, boys sometimes became partners with one another, and females, too. But Michal could not help but remember the hateful, echoing taunts about variants that she heard her entire life: that they were freaks, animals, not really people.

Yet Skar, with all of her delicate toughness, was as human as she was. With Skar, Michal felt emotions she thought had been closed to her forever. What could be wrong with that?

Michal remembered the swaying, treacherous drop, when each of them was lowered by rope to safety. One wrong move and any one of them might have plummeted to her death. Who knew what would happen tomorrow? How long did any of them have to live? And so why did any of the old rules even apply anymore?

To live with death so close was terrible, she realized, *but at least it meant one thing was true.*

She was free to do what she pleased.

"Yes," Michal said.

She took the hem of her robes in order to tear a strip from it. That was how it was done; they would bind their wrists together and speak their vows. But Skar held her back.

"I need you to see something," she said.

The variant girl held out the underside of her right arm. Among the many scars and tattoos that swirled and wound their way around her slender limb, one stood out: a pink ridge of raised skin that flowed its way from wrist bone to elbow.

"This is my partnering scar," she said. "From Tarq."

With a finger, Michal traced it from one end to the other.

"That is over," Skar said. "I am no longer partnered to him. Yet I can't remove this . . . it stays written on my skin."

Michal nodded.

The variant reached into the pouch slung at her side. From it, she removed the hunting knife she had just used to skin and gut the rabbit. She held it out like a question.

"I can give us new markings," she said. "Mine will be on the other arm and it will be deeper and longer than the one Tarq gave me. Yours will be on the same place on the opposite arm. But only if you want."

Michal hesitated.

"It will only hurt for a minute," said Skar. "And it will be beautiful." Skar placed a soft hand against Michal's ruined face. "Though you can never be less than beautiful. Not to me."

"It's not that." Smiling, Michal shook her head; she no longer feared pain or disfigurement. "I want us to do something new. Because *we're* new. We're something no one has ever been before." She thought, then glanced up at Skar. "This will do instead."

She took Skar's face in both of her hands and gently kissed her lavender eyes, her flattened cheekbones, the scars that wound around her throat. Skar did the same to her, brushing her mouth softly against Michal's ravaged features, her golden hair, her brilliant blue eyes. Then the two girls kissed on the lips, lingeringly.

"Now," whispered Michal, "we are partnered." Yet even as she spoke, they heard shouts.

Through the sparse foliage, they could see the diner in the distance. The sounds were coming from that direction.

Something was terribly wrong.

TWELVE

W**HEN** T**ARQ HAD RETURNED HOME TO PICK UP HIS HUNTING EQUIPMENT,** he noted Skar's absence with annoyance.

It happened every time she made a mistake or disobeyed him. After Tarq finished disciplining her, she would go off by herself for a few hours—to cry, he assumed, the way girls did. When she returned, she would invariably be sullen and withdrawn.

He headed back out to meet friends for an afternoon of hunting, and afterward spent time with them skinning and cleaning what they had caught. One of them brought with him a bottle of clear liquid he had found in the clutter of an abandoned store. It was Tarq's favorite drink, the kind that was fiery to the taste, loosened your tongue, and took away your worries. He drank more than his share, and soon grew red-faced and loud, boasting and laughing.

The thought of Skar kept nagging at him, however, prickling like a burr.

Tarq was keenly aware of his place in the community and valued his position above all else. It was, in fact, the main reason he had courted Skar in the first place. She was the younger, beloved sister of their leader, Slayd, and a simple girl, eager to please. Winning her affection had been easy: a few sweet words, some meaningless trinkets, and she—and the status she brought with her—were his. Overnight, Tarq became someone of consequence, a person to be reckoned with. Even now, as he joked and bantered with his hunting companions, he knew that deep down, each was envious of him and covetous of his position.

So Skar's absence was a slap at him that others might see. It was essential that no one notice there was anything wrong.

Tarq had a flash of worry that Skar had gone to her brother: She treated her doting sibling more like a father. Then he dismissed the concern. Skar would never go behind Tarq's back and speak against him; her loyalty to him and shame at her own failings, he knew, were too great. And, until today, Tarq had always been careful to keep her face intact and not to break any of her bones. He also showed her how to cover her bruises with mud so no one would notice the extent of his corrections.

Skar would never involve anyone else in their business.

This time, admittedly, he had gotten a little carried away. The floor was still splattered with her blood, which she would have to clean up once she got home. Yet it was only because Skar had forced him to do it. She had gone against his orders. She had traveled to Prin to see that girl, the norm they called Esther, even after he had forbidden her to speak to her again. After all, Esther had once been cast off by her own kind; knowing her could only bring trouble.

Tarq felt he had acted appropriately, but he was aware that others might not agree. And if one of them told Slayd, there was no telling what the outcome might be. All this added to his sense of uneasiness.

By the time Tarq returned home with the skinned bodies of two squirrels and a woodchuck slung over his shoulder, the sun had dropped low in the sky. He was surprised to see that the main room was still in the same disarray as it had been early that morning, with furniture knocked over and blood blackening on the floor.

Skar had not returned.

The variant boy sat alone in the dark of their shack, his arms resting on his knees. The exuberance that the drink had brought had vanished; now, his head was heavy, his temples throbbed, and he was hungry. *Not having his dinner waiting for him,* he thought muzzily, *was yet another thing to be angry about.* To calm himself, he pictured the ways he would discipline Skar when she came creeping back.

He would put an end to this nonsense for once and for all.

This time, he wouldn't worry about being found out. By now, it was clear he had been wronged; it had been many hours since his partner had left, without permission or explanation. This was unusual in the extreme. Was there anyone who would argue with his right to discipline her?

But when the night deepened, Skar still had not returned.

Might she have run away?

The thought of Skar surviving on her own was so ridiculous as to be downright laughable. She was too small, too weak, too silly.

Tarq was tempted to go outside and search for her himself; but he didn't care to let any inquisitive neighbor know he was concerned about her whereabouts. Instead, he diverted himself by searching for her favorite possessions one by one: a pair of mirrored sunglasses, a blue glass bowl, a battered doll from her childhood, her clothing. He twisted, smashed, and shredded each item, until the floor was littered with trash.

Each small act of destruction gave him a sense of purpose. Yet as the hours continued to slide by he grew less and less satisfied by these escapades. He began to dwell morbidly on the possibilities.

Over and over, Tarq recalled what Skar had told him: something about the norms leaving Prin for good. Had Skar decided to abandon her home and run away with them?

As his incredulity gave way to certainty, it ignited an anger that blossomed until it became white-hot rage. He would not be made a fool of by a girl. And he would kill anyone who disrespected him.

Then Tarq looked down at the broken doll clutched in his hand.

He knew he had to proceed with care.

If he were to hunt down Skar, he would first have to seek permission from her brother. Slayd was a ruthless warrior, harsh and punitive toward all females except his younger sister. He would not stand for any display of anger against her on Tarq's—or anyone's—part.

Sure enough, when Tarq appeared outside Slayd's home early the next morning, the variant leader did not usher him in. Instead, he kept him standing on the threshold like a common stranger, and his voice and manner were cold.

"What is it?"

Tarq averted his eyes.

"It is your sister," he replied, putting on a look of sorrow and concern. "I overheard something the other day, and I am scared it has come true."

The leader didn't answer, which forced Tarq to continue.

"The norm girl," Tarq said. "The one called Esther. I heard her tell your sister that all of Prin was moving away, on account of the earthquake. She filled Skar's ears with some nonsense about a magical place that lies far away, a place full of food and water. Mundreel, it's called. She begged Skar to come with them."

After another long pause, Slayd's voice was weary. "That does not sound like something Esther would say." Then he glanced up, his expression sharp. "Unless she had reason."

Tarq avoided the implication. "I, too, was confused. But I swear upon my mother's grave that was what Esther told her. And although Skar refused at the time, she did not come home last night." The boy squinted, studying the ground, as if taking pains to think. "I think she has run away to join them."

Slayd grunted. "So what is it you want me to do?"

"I want your permission to take two men with me and go after her."

There was no reply at first. Tarq was forced to sneak a peek at Slayd, who was frowning, gazing into the distance.

"You may go," the variant leader said at last. "But you will go alone."

"But—" started Tarq, but Slayd cut him off.

"Right now, I only have your word . . . and I have yet to learn how much that is worth."

Anger flared hot in Tarq's breast, but he fought to control it. "I understand."

"I will want to hear from my sister firsthand why she left us, if that is what she has done. If you harm her in any way on the way back, you will suffer dearly for it."

"Of course. Of course." Tarq was bowing his head, backing away, his hands raised in a show of conciliation. It was only when he was inside his own home that he regained his full height and expelled a sigh of relief. The hardest part was over.

Already his mind was busy. He was deciding on the story he would tell the variant leader after he returned. Perhaps there would be an unforeseen attack by a pack of wild animals. Maybe there would be an unlucky stumble into a fast-moving stream, or an earthquake that swallowed his sister's body forever. For after Tarq tracked her down, there could be nothing left of Skar, no trace that might reveal what he was planning to do to her.

He would make certain of that.

* * *

There was no time to think.

Crouching low, Esther pushed Asha and Silas under one of the booths, where Joseph already cowered, clutching Kai. The child had awakened and was whimpering.

The flaming arrow had stuck, quivering, in the far wall, next to a window; the cheap and filthy curtains next to it ignited and instantly fried to a blackened wisp. Grabbing a towel, Esther tried to yank it out; when she couldn't, she attempted to smother its flames. But the projectile was wrapped in a T-shirt soaked in gasoline and the fire was unquenchable; it was already scorching the towel and she had to drop it. Underfoot, the threadbare carpet was starting to char in spots where orange embers had landed.

All around her, the air was filling with the stink of fuel as, one by one, burning arrows flashed through the broken windows and gaping door. They skittered across the floor, embedded in the upholstered benches and cheap walls, and bounced off the metal counter, trailing smoke and ash. One of them narrowly missed her, its fiery tail grazing her arm. By now, part of the low ceiling was blazing, as were several of the seats. The flames fed on their dry and ancient stuffing; and their cracked-vinyl upholstery burst open with a popping sound, melting and sizzling.

Somehow, Aras found her, his free hand clawing the smoke-filled air as the other kept hold of Pilot's leash. The dog was whining, anxious to get away. She pulled the boy down behind the counter.

"Who's attacking us?" she shouted over the muffled crackling and pops that surrounded them.

"They soaked with gasoline, right? That sounds like variants. A *variant*. They coming one at a time. Ain't no more than one shooter out there."

Stunned, Esther nodded, as the realization hit.

It had to be Tarq.

Skar was hunting with Michal. Esther could only hope that she had found a safe place to hide.

By now, the small restaurant was filled with smoke. Esther could barely see Joseph and the others as they huddled together, choking and coughing. Eli crouched against the front wall, stealing peeks over the windowsill.

"Let's bring everyone out through the back!" he yelled at her.

Esther made a quick decision. "Not yet . . . we don't know if it's a trap."

Even if Aras was right, there was no way of knowing if others were outside, waiting in ambush. The diner still provided a shelter of sorts. But Esther had to control the blaze before it grew any bigger.

As if reading her mind, Aras spoke. "Try to beat it out."

Her eyes stinging, Esther grabbed a blanket. The fire was mostly contained in one area, by the open kitchen doors, but it was spreading swiftly, consuming the walls and speckled tiles, and eating through the wooden planks below. When Esther approached, the heat became unbearable; the air was full of the sounds of unseen items made of glass and crockery popping and shattering. She attacked the flames with the wrap, attempting to beat them down. But she only fanned them higher.

"Not working!" she yelled at Aras.

Desperate, Esther looked around for anything else she could use. In Prin, everyone used dirt to put out fires. She searched farther and as she did, her eye fell on an orange plastic sack: ARM & HAMMER BAKING SODA.

On an impulse, she ripped it open and dug a hand into the soft, white powder. Cautious, she tossed it onto the flames, and they died instantly, sending up a plume of smoke. With that, she hoisted the heavy bag and upended it over the fire, shaking it to spread it evenly. Within seconds, the entire inferno had been extinguished.

"What'd you do?" Aras asked.

"I'm not sure," Esther answered. Yet there was no time to explain.

"Skar!" someone shouted from outside.

Esther took a quick glimpse through the window. A figure stood on the edge of the parking lot. He wore a bow across his wiry chest, and his quiver still held two arrows wrapped in dripping cloth. Although she had only met him twice, she had no trouble recognizing Tarq.

"Skar!" he shouted again.

He sounded more desperate than angry, Esther thought. *Maybe he could be reasoned with.* When she moved to the door, Eli grabbed her arm.

"What are you doing?"

"I'm going to talk to him." When Eli started to protest, she cut him off. "We got no other choice."

"Let me go instead," he insisted. But Esther shook her head.

"I know him. I bet he thinks it's beneath him to shoot a girl." Unsure, Eli turned to Aras, who nodded.

"Let her go," was all he said.

Esther pushed open the metal-and-glass door with a screech of rusty hinges. As she stepped outside, the light of the setting sun blinded her for a moment. Although she had spoken with assurance, her heart was pounding. *I better be right*, she thought.

Back inside, Aras was already scrabbling through their supplies until he found what he wanted. It was the primitive throwing stick Skar had fashioned from wood and a sharpened bicycle spoke.

"Keep it on him," he said to Eli as he handed it over, "in case she turn out to be wrong."

In the parking lot, Esther stood still. On the other side, shimmering waves of heat danced around Tarq, making it seem as if he were standing in a field of tall grass. She held her hands in front of her, palms up, to show she was unarmed.

When he saw who it was, Tarq's face darkened with anger. But he did not raise his weapon, Esther was relieved to see. She crossed the lot, taking care not to make any unexpected movements.

"Where is Skar?" he said.

Esther shook her head. "That doesn't matter. What matters is she wants to stay with us." As she drew even closer, Tarq visibly tensed; still, he did not cock his bow and arrow.

"Answer my question," he said in a harsh voice. He nodded toward the diner. "Is she inside with the others?"

"No," Esther replied. "So you'd better go, 'cause we're not handing her over."

In one move, Tarq was on her. Seizing Esther with one arm, he grabbed an arrow, which he pressed against her side.

"I have no fight with you," he said into her ear. "But I will kill anyone who tries to stand between me and my partner."

Tarq wrapped an arm around her neck. Esther could hardly breathe; although he was not much bigger than she was, it was like a band of steel around her throat. She gagged from the overpowering stink of gasoline that enveloped them both. Now he jabbed her with his weapon; it broke through thin cloth and bit into her ribs.

"Are you going to tell me where I can find her?" he said.

"He's got her." At the window, an agitated Eli drew back the stick as he attempted to take aim. Then he put it aside with a grunt of frustration. "It's no good," he said to Aras. "He's got her too close. If I miss, I'll hit her instead."

Aras only nodded. "Then all we can do is wait." Although he seemed calm, his knuckles were white as he held his dog's chain.

Esther felt the hot spill of blood down her side. She struggled to break free of Tarq's grip, twisting her neck into the crook of his arm and trying to pry his fingers loose, but it was no good; he was too strong. She had always prided herself on finding options when none seemed left. But as her mind continued to race, she realized she had nothing left but the truth.

"Killing me won't bring her back," she whispered. "And you'll have to kill me, because I ain't telling you where she is."

Tarq hesitated.

The girl was right; taking her life would not bring him any-thing. And even if she were bluffing, he could not help but feel a flicker of admiration for her courage. But he was aware that there were faces pressed against the diner windows, watching. He could not bear to look weak, especially in front of others.

"Very well," he said, his voice hardening. The girl had stopped fighting; she hung in his arms as defenseless as a pigeon . . . and just as easy to destroy. She seemed to be daring him to do it, which infuriated him even more.

Tarq made his choice: He had to finish what he started. But before he could shove the steel-tipped arrow between her ribs, he heard a familiar voice.

"Stop!"

Like a ghost, Skar materialized from behind a cluster of trees on the far side of the parking lot, looking taller than her slight frame. Tarq noticed she wore a new bow across her chest and that a skinned rabbit dangled from her belt. Trailing by her side was another norm, apparently a girl, heavily cloaked and hooded.

Tarq hesitated, and in that instant, Esther was able to wrench herself free.

From inside the diner, Eli lifted the stick again. "She's clear," he hissed to Aras. "Should I shoot?" But Aras held his hand up, listening.

"Wait," was all he said.

"Skar," said Tarq, his small teeth gleaming in a wide grin. *How easily he smiled,* Skar thought, *when he wanted something badly enough.* In three steps, he crossed the asphalt lot toward her. "I have come to take you home."

The variant girl stood still. "I already am home," she said.

Tarq made a dismissive sound. Then he went to take her by the wrist. With a swift move, Skar avoided his grasp; she knew better than anyone that it was like a manacle, impossible to break. "I do not expect you to understand."

Tarq stood there, more rattled than he cared to admit. This Skar seemed a completely different person than the one he knew, both stronger and older; and she appeared to mean what she said. For the first time, he felt a flicker of unease and so he decided to change his approach.

"Things will be better," Tarq said. His voice softened and he spoke with as much sincerity as he knew how. "Maybe I have not always done what is best. Maybe I should have treated you in a different way. You are written on my skin and in my soul." He reached an awkward hand to brush her face, but, unmoved by his words, she again evaded his touch.

"And you are also written on my skin," she replied in a toneless voice, "but only because you have done so against my will, and with your fists and your feet. I am no longer yours."

Tarq's eyes grew steely. "You cannot undo what our laws have decreed."

"Then I no longer accept our laws." Skar seemed to spit the words. She held out her hand and the cloaked figure next to her stepped closer and took it. "This is my partner now."

Tarq stared at the obscene sight before him. Skar was openly holding hands, intertwining fingers, with a girl with strange golden hair. His mind could not take it in and he burst into incredulous laughter.

"But she is a norm," he said at last in a mocking tone. As his laughter died down, he could not disguise the disgust and horror in his voice. "And she is a girl. Have you decided you are now a boy, Skar?" He gestured at the circle tattooed on Skar's upper arm. "Didn't you make another decision a long time ago?"

At this, Skar smiled for the first time. "I'm still a girl," she said. "And I love this girl."

Blind rage flared in Tarq's breast. Without thinking, he stepped forward and smacked the female norm once across the face, hard. She fell to the ground, her hood falling back to reveal a face so hideous that Tarq recoiled. The day's unreality increased, and the variant felt faint. Yet he wasted no time.

He seized Skar by the throat so quickly, she had no time to use her weapon; the knife she had pulled from her pocket fell to the ground. "You will not bring me such dishonor," he breathed. "I will see both of you dead first." Then he began to squeeze.

"Tarq," said a voice.

The variant boy looked around. It was Esther.

Standing next to her was a norm, a boy, who stood with a throwing stick pointed directly at Tarq. He did not seem all that comfortable handling the weapon, yet he was standing so close, it would have been impossible for him to miss. On her other side stood a boy with long hair and dark glasses. He held back a wild dog on a chain, an animal that snarled and growled, its sharp-fanged jaws flecked with foam as it struggled to break free.

Outnumbered, Tarq let his weapon clatter to the ground. Then he released Skar. She fell to the side, choking and coughing. With difficulty, she crawled to Michal, and the two girls clung to one another.

The variant boy squeezed shut his eyes, bitter in defeat. Then he raised his head high as he braced for death.

Killing him was certainly what he would have done in their place. He comforted himself knowing he would at least die as he had lived, with bravery and honor, and as a warrior.

Yet after a few seconds, nothing had happened.

The boy holding the wild animal was addressing Esther in a lazy voice. "We kill him or no? Whatever you say."

"No," replied Esther, distracted. She was too busy staring at her oldest friend, Skar, who was now helping Michal to her feet. She should have noticed them growing closer on the road, yet she had been preoccupied with other things. It made all the sense in the world, yet she was still surprised. "Skar?"

Catching her gaze, Skar gave a shy smile. "Yes," was all she said. Michal put her arm around Skar, and Esther smiled at them.

Incensed, Tarq snatched up Skar's knife and again turned to Esther. *This time*, he thought with blind fury, *he would finish the job.* But in the next moment, he was thrown to the dusty ground and pinned there by Eli.

"Give me the knife," a voice said.

Surprised, Eli looked up. It was Skar. Eli forced the weapon from Tarq's grip and slid it over.

"Now bring him to me," Skar said. As the others watched in silence, Eli obeyed, dragging the struggling variant boy to his feet and pushing him in front of Skar, who held the weapon high.

Panting, Tarq faced his former partner with a look of defiance. With one swift movement, Skar reached across with the blade as if to caress his face and Tarq gave a cry of surprise, not pain. She had drawn a new and bloody line on his cheek.

He recoiled when he realized it was shaped like a teardrop.

"You only live because of our pity," she said. "And now everyone will know it."

Eli let Tarq go. Then they all watched as he stood and stumbled back down the highway.

As Skar began slapping away the dust that marred her robes, Michal put her arm around her. "We don't care what others think," she said. Although she saw no judgment in anyone's eyes, she could not help but sound defensive.

"It doesn't matter," Esther said. "Variants and norms, I mean . . . we're all the same." She turned to the others. "I saw it once. Aima's baby, in Prin? They told everyone it died, only they really left it for the variants."

The two girls stared at her.

"I always wondered," Skar said at last, a smile dimpling her face. "We could never make our own babies . . . we always found them. And now I know."

By the time Tarq returned to the variant camp, he could barely remember his original plan to kill Skar and then concoct a reason for her disappearance. All he knew now was that he had been humiliated. He tried to use mud to hide his new scar, as he had once taught Skar. But it still tormented him beneath the dried dirt, itching and burning like a taunt.

When he reached his home, he was told that Slayd wished to see him.

What happened next was a blur. The variant leader spoke to him alone, with poorly disguised fury. It seemed that in Tarq's absence, people had reluctantly at first and then in greater numbers come forward and told Slayd their suspicions, strange things they had noticed. Unusual noises coming from Tarq and Skar's home late at night. Bruises that no mud could disguise. A once-happy girl made fearful and depressed.

"Can you tell me," Slayd said, though it seemed he already knew, "what they're referring to?"

Tarq did not have the will to defend himself; he merely shrugged.

"How is my sister?"

Tarq hesitated. Then he shrugged again, shutting his eyes. "She is living."

Slayd's eyes narrowed. Reaching across, he wiped away the mud caked upon Tarq's face and saw the mark of pity that had spared his life.

Visibly restraining himself, Slayd ordered a punishment he deemed appropriate: Tarq was to be Shamed. Shaming did not entail physical banishment, as the norms' Shunning did; it was more devious than that. For although one who was Shamed continued to live with the others, no one could speak to him or socialize with him. It was the lowest form of existence within the variant community; it was like being buried alive.

As mortified as he was, Tarq could not believe his ears at first. "Please," he said.

Then, weeping, he begged to be beaten instead.

THIRTEEN

After Tarq left, Esther steadied herself against a straggly tree near the restaurant's front door. The air was thick with the stink of gasoline, melting plastic, and smoke.

And yet she was thankful.

It could have been worse, she thought. *A lot worse.*

She glanced at Aras. Beneath the blackened grit that covered his face, the guide looked pale and shaken. "Are you all right?" she asked.

Aras shrugged and bent to stroke his dog. "You?" he replied after a moment.

Esther didn't answer right away. "I think so."

It was the first time Aras had expressed concern for her

or for anyone else. But it was more than that. Today she had depended on him. And he had depended on her, as well.

We were partners, she thought; and the realization made her blush.

Partnering was what happened when two people pledged themselves to each other. Was this what she and Aras had done, only with actions instead of words, and violent ones at that?

The thought made her uncomfortable. Yet it didn't repel or even displease her, which was another shock. It was a natural thing to pledge yourself to another; nearly everyone partnered at some point in their lives. It wasn't just Skar and Michal who had done it; Esther noticed that Eli and Asha had also begun to wear partnering ties, torn from the same piece of cloth. Yet it also made Esther realize how little she knew the boy before her, who now knelt and buried his face in his dog's fur, as if to find a way to avoid speaking.

Making a decision, she approached him. The dog glanced up at her, panting, and its tail thumped once on the dusty ground. By now, she was the only one it would allow to come near like this; if anyone else tried, it would bare its yellow fangs and growl, its matted fur rising in spikes along its back.

"Who are you?" she asked.

The boy laughed, startled. "What you mean?"

"You know." Not for the first time, Esther felt frustrated by the constraints of language; she couldn't find the exact words. "Why are you . . . who you are?"

Aras kept silent for a long time. "It ain't important."

"It is," she said, "to me."

He nodded.

Given everything Aras had been through, answering such a question should have been simple. Yet for the first time since he had joined these people, Aras felt confused and vulnerable. *It was because of Esther,* he realized, *the girl who stood in front of him now, so close he could feel the warmth of her.* A funny expression he had heard once, "heart in your mouth," popped into his mind. *That was how he felt now,* he thought. *Like his heart was in his mouth.*

"It's a long story," he said at last.

"I got nowhere else to go."

He smiled a bit. "Okay. It ain't really that long."

He stood, and with Pilot leading the way, he and Esther headed from the parking lot and down the narrow, two-lane highway. By now, it was dark and a crescent moon hung low in the winter sky. Aras didn't say anything until he sensed they were far enough away from the others to not be overheard.

"I always been a guide." His words came slowly at first. "Even when I was nine or ten. I could still see, and I knew how to find places people wanted to go. Groceries full of food. Restaurants, stores." He picked up a stick and began peeling off the bark. "And I knew how to get by. What to eat. How to make water safe. I don't know why, but I was always better in nature than with people." He paused, then shook his head. "Guess that sounds stupid."

"No," Esther said. "It doesn't."

"Maybe not to you." For a moment, he couldn't speak. "Anyway, I got by. I took people where they wanted to go and they gave me a piece of what they found. Okay life for me and Min."

"Min?"

"My partner." There was a long silence before he continued. "Maybe two years ago, I was leading a group to a place west of here. It was rough, but I got us there. But something was wrong . . . I could feel it. They made excuses, didn't want to share. Turned into a fight, then one of them jumped me. The others piled on. I don't remember anything after that. But it was the last time I could see."

He shrugged. "And that was that. Found my way home, somehow. After I got Pilot, it got better. I was able to get around some. Enough to take care of us. And I grow what I smoke. Ain't much, but it makes me feel better."

Esther spoke up. "What about Min?"

Aras shrugged again. "Guess she didn't want to be with a blind boy."

He turned away now, fumbling with his glasses. He realized he had said too much; he hadn't thought about his past, especially Min, in a long time. To his surprise, it still hurt; and revealing his pain so openly left him feeling raw and exposed.

Yet opening up to Esther also gave him an unexpected feeling: as if he had been relieved of a terrible load he wasn't even aware he'd been carrying. At the same time, his hands shook; he was desperate to light up one of the smoking papers he had stashed in his pocket. With supreme effort, he held back and reminded himself why.

He was doing it for Esther.

"Well," he said with difficulty, "I better go."

"Don't."

The word hung between them, barely spoken. Aras realized that Esther hadn't meant to say it; he heard the intake of breath that followed it, as if she were trying to swallow it. Around them, he could smell pine needles, the rich scent of earth, and smoke. And Esther's hair. There was heat coming off it, she stood so close.

"I mean . . . do you have to?" she asked.

"No," he said. "I reckon not."

They continued to walk down the highway, lit by the faint glow of stars. Aras let Pilot off his chain and the dog bounded off to explore the dark woods. Without him, the boy took Esther by the arm, his fingers barely touching the crook of her elbow.

She told him her story, as well. What had happened to her. The loss of her sister, Sarah. Her friendship with Skar. The earthquake that had forced them to leave Prin.

And Caleb.

Esther hadn't spoken his name in many days. Through sheer effort, she had buried her grief and rage in constant motion and effort. Now, she realized how much she had missed even the thought of him. Talking about Caleb like this to one who had never met him seemed to bring him back to life, if only for a few fleeting moments. And so she spoke, haltingly at first and then so fast, the words tumbled upon one another.

Yet when it came to speaking of Lewt and the murder, Esther trailed off in midsentence and stood in silence. Only then did she realize that her cheeks were wet with tears.

Then Aras did something that startled her.

He raised his hand and placed it lightly in front of her face. His palm covered it, from her brow to her chin, obscuring her own sight; it hovered above her skin, not quite touching. Then his fingers landed upon it, softer than feathers.

"I just want to know," he said, "what you look like." He paused. "Is that okay?"

Esther found that her chest was rising and falling, quickly. She felt torn by so many emotions, she could not even say what she wanted.

"Yes," she said. Her voice was almost inaudible.

"Close your eyes."

She did. Aras started with her hair, feeling along the spiky strands which had grown longer since they'd been on the road. Then he trailed his fingertips around her forehead, and down her nose. They brushed against her cheeks and chin. They reached her lips. He tapped each one, gently, assessing the cracks the sun had made. Then he rounded her chin, cupped it for an instant.

"Pretty," he said.

By now, tears and sweat mingled and dripped from Esther's face to her throat. Aras slid his fingers down its length. He brought his fingers to his nose and sniffed, making her laugh. Then he put the fingers to his mouth and tasted.

"Nice," he said.

It was different from what Esther had ever felt with anyone, even with Caleb. Aras had nothing in common with her partner: He was more like an animal than a human. And yet he was not unpleasing to the eye. She looked at him, as if for the first time. He had a strong aquiline nose, full lips. Dark hair in thick and tangled locks, rangy limbs. He was handsome, in his own way.

Aras moved even closer. He placed his hands on Esther's hips, to steady himself and draw him to her. She found herself pulled into his arms, too shocked and confused to resist and not sure if she even wanted to.

Aras kissed her. Again, he was unlike Caleb; for although he was gentle, he was feral in his sensuality and this made it impossible for Esther not to respond. Without thinking, she moved closer into his embrace and wrapped her arms around him.

She kissed him back.

It seemed to last forever, though it was only a second. Then confused, she pulled away.

"I'm sorry," she stammered. She was blushing, although of course he couldn't see that. "I . . . I just can't."

She knew it was crazy. Her partner was gone . . . gone for good. It made no sense to waste more than a few days in mourning. Grief was pointless and no one, not even Caleb himself, would have blamed her for moving on.

Yet Esther had never known anyone other than Caleb. There were moments when, awakening, she still believed he was alive. Try as she might to forget, she could not dissolve the profound love that kept her faithful to him, even after death.

She couldn't let go of him. Not yet.

She pulled away from Aras's embrace, not noticing the look of hurt that flitted across his face. He gave a brusque nod and then whistled for his dog, which came bounding to him.

Then without another word, he turned and walked into the night.

When Esther awoke, it was still dark. By the dim light of embers still glowing in the firebowl, she saw that the others were asleep, bundled in blankets and sleeping bags in booths and across the fire-damaged floor. In a plastic crate near Joseph, Kai struggled in a dream, then relaxed.

She turned to locate Aras. When Esther had returned from their walk the previous night, he had conspicuously avoided her. During dinner, he and his dog had taken a place by the door, away from the others who had gathered around the fire. Esther now wanted to speak with him, before the others awoke, to apologize for her behavior, and to explain how she felt.

But Aras was no longer there.

On the battered Formica table next to her was a piece of paper. It was the title page from the front of her book, torn out and covered with a broken scrawl. Puzzled, she thought it had been written by Joseph. But this handwriting was unfamiliar: shaky block lettering that was full of mistakes. Holding it up, Esther was able to make sense of some of the words.

Mundreel is 2 dys awy. sty on the mane rud. If yu need to detor, hed north est.

At the bottom of the paper, written in faint pencil, were two final lines: *i no yu can do ths. Lov aras.*

That was when she picked up something lying underneath. It was the object Joseph called a "compass."

Alarmed, Esther rose and left the diner. Ignoring the broken glass that lay scattered across the parking lot, she ran on bare feet until she reached the road. Then she stood in the highway, straining to look both ways.

There was no sign of him.

Esther's heart sank. Aras had not given her a chance to explain and so all she could do was hope that he had forgiven her and had not left out of anger. As for her own feelings, Esther felt as torn as she had been the night before. She was haunted by the memory of his embrace. And already, she missed him with an ache that was almost physical.

Unthinking, she closed her hand around the compass; and when she grazed the delicate needle, the sharp sensation made her jump. *Aras would be alone*, she realized with a flash of fear, *with only an animal to help him.*

Then she realized that she was wrong to worry. He was a guide by nature. Somehow, she knew, he would find his way.

It was herself she wondered about. How would she find *her* way, without him?

At that moment, Aras was already several miles away, heading south in the darkness. Alone with Pilot, he was able to walk at his own pace, down the center of the highway.

It was a relief to be alone again. He had found that his clients were the same as they always were—frightened, needy, and pathetic in their ignorance. It was all so predictable: They were distrustful at first, then resentful, then increasingly dependent.

He thought, *You brought them where they wanted to go and then they were done with you. Your services were no longer needed; and you realized that they always saw you as a job to be paid for and then forgotten.*

And Esther was no different.

What stung the most was the way she had pulled away from him after their kiss. Memories of Min and how she had abandoned him came flooding back. Once again, he had found himself judged by a girl and found wanting. Like his partner, Esther had seen him as defective, as something less than a full human.

There was no way he could bear to stay near her another night. As soon as Aras was sure everyone was asleep, he had gathered his belongings and left.

One thing, however, continued to confuse him.

Aras still wasn't sure what had prompted him to leave that note, as well as his precious compass. Had he thought that doing so would keep them from coming after him? Even now, he regretted his sacrifice.

Then he urged Pilot to a trot, and again, he resolved to put Esther from his mind.

For a little while, anyway.

The air around him grew heavy and Aras knew he had to find shelter before too long. Electricity crackled overhead, followed by a distant rumbling that sounded not like thunder but the growl of an animal, immense and unnatural.

Although he was not superstitious, the guide felt an inexplicable stab of dread.

He didn't know if the danger lay ahead of him or behind.

FOURTEEN

"WHERE'S ARAS?"

Esther had been bracing herself all morning for this question. It was Joseph, ever observant and anxious, who brought it up when they were almost ready to leave.

Esther felt strange revealing the truth: that Aras had left because of her. She knew that, despite the distaste they often felt for him, the group had grown to depend on the guide. She wasn't sure how they would take the news.

Seeing her hesitation, Eli stopped what he was doing and Asha came close to cling to him. One by one, the others glanced around, only just realizing that the guide and his dog were not among them.

Esther took a deep breath. *Sometimes,* she decided, *you just had to lie.*

"He left last night," she said. "He said the trip wasn't worth his while . . . it was more trouble than he counted on. I tried to get him to stay, but . . ." She shrugged. "You can't reason with some people."

Esther caught Skar's eye and held it for an instant. Her friend seemed to understand; she gave the briefest of nods. Still, Esther couldn't help but notice that Skar looked grave as she took Michal's hand. The two girls interlaced fingers, as if for comfort.

But the others took the news as badly as Esther had feared. Agitated, Joseph began talking to himself, clutching his cat close. Asha whispered to Eli, gripping his arm so tightly he had to ease her fingers. Waves of panic rippled and spread through the group.

But before the situation could disintegrate any further, someone spoke up.

"To hell with him," Silas said in a harsh voice, "if that the way he feels." He looked away and spat.

This seemed to inspire Eli, who gave a slow nod. "Yeah. We don't need his help anyhow."

Esther smiled. Aras had not just taught the group how to survive; he had also instilled in them the pride they had been lacking. She folded the note he had written and tucked it in the pocket of her jeans. The faint crinkle reassured her.

"We're almost there," she said. "Maybe two days at most. We just stay on the road when we can."

* * *

Now the caravan was led by Esther alone. She bicycled at the head of the group, pulling the wagon, setting the pace for the others, and guiding the way.

From habit, Esther often found herself turning to speak to the guide, to read highway signs aloud or to report on the road condition. Without him, she instead had to make do with Aras's compass, studying the raised letters as she had seen him do. She was relieved when, later that day, they passed through a row of booths that blocked the road, marked by a sign with the strange word, CANADA; Aras had once mentioned this landmark.

Esther knew that she missed the guide in more ways than one. Like his dog, he could be intimidating, even cruel. Yet alone with her, he had revealed a side of himself vulnerable and full of hurt. And this was the part of Aras she found herself thinking of again and again.

By the time she called a stop for the night, Esther realized they had covered less ground than they had over the previous days. What bothered her more was the lack of choice of where to camp. They had moved out of the mountains into flat land; yet they hadn't passed an exit in many hours. The only structure visible for miles was a large building on the highway itself, something called a "rest station." Aras had taught her the importance of finding small and secluded campsites, places that lay far from the main road and didn't call attention to themselves. This was far too exposed and would leave them vulnerable. Yet Esther had no choice.

While Eli and Joseph collected and boiled water from a nearby runoff, Esther and the others attempted to gather edible nuts and plants, but there were few to be found. Skar and Michal had similar bad luck, returning with only two squirrels and a juvenile rabbit—altogether, a meager dinner for eight.

Inside the rest station was no better. As Esther expected, the kitchen areas of all of the restaurants and stores had long since been gutted and ransacked. The food machines in the central room had also been emptied of their contents, their glass fronts smashed and the ground before them littered with filthy, sodden pieces of paper and small metal discs.

But there was one payoff. Silas spied something in one of the machines, an object that was caught deep inside the mechanism, snagged on a metal coil. He was able to work one of his thin arms inside; and, after what seemed hours of fiddling, he extricated the object. It was a packet of individually wrapped candies. True, they were whitened and dusty, yet they were edible. Esther divvied them up after dinner and everyone shoved them into their mouths, crunching and swallowing ravenously.

Esther did a quick calculation. Although everyone was nearly desperate with hunger, they still hadn't yet been reduced to eating their emergency rations, the dried meat and acorns that they kept in one of their wagons.

With any luck, they'd be in Mundreel before things got that bad.

Sometimes food was more important than anything else.

Lewt was surprised he felt this way. He had never cared much about eating, as long as he had enough. If he managed to fill his belly, that was enough for him. Now he needed to eat, and bad. He needed clean water, too, lots of it.

Since his bicycle had broken down, he had had no choice but to walk. Although the sun had set, the endless expanse of tarmac was still hot. It scorched Lewt's feet through his tattered sneakers and sent waves of heat pulsing upward into his body as he trudged down the middle of the highway.

He hadn't known food and water could go so quick. *Still*, he thought with some bitterness, *it hadn't had to be that way.*

Quell had been a problem from the start. To be sure, his size, brutality, and low intelligence made him a valuable companion, since he posed a threat to everyone but Lewt. Yet his bulk meant he ate a lot, which Lewt found disgusting as well as unfair. It was fortunate that the snake had bitten him when it did, for it saved Lewt the trouble of killing Quell himself. True, he could have tried to save Quell by sucking out the poison; the bite had been where the giant couldn't reach it, high on his shoulder. In the end, Lewt let nature take its course. Once the screaming, vomiting, and bleeding from the mouth had stopped, the worst was over.

After that, it was just him, Tahlik, and Rafe, and that had been fine; neither needed much to stay alive. But when their supplies started to dwindle, Lewt began to hide food for himself. It was easy enough to do; and, frankly, he was surprised Tahlik didn't do the same.

Tahlik discovered the theft after sneaking up on him after dark, when he was supposed to be asleep.

"What you got there?" he said, scaring Lewt half to death.

"Nothing," Lewt answered, his mouth full.

"You ain't got nothing—you got food!" Tahlik had yelled.

In retrospect, Lewt had stabbed him more to shut him up than anything else. It hadn't been easy, either: Although wiry, Tahlik had more strength in his skinny frame than Lewt had imagined, and the blade was dull. He ended up smashing him with a rock, as well, just to make sure. The next day, he made a point of sharpening his knife, rubbing it back and forth against a brick wall until it was as good as new.

And then there had been Rafe.

Lewt knew that the boy didn't have a clue where Mundreel lay; he couldn't read the maps they'd taken and eventually used them to start fires. But that wasn't the worst of it. Rafe couldn't even do what he'd promised: He pulled Lewt's wagon too slowly and tired too easily. What was more, he couldn't cook: his beans were inedible and his coffee a black, soupy mess.

Lewt had been saving his ammunition; there were only a few bullets left and he didn't want to waste them. So he waited until Rafe was asleep, then took care of the problem with a single shot.

Leaving the note had been an impulse. Lewt seriously doubted if anyone had been following them; he assumed that the people of Prin, as helpless and stupid as a herd of mice, had all perished long ago. Yet there was no harm leaving a warning just in case he was wrong. He had a flickering sense that if there were to be any repercussions, it would be because of the other boy he had killed.

Caleb. That was what Esther had called him.

He could see her face now, swimming before him in the hazy night air. She was pretty in the way he liked, dark-eyed and watchful, and feisty, too. In a moment, it was as if she was standing before him on the dark and silent highway. He reached for her, his hands closing on empty air, and he stumbled hard, nearly falling. His hunger was so bad, he was getting light-headed.

Lewt had run into other travelers since that first band and robbed them as well, waving his gun. But how many times could he get away with doing that? How long could one man survive, alone on this road? He felt panic gripping him.

Where was this place Mundreel everyone talked about, anyway? Did it even exist?

Then he smelled something.

Lewt stopped. He raised his nose and sniffed at the still winter air, like an animal. There was no doubt in his mind. Unless he'd gone crazy, someone not too far away was roasting meat.

A smile fell upon his burned and wasted face.

He was going to survive, after all.

As moonlight streamed down through the cracked skylight far overhead, Esther lay on her back, wide awake.

Wretched, she readjusted her blanket and turned on her side. But as exhausted as she was, her mind whirred with a constant chatter of thoughts and questions.

If Aras was correct, they would be in Mundreel in a day or so. But now that they were so close, she wondered for the first time about the fantastical tales of endless food and clean water that they had recited like prayers, the stories that kept them going.

What if they weren't true? What would they do then?

Around her in the cavernous space were the still forms of Joseph and Silas. Eli and Asha slept together, as did Skar and Michal. As if he could read her thoughts, Kai now frowned in his sleep and began to thrash his arms and legs.

She wondered what babies dreamed about. Did they dream of their mothers, as she herself had done? As the boy began to whimper, she made a quick decision. She would take him for a walk before he woke anyone else up. That way, she would soothe his fears and perhaps calm her own worries, as well.

The night sky was dark and overcast; occasionally, the clouds would part, allowing moonlight to stream down, pure and white. Esther paced up and down the cracked sidewalk that surrounded the building, past the rusted metal boxes with glass fronts that still held moldering newspapers, and dandled the child against her chest. Her sneakered feet made no noise. In the still air, she could smell the smoky remnants of the fire Eli had built in the parking lot, against the black silhouettes of trees.

That was where she heard something move.

Esther froze.

With Kai heavy in her arms, Esther stayed still and willed her eyes to grow accustomed to the dark. Within moments, she could not only hear but see something moving by the campsite, something large. There had been little left from dinner; after eating, she and the others had cracked the bones open with their teeth and sucked out the marrow inside. But some kind of animal now seemed to be rummaging through their garbage, rooting in what they had thrown out.

It was most likely a bear, Esther thought; *wild dogs traveled at dusk, and mountain lions didn't eat dead meat.* She knew enough to stay away: A mother bear with cubs could be especially deadly. Keeping her eye on the dark figure huddled over the campsite, she began walking backward one small step at a time, in order not to draw any attention to herself.

The clouds parted. In the sudden light, Esther saw what it was and her heart contracted. Then in the next second, everything was plunged once more into total darkness. Yet nothing could erase the image just seared onto her brain.

It was Lewt.

Could it really be him? She had only caught the briefest glimpse, yet it was impossible Esther could ever forget his shape, his face, his silhouette. A wave of hatred swept over her, one so powerful that she felt paralyzed, rooted to the spot. Then, with a start, she remembered the baby in her arms, as well as the others inside, asleep and defenseless. But before she could slip back in the building, the clouds parted again. This time, the moonlight fully revealed the pale circle of Lewt's face as he looked up.

He saw her. And he broke into a slow smile.

Her eyes swept the parking lot, searching for his companions, but he seemed to be alone. Even so, he appeared sure of himself as he sauntered forward. As he approached, Esther saw why: He still carried the weapon by his side, the thing Joseph called a "rifle."

She had seen up close what the weapon could do; it could kill a person in the time it took to point it. It would be foolish, she realized, to run indoors to awaken the others; the broken doors and smashed windows would provide no protection. Even with Skar's bow and arrows, they would be helpless against such a weapon should he decide to attack.

Esther made a quick decision: She would speak to Lewt alone. If all he wanted was food and water, she could give him what few supplies they had and send him away.

"Well," he drawled as he drew close. "Look what we got here."

Esther smelled the stink of him even before she could get a good look. Lewt had lost weight, like the rest of them; his cheeks were sunken, and his filthy robes and jeans hung off his bony frame, cinched with a cracked belt. There were black holes in his mouth where his front teeth used to be. *Caleb's work*, she thought with grim satisfaction.

Lewt was still eating, gnawing on bone splinters that no one else had found edible. "Hope you don't mind I helped myself. Smell of cooked meat travels far and I'm famished." He set the barrel of his rifle against the ground and leaned on it, picking what remained of his teeth with a greasy fingernail.

"What are you doing here?" Esther asked at last.

The boy smiled again. "What you think?"

Kai stirred. Esther realized she was gripping him too tightly and she forced herself to relax. "You want something to eat."

Lewt shrugged. "That's why I come. But that ain't why I here." He leered in her face and Esther felt ice down her back.

"I don't know what you're talking about."

"I think you do," he replied. "You and me got some unfinished business." He extended a filthy hand, but she yanked away before he could touch her face.

Kai awoke with a start and started to cry.

"That his?" Lewt turned and spat in the dust. His eyes narrowed as he watched Esther pat the child and bounce him on her shoulder. "That the reason you didn't come with me?"

Esther gazed up at the boy. For an instant, she was in danger of giving in to her roiling emotions. Then she regained her composure.

"No," she said.

Lewt shrugged, as if resigned. "I ain't expecting an honest answer. Can I ask a different kind of favor?"

Guarded, Esther nodded.

"My bicycle broke down a few days ago," he continued. His voice was now openly plaintive. "Been walking everywhere, and it wore me out."

"If you want a bicycle," said Esther in a stony voice, "take it and go." She nodded toward the foyer, where they were heaped. It would be a serious sacrifice, but worth it if he left without harming anyone.

Lewt kept his eye on her as he walked to the entry. Even when he turned to rummage through the bicycles, pausing to inspect the tires on one, the handlebars on another, he never took his hand off his rifle.

Finally, he settled on the one that pleased him, their best vehicle. Then Esther watched as he searched the wagon and grabbed the bottles of boiled water and plastic bags full of acorns and dried meat, stuffing them into his pack. It wasn't much, but it was all they had.

When Lewt emerged, he seemed apologetic. "Hope you don't mind, I took a little something for the road."

Esther didn't answer.

"I brung enough for both of us." Lewt nodded at the baby in her arms. "Ain't enough for three, so you best leave it. Runty little thing ain't got long to live, anyways." He had a thought. "You want one so bad, we can have one together. Once we get to Mundreel. How that sound? Have our own family, me and you."

Again, Esther didn't answer and Lewt's face constricted in anger.

"Goddamn it," he said. "I'm sick of this. What so wrong with me?"

He lunged forward to grab her wrist, but his robes became caught in the gears of the bicycle. Cursing, he staggered to the side and struggled to free himself, weighed down by his bag. As the vehicle tipped over, the rifle dropped.

Esther snatched it up before it could hit the ground.

"Get out of here," she said.

Her voice was steady, but the firearm trembled in her grasp and she fumbled to keep it straight. She had never touched one before; it was heavier than she thought and awkward to handle while still holding Kai.

For a moment, Lewt looked surprised. Then he laughed. He bent down to spin the pedal, extricating the filthy cloth from the interlocking wheels. Wiping his hands clean, he threw the bicycle aside and faced her.

"I said, get out," Esther repeated, her voice harsh.

Lewt ignored her. "First her partner, now you. Always something get in the way." He reached into his pocket and retrieved something that glinted in the moonlight. It was his knife—the same one that had killed Caleb. Esther had seen it many times, in her nightmares.

She realized he was addressing Kai, speaking in low tones that were almost tender.

"I can't have you ruin everything," he said.

Esther stumbled back a step. Then in one quick gesture, she pointed the rifle in the air and pulled the trigger. The weapon nearly bucked from her arm as it exploded, deafening her. The sound awoke faraway birds and sent them, fluttering and cawing, into the night air.

Lewt stopped for a second and looked upward, impressed. Then he continued to talk to the screaming child, his blade drawn as he came closer.

"Your mama thinks she going to miss you. But she'll get over you. I swear." He looked at Esther and smiled. "She'll get over you the way she got over your daddy. And it won't hurt for but a minute."

As he lunged forward at the child, Esther brought the rifle down by instinct, squeezing the trigger as she did. There was an explosion of heat and light and Lewt was thrown backward. Esther, covered with a spray of something hot and sticky, clung to Kai, who was shrieking.

Through tearing eyes, Esther saw that Lewt lay on the ground, several feet away. His twitching legs were spread wide, and his head was wrenched to one side. What had been his chest a few moments ago was now a wet and blackened hole, pulsating in the moonlight. His knife lay on the ground between them, shining, useless.

And suddenly, there were torches and sound.

People surrounded Esther. They were all talking to each other, touching her, pulling her weapon away. Throughout it all, Esther could hear nothing, feel nothing.

The world retreated from her. And everything for Esther grew silent.

FIFTEEN

Holding up a torch, Eli stood over the dead body.

It was clear what had happened: Lewt had been tracking them all this time. Esther had found him outside and somehow managed to seize his rifle, killing him with his own weapon. Eli hoped he would have done the same had he been in her place.

Still, he found he was rattled she had done it at all.

"What do we do with him?" he asked, keeping his voice down.

Silas didn't even shrug as he dropped to his knees. "Ain't no difference to me," he said as he began to go through the dead boy's pockets.

Eli found it distasteful and turned away. The body was still warm; the flies had yet to arrive. But before he could say anything, someone spoke up.

It was Joseph. The boy, so serious and peculiar, had always bewildered Eli. Now he stood in front of him, his face full of emotion.

"We have to bury him," he said.

Confused, Eli blinked. Even Silas glanced up as he felt along Lewt's ankles for anything he might have hidden in his socks. "Why?" asked Eli.

"Because," Joseph said, "he's a human, not an animal. It's the right thing to do." When Silas snorted and continued his work, Joseph repeated himself, his voice rising. "It's the right thing to do."

Up close, Eli could see that the older boy was trembling with emotion, his neck flushed a deep red. Eli admired Joseph's sense of morality. But something more important occurred to him.

"He's right," he said to Silas. "What if Lewt's boys show up and find him? They might come after us."

Silas slipped a few items into his pockets as he thought it over. Then he nodded.

"Take his legs," Eli ordered. "Joseph, get the shovel and bring the others. We're gonna need some help."

Then a harsh voice cut through the night air. "Nobody's helping anybody."

It was Esther.

Still holding Kai in one arm and the rifle in the other, she shook free of Skar, who tried to hold her back. As the child wailed, Asha rushed forward to take him. But before she could wrestle him from his mother, Esther lashed out without looking. Asha screamed as the rifle butt hit her glancingly, knocking her down.

"Asha!" shouted Eli.

The girl looked up, stunned, from the ground. As her lower lip trembled and tears began to well up in her round eyes, she scrambled to her feet. White-faced, she bolted away, into the woods.

"Asha!" Eli called again, but it was no use. He would have to find and soothe her later.

In the flickering circle of torchlight, Esther now loomed over the dead body. Against the darkening flecks of Lewt's blood, the pallor of her face stood in shocking contrast.

"How do you mean?" Eli asked her.

"I mean," Esther said, "nobody's burying him."

Eli exchanged glances with Silas. A similar look passed between Skar and Michal, yet no one said anything. Then Joseph spoke up.

"But Esther," he began, "he's—"

"I don't care." She spat the words, making her friend recoil. "Leave him for the wild dogs. They could use the meat."

Then she turned to go. As she passed, Skar attempted to touch her arm. But Esther jerked free of any contact before disappearing inside.

She needed to be alone. *There was something as poisonous as rainwater inside her now,* Esther sensed, something she feared would splash out and hurt those she loved. She still felt gripped by hatred, caught up in the same trembling sickness she had felt after she pulled the trigger.

She paced the building like an imprisoned animal, swiftly and with unseeing eyes; but the movement gave her no relief. She realized there was something else bothering her. It, too, repelled her and made her weak, like cold metal in her stomach.

It was guilt. Wretched, she felt remorse at having taken a life, even one as debased and worthless as Lewt's.

A sound made her turn her head. A familiar silhouette stood motionless across the echoing space: Skar.

"I think I can help."

"Can you?" Esther could not keep the desperation from her voice.

"I can try. Come with me."

Obeying a new instinct, Esther reached for the rifle.

"Leave that," Skar said. And after a second, Esther did.

Once they were outside, Skar took Esther and Kai in a different direction, away from the others who still clustered around Lewt's body. "Wait here," she said.

Running on light feet, Skar crossed the parking lot and slipped into the dark woods behind the rest area. The sky was touched with the palest hint of dawn; and her eyes soon adjusted to the gloom.

After several minutes, she returned carrying a few objects in her cupped hands. They were small mushrooms, gleaming white with purple gills, as well as a few ferns with feathery leaves. They all looked ordinary, the kinds of thing you would find underneath any fallen tree or boulder. Yet Skar placed them all on the ground with great care, making sure to wipe her hands thoroughly on her tunic after handling them.

"Don't touch these," she instructed Esther.

Skar darted away again, this time deeper into the parking lot, where a dozen cars and trucks were arranged in an orderly fashion across the asphalt. Each was in its own diagonal space marked by faded white lines. As Skar ran up and down the aisles, her eyes flickered over the rows of rusted and dented vehicles, scrutinizing each one until she found the one she wanted.

It was a box-shaped thing in a dingy color that must have once been a vibrant silver, with sliding doors on the sides. Unlike most of the other cars, its windows were still intact, although obscured by a heavy crust of dust, mud, and bird droppings. Stuck to the low, rusted metal bar in the rear was a rectangular piece of paper, barely legible. On it, in faded letters, were the words VIRGINIA IS FOR LOVERS.

It was what Tarq called a "van."

Perfect, thought Skar.

She tried the handles and, to her relief, one of them released with a loud metallic clunk. She managed to slide the door open, and a rush of hot, stale air surged to greet her.

Skar crawled inside. As she had hoped, it was almost pitch black inside, with only the faintest glints of morning light showing through the cracked mud. There was a wide, padded seat of ancient leather with armrests attached to the floor; with effort, she found she could tilt it forward. This created more room in the back, a place where a person could sit cross-legged.

Skar cleared away the trash that cluttered the floor: musty clothing, a few stuffed animals, empty soda bottles, and a small plastic object called iPod. A dusty stack of browned and crumbling newspaper she decided to keep, pushing it into a large heap. Then she sat on her heels and examined the space with a critical eye.

It wasn't ideal, but it would have to do.

"Get in," Skar said, crawling out. She gathered up the plants she had found in the forest and followed Esther back into the van. "Sit in the corner," she instructed, and Esther obeyed like a small child. Then Skar arranged the pile of newspaper so it was farthest from Esther, in the opposite corner.

"This is a Spirit Room." Skar chose her words with care. "Only our eldest females are allowed to attempt it. And that is after many months of training and fasting. I know how to build it, since I have seen that many times." She sighed. "But I cannot lie to you, Esther. That is all I know."

Esther did not answer.

"I'm going to leave you now," Skar said. "There's going to be smoke, and in a few minutes, it's going to be hard to breathe. You might even think you're dying. But you're not."

Esther spoke for the first time. "What should I do?"

"Nothing," said Skar. "Just don't fight it. If you keep breathing, you'll be fine."

Don't be frightened, Skar wanted to add. But she knew it would be useless.

Using a purple firestarter she dug from her pouch, Skar lit the heap of newspaper. The ancient newsprint caught quickly; within moments, the air filled with acrid smoke and ash. She waited until the flames died down; and when they were reduced to crumbling orange and white flakes and the haze cleared a bit, she scattered the handful of mushrooms and ferns across the embers.

"Remember," she said. "I'll be right outside."

Then Skar took Kai in her arms, backed up, and jumped free of the van. When she slid the door shut with a bang, Esther's world was plunged into darkness.

Esther brought her knees to her chest and leaned against the warm metal wall. Mixed in with the scent of burning paper was something unfamiliar that grew stronger every second: a heavy, vegetal smell that seemed to cling to her skin and hair, burrowing its way into her eyes and nostrils like something alive.

As the minutes passed, it only grew worse. Taking in shallow sips of air made it no easier to breathe. Feeling the start of panic, Esther sensed that her body was starting to seize up, as her lungs began to fight for air and adrenaline coursed through her throbbing veins. A distant rhythm grew stronger and quicker, until it seemed to shake the van itself. Dimly, she realized it was the pounding of her heart, beating faster and faster. In the darkness that surrounded her, her eyes began to glaze over with a faint red miasma that pulsed in time with the accelerating beat.

I will not die.

And as the words formed in her mind, Esther realized she was not alone.

Someone or something was sitting in the far corner, where the blackness was absolute. Whatever it was gave off the faintest glow, the palest of outlines that dissolved as soon as Esther tried to fix her gaze on it and pin it down. After a while, she stopped, and only then did the vision begin to grow clearer, viewed from the corner of her eye.

It was a slim figure shrouded in robes, sitting cross-legged and watchful, hands folded in its lap. Esther blinked rapidly, trying to clear the red fog.

"Sarah?"

Sarah sat, looking the way she had when she was radiant and alive, her long, dark hair framing her pretty face and streaming past her shoulders. With a surge of joy, Esther reached forward to seize her sister by the hands. Yet even as her hands closed on air, the swirling vapors began to darken and coarsen, transforming into something altogether different.

It was now Lewt.

And she could not pull herself away.

His chest was torn open by his massive wound and blood pumped out, staining his shirt and jeans black. To her horror, Esther could feel the thick heat of it pouring over her arms, making her hands sticky with it, as the stink of copper filled the air.

Esther, he said. Or was she imagining it?

The boy leaned his face forward in a parody of a kiss, and every nerve in Esther's body recoiled. He only seemed to gain in substance as she fought him; the more she struggled, the more real and corporeal his spirit became and the more she felt her life drain out of her. His grip tightened and he pulled her closer and closer.

She realized he would never let her go, no matter how desperately she wanted him to.

You had no choice.

Although no one had spoken them aloud, the words rang through her mind as clearly as if someone had. The voice, too, was familiar somehow, yet Esther could not place it. Was it Skar? Sarah?

Esther stopped struggling.

You had no choice.

It was neither a curse nor a threat, but the truth: a terrible reality she had to face and own. It was the only thing that could take the place of the guilt that threatened to consume her.

As she took in this thought, a great weight seemed to lift from her and the strangling grasp of Lewt's arms dissolved to nothingness.

Esther sat in the darkness, gulping for breath. And as her thundering heart quieted, she became aware that another apparition was waiting.

Someone sat across from her, head tilted to one side in a familiar way, as if appraising her. And even before she could discern his features, Esther already knew who it was, could tell without even looking, the way she could in real life, whenever she walked down a road or entered a room or woke in the middle of the night. It was him. He was there, and she was already crying out and stumbling across the floor and lunging into his arms, arms that for a few precious moments felt real and solid and strong.

Caleb.

Caleb was holding her the way he had thousands of times before, his face buried deep in her hair as she clung to him.

He raised his face to hers and caressed her cheek; and as their lips touched, it was as if all of him poured into her. As she received him, she sensed a similar force within her, something she never knew she possessed, reaching to join him. Their spirits—for what else could they be?—began dissolving into one another, and Esther felt what it had been like to physically love Caleb, only more intense, more profound, more sacred.

She had no idea how long it lasted; and when it was over, she found herself alone, curled on her side and bathed in such love that she could hardly breathe.

And she was tiny, so small that she barely filled the soft, gigantic arms that now enveloped her, rocking her.

Whoever held her must have been a giant, a monster of enormous size. Yet Esther wasn't afraid; in fact, she realized with a sense of wonder that she had never known such peace before, such trust.

It was her mother.

As Esther struggled to see her face, the face that had haunted her for years, she could sense the specter dissolving, fleeing as the others had.

Yet even as it vanished, it left a piece of itself behind, a tiny seed of strength deep within Esther.

It was time to join the others.

After Esther had pushed her to the ground, Asha had stormed through the dark forest by herself.

She knew she wasn't supposed to wander off alone like this.

Eli had spoken to her about it, using the stern voice that sometimes annoyed her. But she didn't care, not even if he got mad at her. She picked up a leafy branch and lashed it against a mossy boulder again and again until it splintered in her hand. For extra measure, she kicked pinecones and rocks and anything else she could find as hard as she could.

She was so mad at Esther.

Before, Esther had always been nice to her, even in Prin. One time, some of the bad boys from an Excavation had teased her and Esther had stuck up for her. *She wasn't scared of them at all,* Asha recalled with wonder, *even though there were three of them and one of her.*

For a long time after that, Asha had wanted to be like Esther. She wanted to be brave like her, she wanted to not care what others thought, and mostly she wanted to seem as grown-up as she was.

But now Asha *was* grown-up. She had found a partner, just like others had. The blue partnering tie she wore around her wrist made her just as good as everybody else, maybe even better. Joseph, for instance, had never been partnered even though he was the oldest of them all.

It turned out Asha didn't need Esther, after all. She was fine all by herself, just her and Eli.

If only they had a baby, then everything would be perfect.

At the thought of babies, Asha grew even more angry. There already *was* a baby, and it seemed impossible and unfair that she couldn't have him to herself. After all, she loved Kai the best, more than anybody else did. She longed to keep him with her all the time, to sleep with him, to see his little face first thing when she woke in the morning. But no . . . he was Esther's. That was what everyone kept saying, and she was sick of hearing it.

"We can make our own baby," Eli told her again and again.

Yet so far, nothing had happened. Asha wasn't dumb; she knew girls and boys made babies together, and that they were supposed to grow in your belly. But every morning before Eli awoke, she would pull up her T-shirt and check herself. Her white stomach would be as flat and pinched as it always was.

Asha glanced around. The sun had almost risen and there was enough light to see that she was deep in the forest, so far from the others she couldn't hear them. This worried her for a moment; the last time she had wandered away by herself, she had run into the bad boys. But the woods here were peaceful and quiet.

Then something caught her eye.

It was a flicker of movement past the trees; it made Asha pause and cock her head. At the same time, there was a distant crunch, the faraway sound of twigs snapping.

"Hello?" she called.

Asha approached carefully. She didn't want to scare it away, whatever it was. But as she drew closer, curiosity overcame caution.

It was hidden from view, tucked beneath the sprawling roots of a large tree. The underlying earth had been dug away, forming some kind of underground warren or den; there were flattened piles of dirt on all sides, marked with deep horizontal grooves and footprints that looked almost human.

This was where the sounds were coming from.

Asha squatted down in front of the tree, taking care to avoid the piles of scat and tufts of coarse black hair that littered the ground.

"Hello?"

Something moved in the dark recesses beneath the roots, and a pair of shiny black eyes blinked at her. Asha waited. Sure enough, a small head soon emerged. It was black, with softly rounded ears and a long snout that sniffed the air.

The entire animal was not much bigger than Kai. And it was adorable.

"Ohhh," breathed Asha.

She reached forward and touched the animal's brushy black fur. It reached up to smell her hand, then licked it with a tongue that was warm and surprisingly soft. Asha giggled.

Then she made a decision.

She reached into the den with both arms and took hold of the animal. It was plump and warm and when she lifted it clear of its bedding, it let out a series of piercing squeaks.

"Shhh," said Asha. "It's all right. It's all right."

She knelt down and cradled the creature, holding it close. It seemed to trust her and reached up to lick her nose. Again Asha laughed out loud as she thought about what she should do.

It was soft and cuddly, something Asha could carry around. Perhaps it could ride in one of the wagons with Joseph and Kai. It was so small, it probably wouldn't need too much to eat, either. And she was certain Eli would grow to love it, as she already did . . . or at least until they had their own, real baby.

Besides, it was alone and needed a mother.

Holding it with both arms, she stood up.

Then she turned around.

"Asha!"

There was no reply from the woods, and Eli felt his usual anger and embarrassment. How many times could the girl keep running away? He was annoyed with her and not proud that he felt that way. Still, Asha's erratic nature exasperated him. With all the patience in the world, he had still not been able to tame it.

Silas had offered to come along and find her, and that made it even worse.

"It's okay," Eli had said, his voice tight. "I can handle it."

Silas shrugged. "Maybe I can help."

His response mortified Eli: It suggested that the others saw Asha as a liability. This reflected on Eli, and not in a good way. It made him even more determined to improve the situation: He would lay down the law for Asha once and for all when he found her.

"Okay," he sighed. "Come on."

Now the smaller boy moved ahead of him through the dense trees, whistling through his teeth for the girl. That was also humiliating; it reminded Eli of the way Aras used to summon his dog. He made a point of calling her name, instead.

"Asha!"

Far ahead, he could only dimly hear the boy's whistle. Then it stopped.

Moments later, Silas came crashing back through the underbrush. His face was white and his mouth kept working, although no sound came out.

"What is it?" Eli asked.

Silas was trembling and short of breath, unable to speak. Unnerved, Eli tried to step past him. But although Silas was nearly half his size, he cut Eli off, grabbing him by the arm.

"No," he gasped. "Don't go. It's bad. It's—"

Now frightened, Eli grabbed Silas's narrow shoulders and pushed him to one side. Then he broke into a run. He crashed through the underbrush, branches and vines whipping his face.

"Asha! Asha!"

Then he stopped.

He saw a large tree, its roots half exposed and reaching from the ground. Beneath them was a hollowed-out area. The tree and the earth around it were wet and glistening, stained a vivid red.

Eli took it all in without comprehension, seeing what lay scattered in and around the area, yet not understanding what he saw. Then his eye caught something lying trampled on the ground nearby.

It was a purple Swatch with a daisy pattern.

He reeled back with horror, his hand to his mouth. Then, dropping to his knees, he vomited heavily.

Silas had followed and now ran to him. He grabbed the larger boy under the arms and attempted to pull him to his feet. But he was not trying to comfort him.

"We got to get going," Silas kept saying. "Before it comes back."

It was only later that Eli was able to understand what had happened. Asha had interrupted a bear cub and its mother in their den. Or perhaps she had stolen a cub and paid the consequences. Nature had its own rules, as Aras had taught them, and woe to anyone who violated them.

But, at first, Eli could only cast blame.

When the two boys returned to the camp, he found the others near the opening to the woods. With Skar watching, Esther stood over a grave, freshly dug and filled, patting down the earth with their one shovel.

Eli could not bear to look at her. Because of her, Asha was dead. He kept silent as Silas told the others what they had found in the forest. Then as everyone glanced at him in shock and sympathy, he spat out what was on his mind.

"Why the hell did we leave Prin in the first place?"

No one answered.

"Why? Just tell me that!" His voice was choked.

Esther didn't shrink from the question.

"We had no more home there," she said in an even voice. "We had to find somewhere better."

Eli pointed at her, his hand shaking. "It was all you, from the start. Your idea!" His voice broke. "If we hadn't left—" He couldn't finish. But Esther stood her ground.

"We tried to take care of her," she said. "We all did, and you above all."

At this, the boy reeled backward, as if struck. Then his hands rose to cover his face, the truth hitting him. It was he who had failed to protect Asha. It was his fault that she was dead.

Eli began to sob.

Esther watched him. For a second, she wavered, not sure how to respond. Then she approached and put her arms around him. He fell into her embrace.

"It's all right," she whispered so only he could hear. "It's all right. It's all right."

When at last Eli pulled away, Esther looked up and addressed everyone.

"Let's get going," she said.

Within the hour, Esther had taken her usual position at the head of the caravan, pulling the wagon that held Joseph and Kai. Yet something had changed.

Although no one could see it, the rifle was also in the wagon behind her, within easy reach.

And by late afternoon of the same day, they caught glimpse of the sign that they had seen only in their dreams.

MONTREAL.

PART THREE

SIXTEEN

THE NAME WAS FEATURED ON A SIGN THAT WAS ATTACHED TO A PROMI-nent beam above the highway; the word was nearly rusted over and the placard hung at a crooked angle. Those who could read sounded out the letters and spoke it aloud, with wonder.

The highway funneled onto a seemingly endless bridge. It was flanked on both sides by low concrete walls covered with spray-painted obscenities and sections of chain-link fence. It spanned what had once been a body of water far below. On either side in the distance, Esther could see the remains of other bridges that had also once crossed what was now a bed of baked red clay, crazed with millions of cracks. Yet to the seven travelers—Esther, Skar, Michal, Eli, Joseph, Silas, and perhaps even little Kai—the barren landscape was the most beautiful thing any of them had ever seen. For far across it lay a shimmering vision of glass and steel.

Before they were even halfway over the bridge, Esther could see that Mundreel was unlike any of the other places they had passed through. This was no small town with a main street and handful of shops and gas stations. It was not even like Prin, with its two- and three-story buildings and destroyed mansions.

This was a place of endless avenues and wide, hilly roads that bristled with stoplights, street lamps, and signs pointing to still more destinations. As they entered the city, it appeared to be a man-made canyon, arranged in neat, geometric blocks that were bordered with glittering sidewalks and separated by asphalt. Gargantuan buildings towered above them, some that seemed a hundred floors high. Their glass and metal shone in the brilliant pink rays of the setting sun, reflecting so strongly that even with their sunglasses, they had to shield their eyes.

One by one, all of them fell silent, cowed. Even Kai could not be heard to laugh or cry: He, too, in his own small way, seemed overwhelmed.

Yet a single question nagged at Esther: *Would this be the place they had hoped?* Tall tales had cheered them up and kept them going during even the bleakest moments. *Mundreel held more food than they had ever seen or could eat in a lifetime. The water was clean and so safe, you could stand in the rain and catch it in your mouth, drinking from the sky. And the people there lived forever: to thirty, forty, even fifty years of age.*

But despite the magnificence of the cityscape, there was no sign of anything like that. As they rounded yet another corner and turned onto a new thoroughfare, Esther and the others grew aware of something else.

They were alone.

The streets and alleys, striped with lengthening shadows, were empty. Esther heard only the occasional crunch of gravel and broken glass beneath their feet, and the far-off baying of a dog. When they gazed up at the gleaming buildings, they saw no faces watching and no movement of any kind behind the panes of glass.

Cars sat everywhere: parked at meters and in lots, and rusted by decades of rain. But they, too, were empty.

Esther said nothing to the others. Yet she sensed that they also wondered: *Had they been misled? Had they made this trip for nothing?* Even in silence, she thought she could detect disbelief and with it, growing fear.

Then Esther stopped. Several blocks away, a building caught her attention.

Compared to the monoliths that surrounded it, this one seemed distinctly older and less impressive. It was made of polished gray stone, with pillars on either side of an entry. Above the front door, three poles pointed outward, one still bearing the ghostly tatters of what had once been a flag. But that was not the only thing that drew Esther's eye.

A solitary figure stood on the roof, watching them.

It was impossible to tell its age or gender. It was wearing white clothing and held what looked like a pair of binoculars to its eyes, clearly aimed at them. Esther gave a tentative wave, and an instant later, the figure lifted its hand in return. She realized it was beckoning.

"This way," she said to the others, relief in her voice.

As they started down the street, Skar lashed out a hand and grabbed Esther. "Listen," she said.

It took Esther a moment to hear it. It was a sound they all recognized, one that filled them with senseless dread: the thump of multiple bicycle tires on pavement, approaching fast.

There was no way of telling whether or not the riders were friendly. Yet by instinct alone, they all responded as one.

"Go!" shouted Esther.

Eli, Michal, and Silas took off on their bicycles, the wagons bumping along behind. Esther and Skar began to run, much as they had raced each other through the broken streets and fields of Prin. Despite their exhaustion, they matched each other stride for stride, arms pumping as they sprinted for the building three long blocks away.

Out of the corner of her eye, Esther saw their pursuers bearing down on them from a side street and her heart tightened in disbelief and terror.

It was an army of skeletons.

There were anywhere from six to ten of them, all on bicycles. As they came closer at a surprisingly fast pace, Esther realized that they were alive, but just barely. These people were so thin, they were little more than bones, with heads like naked skulls with staring sockets. All were dressed in tattered black, with fluttering cloths tied to their arms and legs and wrapped tightly around their heads. Some wore mirrored glasses that reflected the dying sun, casting a blinding light.

Their leader, a boy who rode in front, was screaming to those behind him. He had tangled red hair that streamed past his shoulders and pale skin pulled over sharp cheekbones that stood in shocking contrast to his black headgear and vest.

"Stop them!"

Pure adrenaline flooded Esther. Without breaking her pace, she shot a panicked glance at the roof: The figure with the binoculars had disappeared. In the next moment, she and Skar managed to catch and then outpace Michal and Eli, who were hindered by the heavy wagons they were pulling. Only Silas, alone on his free-bicycle, stood a clear chance of making it with them to the building.

There were only two blocks left. By now, Michal was falling far behind. When Skar noticed, she slowed and then stopped.

"I have to go back," she panted.

Esther spotted a sign at the corner: RÉSO, with a downward-pointing arrow in the center of the O. The word meant nothing to her, but she decided to take a chance.

"No," Esther shouted so the others could hear. "This way." Without slowing down, she swerved and then raced around the corner.

She wasn't sure what she was expecting. But in the middle of the sidewalk, there was a large metal door that swiveled open to a dark entryway. Inside was a short staircase. Esther ran straight at it, grabbed the handrail, and vaulted down into pitch-blackness. Behind her, she could hear the others following and a moment later, rattling down behind her on their bicycles.

Eli fumbled with a firestarter and lifted it overhead for a few moments. The seven were in a seemingly endless space, musty from disuse. Shuttered stores were everywhere they looked: They were in the remnants of an abandoned underground city. At the far end were two descending metal staircases; it was impossible to see where they led.

The steps were the type they had seen before many times at stores in Prin: steep, made of thinly grooved metal, with dangerously sharp edges. Yet there was no other way to go; already, they could hear their pursuers on the street above them.

"Spread out!" Esther shouted.

They did; and together, Eli, Michal, and Silas launched their bicycles down each staircase and into the darkness that lay beyond.

Esther and Skar started after them on foot, until Esther had a better idea. She indicated the handrails and her friend understood. It was something they used to do for fun in Prin; now, the stakes were much higher. They leaped sideways onto the hard rubber and slid, overtaking the others and making it to the lower level first.

Their friends, however, had a much harder time.

As the bicycles and the attached wagons banged down the steps, they threatened to fly out of control or break apart with every impact. Riders crouched on their pedals in a vain attempt to absorb the shock as they bounced dangerously high down the treacherous steps; the distance to the bottom seemed end-less.

Moments before, Esther had heard the far-off sounds as their pursuers reached the entrance and began to head after them. Now they, too, divided themselves among the staircases and were riding down. The thud of rubber tires and the clanging of metal reverberated above them through the cavernous space.

But the seven travelers had made it to the bottom. By now, the bicycles were useless: Their tires were shredded and their rims bent and mangled. As Eli, Michal, and Silas kicked free of them, Skar pulled a badly shaken Joseph and Kai from their wagon. Esther grabbed her rifle, although it was much too dark to use it.

"Let's just move," she called.

Again, Eli lit his firestarter. They were standing in the middle of a long and narrow subterranean platform; the ground dropped off abruptly on either side to train tracks below. As the tiny flame guttered out, everyone grabbed hands for safety in the dark. Then Esther took off, leading the way as they ran down the path, skidding on debris and broken glass. Dozens of unseen vermin—rats? snakes?—skittered away in front of them.

Behind her, Esther heard the first bicycle hit the ground at the end of a staircase, then another, then another. Their pursuers had not given up but were now chasing them through the underground passageway, some still astride their damaged vehicles, the rest on foot. The boy leader was shouting, his words urgent yet lost in the echoes of the dark corridors.

Then an unholy noise filled the air.

A blaring, inhuman roar reverberated off the floors and walls, shocking the system. Everyone pressed their hands against their ears in a frantic attempt to block the piercing sound, and against her back, Esther felt rather than heard Kai scream in his harness.

And then it stopped.

Esther whirled around. In the echoing silence, she could still hear their enemies. But the sounds they made were fading.

They were in retreat.

Confused, she turned back toward the source of the sound. In the distance the spark of a firestarter broke the darkness. Then it blossomed into fire, and Esther caught a whiff of gasoline and burning cloth.

A silhouette emerged from the shadows, holding aloft a lit torch.

The stranger had on billowing white clothes that were so clean, they seemed to glow in the dark: pleated trousers, shirt, gloves. It wore a wide-brimmed hat with a gauzy cloth tied at the throat that masked its face, as well as a large pair of binoculars around its neck.

It was, Esther realized, *the person who had waved to her from the roof.*

"Hello!" it called. It was a boy, and the relief in his voice was obvious. "You're lucky I saw you in time."

Frozen in confusion, Esther and the others could only wait for him to reach them. Next to her, she could feel Eli tensing up, in anticipation of a fight.

"Hold on," she whispered.

As the boy drew near, Esther could see he was unarmed. To her shock, he reached up and seized her hand not holding the rifle. Then he pumped it up and down.

"My name is Ramon." The voice that emerged from beneath the face scarf was deep and warm. "Welcome."

Moments later, the group huddled together in the entrance, gaping in utter shock.

The place was beyond anything they could have imagined.

Before it had been destroyed, the Source in Prin was the most opulent place any of them had ever seen. It had a supply of electricity and the miraculous luxuries that went with it: indoor lights, a moving ramp, and a functioning freight elevator that rode up and down between floors.

Still, the Source was nothing more than a warehouse, a windowless cement box with gloomy aisles of industrial shelves, cardboard crates, and cracked, gray floors.

What lay before them now seemed nothing less than a magical empire.

The light alone was extraordinary. It gleamed down from massive panes of glass that surrounded them and reflected off the different open levels, marked off by rounded pillars and curving staircases that were a uniform and brilliant white. The huge rectangular window set in the high ceiling seemed like a separate sky; it was framed by colorful designs etched in plaster. The late-afternoon sky itself, streaked with purple and magenta, appeared through the glass like a brilliant, painted decoration. Giant creatures, fanciful sculpted birds with human heads, were poised in the air above, stirring faintly on invisible threads. And everywhere Esther looked, she saw shining surfaces—counters, archways, railings, displays—made of steel, brass, and mirrors.

As Ramon herded them farther into the structure, Esther and the others moved as one, struck dumb. As Eli gasped, Skar stepped closer to Michal. Joseph clung to his cat carrier, breathing fast. Everyone was stunned by the grandeur that enclosed them.

Esther felt it, too.

She had never seen anything so immaculate and felt self-conscious, for the first time in her life, about how filthy she was. Esther could see their images reflected a thousand times, on scrubbed walls that flanked long, metallic staircases, spotless glass cases that contained merchandise, and gigantic, glittering objects that hung directly overhead, higher than the strange bird-men. Even the smaller ones were so enormous, it would have taken three people to encircle one of them with their arms. They looked like fiery stars suspended in midair, sparkling.

Seeing their reactions, Ramon laughed.

"It's nice, isn't it?" he said. "We turned on the power so you could actually see it."

Esther took note of the building's layout. While clearly a single structure, it was more like an indoor mini-city built in the valley between adjoining buildings. Four open levels, including a basement, were made up of shops and restaurants

connected by tiled floors, sweeping staircases, and marble pas-
sageways. Esther noticed something incongruous across the
lobby: a large gray truck parked near the revolving doors that
led to the street. It emitted a low, constant roar and she could
make out the familiar smell of gasoline.

"That must be a generator," Joseph said.

Above were seven more stories, each filled with dozens
of windows that faced unseen corridors. Most were dark,
although one at the top gleamed with light.

It dawned on Esther that this was a kind of "mall," where
many stores occupied a common space. There had been one a
few miles from Prin, where she and Skar had often played. Yet
there, the windows had been smashed, the doors torn off their
hinges, and the stores empty of everything but trash, dead
leaves, and foraging animals.

This one was completely different. It was, she realized,
beautiful.

In silence, she and her friends followed Ramon past store
after store. Each was filled with items that were not only new,
but rare and expensive. Shelf after shelf was stacked with piles
of sweaters, blouses, scarves, all arranged by color; the clarity
and richness of the purples, pinks and oranges were astound-
ing. Delicate, fanciful shoes were arrayed on tables; sunglasses,
jewelry, belts, and things Esther couldn't even identify filled
entire cabinets, exotic and lovely items that somehow you
wanted just for the sheer pleasure of ownership.

Joseph leaned on a window, staring at a display of wristwatches; they were in every color of the rainbow.

"Please don't touch anything," Ramon called out, although his voice was light. "You'll smudge the glass."

Too abashed to even apologize, Joseph pulled away, wiping his hands on his filthy robes.

Now their guide stood at the base of twin stairways. They were similar to the kind they had ridden down to escape their attackers, yet with one difference.

These were moving by themselves.

Esther and the others recoiled in fear as Ramon stepped on.

"Come," he said, turning to them with a smile. "Just get on. It's fun."

When no one else moved, Esther was the first to try it. With Kai on her back, she stepped onto the moving stairs and staggered to the side. Clinging to the rubber handrail in terror, she rose swiftly upward and within moments, found herself on the level above, where Ramon helped her stumble off. After a few false starts, the rest of her friends finally joined them, red-faced and panting with agitation. Yet it was easier the second time. When they reached the third floor, even Joseph managed without falling.

Ramon led them to a metal door at the far end of the slippery marble hallway, which he pushed open.

"I'm afraid we have to climb from here," said Ramon.

Esther and the others found themselves in a dark and stuffy space. Their guide had relit his torch, revealing a windowless stairway with metal railings that threw dancing shadows on the bare cement walls. Ramon was already a flight above them and they scrambled to catch up.

As they passed landing after landing, Esther kept silent count; by the time they stopped, they were on the tenth floor. "Here we are," said Ramon, holding open a metal door. They filed past him into a dim hallway, lit by windows on either end.

Thick carpeting underfoot absorbed their steps as the travelers followed him. Esther noted that the passageway was square; if you continued walking, you would find yourself back where you started. To her left, the wall was lined with windows that faced inward, looking down over what she assumed was the mall far below. To her right were closed doors, nearly all identical.

Finally, Ramon stopped in front of the one set of double doors and indicated that they should enter.

Stepping into the room, Esther was blinded by the last rays of the setting sun. Raising a hand to her eyes, she saw they were in a large chamber, paneled in dark material. A table of golden wood as shimmering and immense as a lake took up most of the space. It was surrounded by at least two or three dozen matching chairs made of chrome and black leather. Facing them, an entire wall of windows revealed the tall buildings of Mundreel and the brilliantly colored sky.

That was when Esther noticed them.

Perhaps a dozen people were seated across the table. It was hard to see them at first; with their backs to the giant window and its blinding light, they were no more than silhouettes. Still, Esther could not help but notice that at least one of them was armed, a rifle held loosely against his shoulder.

This boy was leaning forward, gesturing out the window

with his free hand, and although he was talking in an animated way, the words coming from his mouth seemed to be nonsensical, gibberish. Confused, Esther remembered what Joseph had told her about the signs on the road. *It must be the other language,* she thought. The guard was addressing the one who sat at the center, the one whom everyone seemed to be facing.

It was a girl. And she was already rising to her feet.

"You must be our visitors," she said. "Welcome to the District. I'm Inna."

Esther was relieved to find that their hostess spoke in words she could understand. Yet Inna's voice, musical and low, had a slight hoarseness to it, an odd quality that Esther could not identify.

"I'm so glad you managed to get past the Insurgents outside," Inna said. "Not everyone does, you know. We haven't had visitors in months. Over a year, I think." She had moved around the table as she spoke, and Esther could finally see her in full.

The girl was of medium build, with large dark eyes and black, curly hair held away from her face with a silk cord. She was dressed in strange and luxurious clothing: loose-fitting garments of pink and coral and cream that flowed and shimmered with her every move. Gold chains and sparkling stones dangled at her throat and ears, and a sweet smell arose from her skin, the faint scent of roses and jasmine.

But as she drew closer, Esther recoiled.

Something was wrong with her.

The skin on Inna's face hung slack off her jawbone and in folds across her throat. There were fleshy swags around her eyes and on either side of her nose and mouth. Horizontal lines were etched into her forehead, and her hair, at first glance as dark as her eyes, had streaks of gray in it.

As Skar and the others also drew back, horrified, Esther's first confused thought was that Inna had contracted the terrible wasting disease. Yet she seemed to be free of the telltale lesions, the purple, black-edged sores.

Only Joseph had no fear. He stepped forward, squinting in order to see the girl better. Then he had a visible reaction, one of shock, followed by excitement; and when he spoke, his voice quavered.

"You're *old*," he said.

A murmur of amusement passed around the table and Inna smiled even wider. This deepened the lines around her mouth and eyes.

"Yes," she said. "We all are."

She pointed at the others. "Ravi and Liat are the youngest. They're thirty-seven and thirty-nine, respectively." The two bowed their heads. "I recently turned forty-four. The rest of us are also in our forties and early fifties, including Ramon, my partner, whom you've already met."

She nodded at the boy who had served as their guide. He had unwrapped the gauze cloth from his face and joined the others. To Esther's shock, she saw that his hair was silver and his face as creased as Inna's.

What they had heard about Mundreel was true. Even Joseph, the oldest of them all, was only twenty-six; and that, Esther realized with her shaky grasp of arithmetic, was far younger than these people claimed to be.

"But how did you—" Esther began, then stopped.

Inna had stepped in front of Esther and, unexpectedly, took her hands in hers.

Her touch was astonishingly soft and cool, like an infant's. Esther had a pang when she noticed how dirty and rough her own hands were by comparison, and how torn her fingernails were. Yet Inna didn't seem to care.

"There'll be time for explanations later," Inna said.

Up close, her face didn't look frightening; and her expression was kind and direct. Yet Esther noticed Inna was looking not at her, but at Kai. When the woman reached across her shoulder and stroked the side of his face with a finger, Esther found herself tensing up.

"A baby," Inna was saying. "It's been so long since we've had one here."

Then she smiled.

"But I'm forgetting my manners. First, let us get you settled in."

Esther sat with her knees pulled close to her chin, shoulder-deep in bathwater that was already black with dirt. She had seen such tubs before—there had been one in her apartment in Prin—yet she had never understood their purpose and always assumed they were meant for storage. It was a strange and even frightening sensation to find herself immersed in warm water like this.

She wasn't sure if she liked it.

Inna had brought her, Skar, Michal, and Kai to a private room on the top floor, fenced off by an ornamental silk screen. A stack of clean towels and a cracked block of soap were set to the side. Then as the girls watched, two adults came in, carrying large buckets of scalding water. As they poured them into the tub, Inna added several handfuls of what looked like salt, stirring them with her hand until they produced a thick froth of perfumed suds.

Esther and her friends recoiled in terror.

"It's called a bubble bath," explained Inna.

Since there was only one tub of hot water, the girls took turns bathing. Michal went first, holding Kai, and then Skar, each girl exclaiming when she lowered herself in. It was only when both girls had finished and stepped out, shivering, that a reluctant Esther took the plunge.

By now, the lukewarm bathwater was so filthy, Esther doubted it would do anything but make her dirtier. And most of the bubbles were gone as well, for which Esther was thankful; they were peculiar and bitter-tasting. When some got into her eye by accident, she was convinced that she had blinded herself. The pain was excruciating.

Despite her skepticism, however, the bubble bath cleaned away much of the deep-seated grime, the dust of the road she had assumed was permanently inked onto her elbows, knees, feet, and neck. Afterward, when Esther stood and toweled herself dry, even she had to admit she had never felt so clean.

Thinking about it that way, however, made her uneasy.

What bothered her most was that their clothes had been

taken away. Esther knew that her red hoodie and jeans were torn and filthy and that her sneakers were shredded and full of holes. Still, they had been as much a part of her as hair and skin.

"Hello?"

Wrapped in a towel, Esther gathered enough nerve to poke her head around the screen. One of the adults, a tiny woman named Bao, was seated outside and looked up with a smile.

"Yes?"

Esther felt self-conscious, even shy. "Do you know where our clothes are?"

Bao laughed. "Don't worry about those. Here are your new ones."

She picked up a pile of clothing and tried to hand it over. But Esther demurred.

"We can't," she said. "Thank you. We can keep our old ones." Yet Bao, still smiling, shook her head and insisted.

"Nonsense . . . these are so much nicer. Just tell me if they're the right size or if any of you want a different color or style."

"But we don't need—"

"Don't think of it . . . it's our pleasure. And besides, we insist." Esther wasn't sure, but Bao's smile seemed steely now. "Anyway, your old things have already been disposed of."

Esther had no choice but to thank her again and bring the clothes to the others.

Before she could say anything, she was startled by Michal's response. Excited, the girl pounced on the items with a squeal of delight.

Of course, Esther realized as she watched her sort through the things with swift and expert hands; *she used to be Levi's girl. She knew all about nice things.* In an instant, it was as if all of the hardships and cares of the last few months had vanished for Michal. For now at least, she was once again a beautiful young girl, happy to pick out what to wear.

For that, Esther was glad.

Michal found a sundress for herself, bright with swirling designs, and gold sandals with straps that wound around the ankle. She also selected a colorful, sheer scarf, which she draped across her damaged features and fastened around her throat.

Then she turned to her partner, taking her by the hand.

"Let's find you something good, too."

Bashful, Skar was shaking her head and smiling, as confused as Esther was by the profusion of choices. But Michal was insistent. First, she had the variant girl try on a pleated skirt, then a pair of pants with baggy pockets, then some thick leggings, as well as a variety of tops and shoes. As Skar turned and modeled the different outfits, the two broke into frequent peals of laughter.

Esther watched them, puzzled yet happy that they were having a good time. Finally, Skar found some shorts she didn't mind, as well as a sleeveless top, while Michal dressed Kai in a pair of red overalls and matching socks.

Esther settled on a black T-shirt and jeans, the plainest things she could find. She located Skar's necklace, the one her friend had given her as a going-away gift, which she had put aside for safekeeping. Thankful Bao hadn't thrown it away, she slipped it into her pocket. *It's only clothes*, she thought as she put them on. And the items *were* nice, she had to admit; even she could tell they were of high quality and made to last. Perhaps she was being foolish to be so leery of such generosity.

Still, until she knew more about their hosts, she disliked the idea of being beholden to them.

After they had finished dressing, the girls and Kai went into the hall, where a smiling Bao was waiting. She led them down to an open area on the second floor, where a long table was set with a blue cloth, white plates, and crystal goblets.

Eli, Joseph, and Silas were already seated there. Esther almost didn't recognize them; they too looked much cleaner, their hair still damp. And like the girls, they were dressed in unfamiliar new clothes: colorful shirts, baggy belted shorts, and running shoes.

There was something else about them that seemed strange. Esther had to think about it for a moment before she figured it out.

For the first time in her life, her friends looked *young*.

"Look." As the girls took their seats, a beaming Joseph, dressed in an unfamiliar jacket, modeled two new watches he wore on his arm. "They said I could take as many as I wanted, but I didn't want to be greedy."

"And I got new shoes," added Silas, sticking out a foot. Even Eli seemed proud of how he looked, his hair slicked down and his face shining. He smiled at Esther as she slipped into the chair to his left.

Several adults were already bringing in large platters, which they placed in front of the travelers. Famished, Kai was already fussing, sucking on his fist and squirming in a plastic baby seat. Yet when everyone picked up their forks to eat, they hesitated, confused and appalled.

It wasn't food.

Eli prodded the objects on his plate with his finger. They were colors food wasn't meant to be: orange, green, yellow, red. And everything had a peculiar odor, too.

It smells like wet leaves, Esther thought with dismay.

From where they stood, the adults chuckled.

"They've never seen vegetables before," whispered one man. Another murmured in the strange language and again, they all laughed.

Silas overheard this, and his face flushed with annoyance. With his fork, he stabbed a small, brown sphere from a bowl full of them. Defiantly, he popped it in his mouth and chewed as the others watched.

"It don't taste like much," he said, his mouth full. Then he swallowed and smiled. "But it ain't bad."

After that, everyone began eating, at first with caution, then with desperate hunger. Within moments, there were no sounds but chewing and swallowing, and the clank of silverware on plates.

Yet although she too was starving, Esther could only manage a few bites, chewing over and over before she could swallow.

Being here felt unreal, like a hallucination brought on by a bad fever. She and her people had traveled for weeks on the open road, suffering unspeakable losses to get to this place, fueled by dreams of its perfection. But what had they found?

Yes, there was great wealth here, the kind Esther had never imagined possible. The dinner alone could feed three or four times as many and the stores could clothe hundreds, if not thousands, more. The adults had even discovered how to procure the most valuable luxury of all, old age. Yet mere feet away, the city outside seemed a terrifying wasteland of the walking dead.

If there was abundance, it was obviously reserved for the very few. And there was no guarantee that it was meant for *them*.

Esther's thoughts were interrupted by the distant sound of gunfire. She glanced up, startled, but none of her friends seemed to have noticed. Only Inna, who stood with the other adults, caught her eye and smiled.

"Don't worry," she said. "You're safe here. We're very vigilant."

Esther smiled back. But knowing the woman was now watching her, she became self-conscious about not eating and so picked up her fork again.

She wasn't the only one having trouble with what was served. Joseph, seated across from her, was fussing with something in his lap. It turned out to be his cat. Released from her carrier at last, Stumpy was wriggling about in a desperate attempt to escape as Joseph tried to get her to eat.

"Excuse me." Flustered, Joseph turned to Inna, who came forward smiling. "I'm afraid my friend doesn't like vegetables. Do you have anything else I could feed her?"

"Your friend?" When Inna saw the animal, her smile froze and a look of distaste crossed her face.

"No," she said. Her voice was stiff. "I'm afraid not."

Joseph was too distracted by Stumpy to notice. "She likes meat," he explained, extricating his cat's claws from the table-cloth. "Do you have any meat around here? Squirrel or rabbit?"

"I said, no." At the sharpness of her tone, Michal and Silas glanced up. Inna lowered her voice and continued. "What I meant was, we almost never go outside anymore . . . it's much too dangerous. So we only have it on very rare occasions, when we're lucky to come across it. It's a real treat."

By now, it had grown dark, and candles were brought in and lit. Everyone had eaten their fill and as the adults led them away from the table, there was much talk and laughter—the first Esther had heard in many days. Her friends were so happy, it seemed wrong to share her concerns with them.

Esther was the last to leave; she was having trouble unfastening the straps that held Kai in his special chair. Much of his food was still on his face, and he was falling asleep. The others had disappeared up the stairs, casting long shadows against the walls as their voices echoed and faded. Esther was about to join them, when out of the dimness, Inna spoke.

"Esther," she said. "May I?"

The woman stepped into the light. Smiling at Kai, she extended her arms. "Just for a few moments?"

Esther hesitated. Ever since her encounter with Lewt, she had been loath to let the child leave her arms for even a moment. Yet Inna seemed so gentle that Esther handed him over.

The woman took him as if he were a precious gift, nuzzling into his neck as she held him close against her shoulder. Then she rocked him, stroking his head and murmuring words Esther could not hear.

"Aren't there any babies in Mundreel?" Esther asked.

Inna glanced up, puzzled, then laughed.

"Montreal," she corrected. The word sounded strange to Esther, yet exotic and pretty. *Montreal.* "And no . . . at least not in the District. We've all tried, of course. But now that we're older, we've pretty much given up."

Esther nodded. In Prin, pregnancy had been a rare event, too. "I'm sorry," she tried to say, but her voice was faint.

Watching Inna and Kai gave her a strange feeling. The image of woman and child seemed both familiar and foreign, comforting and disturbing at the same time. Without warning, a wave of nausea passed over her. She gripped the arms of her chair, to steady herself.

The candlelight threw deep shadows across Inna's face. She was now speaking of the other adults and their home together, and Esther did her best to listen. But a distant buzzing sound obscured Inna's words. Esther had the impression that she was standing far away, at the end of a dark tunnel. Without warning, it tilted to one side.

Esther's insides lurched, and a sour taste flooded her mouth. She pushed away from the table, but it was too late. Retching, she threw up the meager contents of her stomach on the linen tablecloth, the brocade chair, and her dinner plate. Even when there was no more, her insides continued to heave.

When it was over, Esther sat back, appalled. "I'm so sorry," she stammered. The beautiful remains of the dinner party were now sodden and reeking. Mortified, she picked up her napkin and attempted to wipe the table clean. But Inna took it away from her, gently but firmly.

"I'm the one who should apologize." The older woman dipped a clean corner of the cloth in a water goblet and, without asking, used it to blot Esther's mouth. "You haven't eaten in days, and you're not accustomed to vegetables. I should have been more careful."

"Thank you," Esther tried to say. But instead of feeling better, she only grew dizzier. When she tried to stand, her eyes rolled up in her head as her knees buckled. Without a sound, she dropped to the floor.

When she woke up, Esther had no idea where she was.

In the darkness, she was being carried in arms that were strong yet soft, cradled against a breast that smelled of roses. Instinctively, she tried to struggle her way free. Yet as she stirred, a voice from above spoke to her.

"Shhh." It was Inna. "You need to get some sleep. Just rest."

"Where's Kai?"

"Don't worry . . . he's right here. Everything will be all right."

"Give him to me. I can walk." Stubbornly, Esther attempted once more to break loose, yet found she lacked the strength. Weak as a newborn, she had no choice but to allow herself to be held.

And to her surprise, it felt good. For the first time in months, Esther sensed her tension and suspicion start to ease, lulled by the rocking motion of Inna climbing the steep steps, one at a time.

Inna brought her to a darkened room on the top floor of the mall. With Kai strapped onto her back, the older woman set Esther down on a bed that had been freshly made with clean sheets and a thick blanket. Esther noted two other cots nearby holding motionless silhouettes, probably Skar and Michal.

As Esther sank into the exquisite softness of the mattress, the woman sat next to her, a sleeping Kai still in his harness, and stroked Esther's hair with a gossamer touch.

"Inna." Still weak, Esther could only whisper. "Have others lived in the District with you?"

Inna exhaled. "Many have wanted to."

"Can we?"

"We'll see," was all she said.

Was she dreaming? Esther wasn't sure. In the dim light, it seemed that the older woman smiled. As she fell asleep, Esther realized she was smiling, too.

She did not stop to wonder where her rifle was.

SEVENTEEN

JOSEPH HADN'T INTENDED TO WANDER OFF.

He, Eli, and Silas had been assigned the job of polishing the intricate metal railings that bracketed the mall. Eli had been accustomed to much harder labor in Prin. Even Silas seemed to have no problem with the arrangement. But Joseph was unused to chores of any kind and soon decided it was tedious and unpleasant.

Cleaning was one of the work assignments Esther had handed out that morning.

"Inna says we can stay, but only if we work for it." When Esther made the announcement, the travelers were eating breakfast by themselves, an enormous feast of flatbread and honey, coffee with sugar, and sweet, slippery objects called "fruit." Her face was flushed with excitement and her eyes sparkled as she continued. "They tried it a few times with others, only it never worked out. So this is our chance."

Her joy was contagious. Save for Skar, everyone smiled and exclaimed, grateful for the opportunity and determined not to fail.

Half an hour later, Joseph and the other boys were on their knees, outfitted with soft cloths and rectangular cans of a strong-smelling cleaner.

Two men named Tahir and Uli supervised their efforts. Although he tried not to stare, Joseph was fascinated by their clothing. Both men wore pants and matching jackets in dark blue or gray, with black shoes that shined as brightly as the handrails. Their soft, silk shirts were each fastened at the throat with a thin, colorful cloth. *A necktie.* The word popped into Joseph's mind from some forgotten source, probably an old magazine he had once read. The men did little but sit on benches against the wall and chat with one another, only getting up when the boys were ready to move on to another section.

Joseph had just finished cleaning an especially ornate piece of scrollwork. Now he stood, easing his back and knees and flexing his fingers; the work was painful, as well. While two floors were nearly done, that meant two were left. As Joseph wondered how soon it would be until lunchtime, his eye was caught by something farther down the hall.

The men were not watching him, so he ambled toward it.

The window display featured large, faded photographs of pretty girls with big eyes, tousled hair and pouty lips, all wearing minuscule pieces of clothing. Such pictures made Joseph blush, and they were not what had drawn him there. Going closer, he saw that his first impression had been right. In the store, all of the crowded display racks across the far wall had been pushed to the side. In their place was a desk with equipment on it, as well as several big metal filing cabinets. Next to them were four sets of shelves.

They were full of books.

Joseph was thrilled. Other than Esther's copy of *The Wonderful Wizard of Oz*, he had not seen a single book since leaving Prin. Surely no one would mind if he went in and took a quick peek. The security gate had been pushed up and locked into place. Glancing around to make sure no one was watching, he slipped inside and stole his way to the back.

After several minutes of skimming the titles, however, his joy evaporated. For although Joseph wasn't a picky reader, even he had to admit it was a horrible selection.

Joseph liked books that involved history, cats, Vikings, large families, clocks and clock-making, ghosts, or time travel. He also had a soft spot for dictionaries, cookbooks, and collections of jokes and riddles. Yet the titles he found were tedious instruction manuals on subjects he had never heard of: mechanics, electrical wiring, hydroponic gardening, water filtration systems.

It was very disappointing.

Joseph continued to scan shelf after shelf, looking in vain for anything of interest. He was about to give up when he saw something perched on the very top: a large cardboard box pushed into the far corner. It was heavy; standing on a chair, he was only just able to lift it down, sneezing at the dust he stirred up.

It was crammed full of old magazines and newspapers. They were yellowed and crumbling and smelled of mildew; still, they were in far better shape than the ones he had once collected for his library.

Excited, Joseph lifted out an assortment of periodicals: *Time*, *USA Today*, *The Washington Post*. Many consisted of only the cover or front page, which served to store smaller clippings inside. Intrigued, he opened up one, then another. Headlines floated past his eyes, with names he didn't recognize and words he didn't know. But as he examined one article after another, he found that laying them out in front of him and putting them in order made them easier to read and even understand.

Two in particular caught his eye:

SPANISH FLU FELLS MILLIONS

New York, NY—Doctors worldwide have declared themselves helpless against the spread of an illness they had hoped never to see in their lifetimes. First unleashed in 1918, the Spanish flu is once more wreaking havoc on world populations.

Having mutated in frozen dormancy, the disease is now of an unparalleled ferocity. Finding a conductor in the Earth's water supplies, it has been borne everywhere through the planet's oceans, rivers, lakes, even raindrops.

LIFE EXPECTANCY SOON TO BE TWENTY

Atlanta, GA—Doctors are now predicting that, in the aftermath of the flu devastation, the life expectancy of survivors will drop to as low as twenty years. "It's conceivable," remarked Dr. Albert Frake of what was once the Centers for Disease Control and Prevention, "you could within a few years see a world populated entirely by children and teenagers."

"What are you doing?"

Joseph jumped.

He had been so absorbed in what he was reading, he hadn't been aware of anyone approaching. He whirled around and saw a furious Ramon standing in the doorway.

Joseph broke into a nervous smile. "I, um, uhh—"

Ramon had already crossed to him and yanked the clippings away. One of them tore down the middle and Joseph let out an inadvertent cry.

"No one's allowed in here!" snapped Ramon. He was already sorting through the clippings, as Joseph tried to stammer his apologies. Too late, he realized what he had done: *While he and his friends were supposed to be proving their worth, he had just ruined everything with his stupid curiosity!* Wretched, he wondered if Esther would ever forgive him.

"I'm sorry," said Joseph as he wrung his hands, his voice

trembling. "I didn't know it was wrong. You see, the door was open and I—"

Ramon waved his hands. "It's all right." He seemed to be calming down; his voice was gruff yet civil. "Nobody told you that this place was off limits. You didn't know any better. But it took me a long time to put my archives together, and I'm afraid I get a bit protective. The paper is very fragile."

"I'm sure," Joseph said. He was wiping his sweaty hands on his shirt, rocking back and forth. "I was trying to be careful. I hope I didn't disturb anything."

Ramon grunted. "So. You read?"

"I do." Joseph tried to keep pride out of his voice; he didn't want to sound like he was boasting. "A little."

The older man nodded, as if in approval. He seemed satisfied that nothing was missing and began checking dates and putting the articles in order. "You see, I'm the resident historian and scribe. And librarian, too, I suppose you could say."

At the word "librarian," Joseph perked up and nodded several times; he could already feel his panic starting to subside. "I always wanted to be a historian," he said in a humble voice. "I even had my own library. But of course, it was nothing compared to this."

Ramon gave a grudging smile. "I've been collecting books and articles since we first moved inside," he admitted. Then he indicated the shelves. "These are the ones I refer to the most frequently. The rest are in storage." The man seemed to think and tilted his head. "Would you like to see my records?"

Not believing his good luck, Joseph nodded.

Ramon went to the equipment that lay on his desk. Scattered across its surface were various thin rectangular boxes in black and silver. A chunkier machine, tan and metallic, lay nearby; it had buttons with different letters in orderly rows across the front. Joseph only now noticed the whirr of a small generator in the corner, as well as the distinct smell of fuel. All of the devices were attached to it by long rubber cords.

"This is a typewriter," said Ramon. He pushed a button on the larger device, which produced a low hum. Then with great care, he scrolled in a sheet of paper and tapped on a few of the buttons. It produced a loud rattling sound, and when Joseph leaned forward, he was astonished to see that faint black letters had been stamped on the sheet.

"I've been keeping detailed records of our stay here," said Ramon. "Together with my clippings, they should provide quite the archive for future historians." He gave Joseph a hooded look. "You're interested in the past, are you?"

Joseph nodded. "Very much."

The older man seemed impressed. "Most people don't care about it. They just slog along in the present, unconcerned about what came before."

"It's true," Joseph said. He had often thought the same thing about his friends.

Ramon sized up Joseph, as if seeing him for the first time. Although he had seemed so angry a few minutes ago, he now opened up, like a little boy.

"You see, there was a terrible catastrophe," Ramon said. "It didn't happen all at once. It started when the president—that's the leader of your country, which used to be called the United States of America—loosened rules on where to dig for resources—"

"Like oil?"

Ramon nodded. "Exactly. She allowed drilling in places that used to be forbidden. Like the Arctic, which is north of here. That's where they dug up the bodies of soldiers that had been frozen for almost a hundred years. They had died from something called—"

"The Spanish flu?" Too late, Joseph bit his lip; he knew interrupting was rude, but he couldn't help himself. Still, Ramon smiled.

"You're a quick study." Although Joseph didn't know what this meant, it sounded like a compliment, and he blushed with pleasure. "Yes, it was the Spanish flu. You see, the cold kept the virus alive. But it had changed. Once loose, it began spreading in ways nobody thought was imaginable. Like—"

"In the water."

"Right. The oceans and rivers. And the rain."

Joseph's mind reeled at the enormity of this. He spoke slowly, as the full meaning of it sank in. "So water wasn't always deadly."

"No," Ramon exclaimed, "far from it!" Agitated, he ran one hand through his gray hair. "We used to swim in it. Can you believe that? We used to have water fountains, and go sailing on lakes, and water ski. And we had those things"—his hands described a sweeping motion—"those things we used to keep the grass from drying out—what did we call them? Sprinklers!

We'd put on our swimsuits and run under them in the summertime." Ramon laughed and, for a moment, looked far younger than his years.

"So you were alive then," Joseph said with wonder.

"Oh, yes," said Ramon. "I remember it all. Things like cars, and television, and . . . airplanes, and ice cream, and the internet, and . . . oh, so many things you can't imagine. Inna and I were twelve, thirteen when it happened, so we already knew things. We all came from good families, so we were educated. We *knew* things. And that's how we managed to survive. Right from the start, we could see how things were going. It wasn't just the water, but the sun, the earthquakes. The food. Everything. So we broke in here, got to work, and never looked back. In fact, we—"

From outside, they could hear the distant sounds of shouting. Then a siren drowned out the noise—the same one they had heard down in the underground tunnels. There was a single gunshot, followed by silence.

"The Insurgents." Ramon's expression changed. "They hate us. Because all they do is envy and destroy. They don't read. They don't work. They don't have a clue what we do in here. What we've had to sacrifice. That's why they hate you and your friends . . . because you want a better life, too. That's why you came here, right? Well, they want to drag you down with them. They're as dangerous as the water, only worse."

But Joseph had stopped listening. He was still mulling over what Ramon had told him.

"I always thought something had happened," he said,

"something big. But I had no proof. And no one believed me."

Ramon smiled once more, his expression that of a pleased teacher. "This is only the beginning, you know. There's a whole other room with even more material. I could use someone to help me organize. Would you be interested in being my assistant?"

Joseph was so thrilled he could barely speak. He nodded so many times it made Ramon laugh.

Then someone appeared at the door: It was Esther, looking anxious, a streak of dirt across her cheek. Joseph was surprised to see her without Kai and was about to ask about it when she cut him off.

"Joseph," she said. "We've been looking all over for you."

Joseph quailed when he remembered the job he had abandoned. But, impatient, Esther was already tugging on his arm.

"Inna wants to see us all on the roof," she said, "right away." It was impossible for her to keep the excitement from her voice. "She says she has something to tell us. Something important."

As hot as it was in the enclosed staircase, the temperature soared the moment Joseph and Esther stepped onto the roof, with Ramon trailing behind.

They were in the middle of a jungle: a dense profusion of greenery, leaves, and foliage that surrounded them with a rich and loamy smell. Extending as far as the eye could see were orderly rows of wooden tables that supported hundreds if not thousands of shallow plastic tanks. Each one contained water and lush growth, corralled with wire and wooden stakes. The air was so thick with humidity, it was hard to breathe.

Joseph saw that the roof was encased in a single and immense house of glass. A network of transparent panels edged in thin black strips formed the walls, as well as the low ceiling. The structure extended for hundreds of feet in all directions, with narrow metal beams holding it up at regular intervals.

Eli and Silas were already there, waiting for Esther as she confidently led the way. "This is where they grow their food," she told them over her shoulder. "They save the seeds from everything and use them to grow the next crop. They're so important, they lock them up."

Skar was crouched by a large plastic tub, twisting off fleshy red growths as big as her fist off a vine and adding them to others. "Come on," said Esther, and her friend put down her basket to join them. Farther down, Michal was sorting through a leafy tangle, snapping off fat green pods; she too stood up and fell into step.

On and on they walked. Joseph marveled at not just the size of the place but the orderly way everything was laid out. It seemed that every square foot of the roof was utilized, save for a large glass field in the center. Staring down at it, he realized it was the ornate skylight, the one that lay hundreds of feet above the main entrance. The thought of it made him dizzy; blanching, he hurried to catch up with the others.

Inna was at the far end of the roof. She was with Bao, examining one of the many pipes that led from the glass ceiling and down the wall. She looked up as Esther and her friends approached.

"Be careful of this." In the midst of the garden, Inna wore what Joseph thought was an incongruous outfit: a silver dress and, around her throat, a rope of exquisite white beads with a luminous sheen. She was indicating something by her feet: a large metal bucket half filled with brackish water. "Our system funnels all of our rainwater from the roof so it can be boiled and filtered, but sometimes, there are leaks. Whatever you do, don't touch."

At that moment, something bright blue stumbled past. It was Kai, and at the sight of him, her face lit up.

"That goes for *you* above all!" Scooping him up, Inna nuzzled his neck. Then she raised her head and her tone sharpened. "Bao! Make certain the boy never gets near the pipes again. Is that clear?" The other woman bowed and nodded, murmuring apologies.

By now, everyone had gathered on the roof: not only Esther and her friends, but the other adults, as well. Inna waited until everyone settled down. But before she could begin, she was interrupted by a soft yet terrifying sound.

It was rain.

Fat drops splattered the glass directly above their heads. Joseph could not help but flinch; he saw Esther and the others recoil as well, some throwing their arms up in an instinctive attempt to protect themselves.

Yet Inna remained unperturbed.

"Look, Kai," she exclaimed as she gazed upward, "isn't it wonderful? We haven't had a good rain for weeks." She bounced the boy in her arms, then cradled him so he could watch the sky. "You've brought us luck!"

With flushed cheeks and sparkling eyes, the woman now turned to face the others. "And that's what I wanted to speak to you about. I know you've only been here such a short time. But you've been doing fine work today. We all have a good feeling about you. If you'd like to, we'd be honored to have you stay with us."

A look of immense relief and joy passed among all the travelers except Skar.

"Thank you," Esther replied. She was clearly trying to keep her feelings in check, but like Inna, her face was radiant. "We hope you won't regret it."

"Oh," said Inna. "I know we won't."

Joseph kept his gaze on the ceiling. It was strange, but true. The glass not only held, but he could see rainwater running along the clear panes and forming a large pool in the center. It would drain through pipes, disappearing into the system that would soon make it drinkable.

The idea was clever yet so simple.

The adults had so much to teach them, Joseph thought.

He only hoped he had enough time to learn it all.

Miles away, the rain came down in torrents.

Aras stood in the doorway of an abandoned home, his heart pounding; he had only just missed being drenched. He took a dry cloth from his backpack and ran it over himself with care before flinging it aside. He had known the storm was coming; over the day, the heavy air had grown even thicker, and stiff winds had begun to kick. Still, it had come on with surprising speed, catching him unawares.

After leaving the others, Aras had made his way back south until he found a village off an exit. He still had a good sense of how towns were laid out. With Pilot, he managed to make his way through a cluster of houses, finding a few edible items in the destroyed kitchens.

Now supper could wait; for although he trusted Pilot, Aras didn't much like the idea of investigating an abandoned home in the rain. When it stopped, he would be able to find a dry corner and build a fire. Until then, he would have to pass the time.

Normally, he would roll up a smoking paper. Yet something held him back, as it had for days now.

It was the thought of Esther.

When he least expected it, he could sense her presence next to him. And she haunted his dreams: He could still feel her features, fine and delicate, beneath his fingertips, and the softness of her lips. Tormented, he wished that she would leave him, as he had left her.

By now, the rain had stopped. And in the silence, Aras heard something he hadn't before.

It was the sound of breathing.

Someone else was in the room.

He whirled around, wondering why Pilot had not attacked. Then he noticed it was an uneven sound, shallow and rapid. Taking Pilot by the collar, he took a tentative step toward its source.

"Don't."

The word, tiny and dry, was the sound of a dead leaf brushing the ground. It was impossible to tell if it was boy or girl, someone young or old. And Aras realized with sudden clarity that it didn't matter.

The stranger was sick. Whatever it had been once upon a time, it was near death now.

Aras instinctively pressed the crook of his elbow hard against his mouth and nose and turned to go. Then he hesitated. In his mind, he saw Esther again, racing to help Rhea after she plummeted into the pool. He knew what she would have done.

Aras set his backpack down. Then he unzipped it. Rummaging through his belongings, he removed some of the food he had found, as well as a bottle of water. He clicked a command to Pilot and the dog led him forward.

"Here," he said, his voice still muffled. He crouched down and offered up the supplies, taking care to keep a safe distance. Whoever it was didn't take them and after a moment, Aras returned them to his bag. "How long you been here?"

"Don't know."

"Where you come from?"

There was silence. Then the word came out as an exhalation. "Mundreel."

Aras was startled. He couldn't help but ask, "How come you left?"

More silence. Aras waited, then after a minute, got to his feet. As he stood in the doorway, he heard behind him three distinct words.

"Didn't leave. Escaped."

Aras swung around. "What you mean?" But this time, there was no reply.

The hair on Aras's neck was standing up. Twice he had ventured to the edges of the city yet never entered.

Who lived there?

What had he delivered Esther to?

Aras stayed in the house for several hours, until he knew it was safe to venture out. By then, he could feel the relative coolness of the evening air. He didn't mind traveling at night.

Aras no longer had his compass, of course; he had given it to Esther. Yet he hoped that as long as he kept to the major road, he would be all right.

Without detours, he figured he would be in Mundreel in a few days.

Something told him there was no time to waste.

EIGHTEEN

Several days later, Inna hosted a party.

Feeling shy, the young people stood by themselves to one side of the big room on the top floor of the District. The large table had been moved, pushed against the wall by Eli and Joseph. Now it was heaped with food and drink.

Like her friends, Esther had put on her nicest clothing. She wore a floral skirt that twirled and billowed when she walked, a pink sweater, and a delicate choker of the white beads called "pearls." The outfit felt strange to her, and what's more, it was nearly impossible to walk in the red shoes she wore, fastened with a tiny buckle at the ankle. Yet the clothes were a gift from

Inna, and Esther was determined to show her gratitude. As she entered with Kai, she combed his hair with her fingers; she wanted him to look presentable for the woman who had been so nice to them.

The adults were clustered on the other side of the room, laughing and chatting to one another in their odd language as they handed around thin silver discs, which they examined and compared. In their midst was a peculiar device Esther had seen earlier: a metallic box with buttons on it. Now one of the grown-ups inserted a disc, pressing a button with a loud click; and within moments, a strange sound filled the air.

It was unlike anything the younger people had heard before: rich, rhythmic, complex. Esther cocked her head, frowning with concentration, and decided she liked it.

"Why don't you dance?"

Esther looked up and saw Inna smiling at her. "I don't know what that is."

"It's what people do when there's music," Inna explained. She waved her hand at the sound. "You see? This is music."

"Oh." Esther felt self-conscious about her ignorance. "Is dancing a ritual?"

"No." Then Inna corrected herself. "Well, I suppose it is, sometimes. But mostly, it's for fun. Like this."

The older woman closed her eyes and began to sway in time to the music. Esther thought she looked beautiful.

"See?" Inna stopped, with a laugh. "It's kind of like that. Only a lot of people can do it better." Now she was the one to appear self-conscious, tidying away a piece of her hair that had become untucked. "And it's even better when you don't do it alone."

"You mean with other people?"

"With someone else. Yes."

Frowning, Esther turned and shot an inquiring glance around the room. Her gaze landed on Joseph. Her friend, who had been studying the floor, looked up and by accident locked eyes with her. Then he cleared his throat, with great discomfort.

"I have to talk to Silas," he said, and bolted.

Esther sighed and Inna patted the girl's shoulder. "Girls like to dance more than boys do," she remarked with sympathy.

"*I'll* do it."

Esther turned to see who had spoken. Standing in front of her was Eli, looking nervous yet eager.

"Do you want to? Really?"

"Maybe." Eli became sheepish. "I mean . . . if you want to."

Esther was surprised to find she really did want to dance. Yet for some reason, she felt embarrassed to admit it.

Still, this was enough for Inna. "Just wait here," she said. "I'll switch the music."

She held out her hand for Kai and led him across the room. There, she too fumbled with the discs, holding them close to examine them.

Esther and Eli looked everywhere but at each other. When the new music began, both glanced up, startled; yet within seconds, they found themselves smiling. This new sound was different from the first. It felt quicker, stronger, even thrilling.

Hearing it, you *had* to dance.

"Watch!" Inna shouted, startling and embarrassing them both. "Watch us!"

She and Ramon stood facing each other. Inna put one hand

on his shoulder, while he held her waist. They raised their other arms, and hands clasped, they began to move together in time to the music.

Esther and Eli watched them, spellbound.

"Now it's your turn!" Inna called.

Panicked, Esther looked at Eli. She thought he seemed more frightened than he ever had on the road, even when their lives were in danger.

Then he swallowed and raised his arms stiffly.

"Ready?" he said.

Esther nodded. She clutched his shoulder and, lifting her other arm, took his extended hand, which was rigid and sweating.

There was a pleasant twanging quality to the music, and its pulsating rhythm was accented by a steady clashing sound. Two or three boys seemed to be singing, their voices interweaving in a strange way; sometimes, it was hard to tell there was more than one.

The words were simple and repetitive:

If I gave
My heart away,
Would you be
My girl today?
And make me
Feel that bliss?
'Cause I've never
Been a boy
Who's ever

Known the joy
That comes
With a kiss . . . .

At first, Esther and Eli lurched and shuffled, their desperate eyes locked on Inna and her partner across the room. The older people made it look so easy, while Eli and Esther rocked back and forth in an agony of clumsy anxiety.

But as the song continued, Esther began to ease into it, as did Eli. It was not that they made fewer mistakes; both had begun to relax and actually listen to the music. Instead of clutching Eli like they were both drowning, Esther held him lightly, his chest pressed against hers. It was an odd sensation, to cling to someone so close in public as they both swayed to and fro. Still, she found it pleasant to lean against his warmth, to feel her waist encircled by his arm.

Up close, Esther could smell Eli now, his hair, his skin; it was nice. Esther looked into Eli's eyes, really looked, something she had never done before. Dark brown, with flecks of gold in them, they were limpid, open, and appealing. She remembered that he had once asked to be her partner in Prin. What if he were to ask again?

With a start, Esther realized that these feelings weren't genuine. The music had made her see him in this way.

'Cause I couldn't
Take the shame
If you

Told me no
And you did not
Feel the same.

Esther glanced over Eli's shoulder. Skar and Michal were on
the floor as well, finding a rhythm in each other's arms. Michal
had her head resting on Skar's shoulder, her eyes shut. The two
seemed natural, comfortable together, and Skar looked happy
in a way Esther had never seen before.

Inna and Ramon had finished dancing. The older woman
now walked over to Kai and took him from Bao. As she led him
into the hall, she caught Esther's eye across the dance floor.
She winked and made the boy wave; and then they were gone.

That was when the full meaning of what had happened hit
Esther.

This was our life now, she thought. *No more worrying about food or
water or a safe place to sleep. No need to fight every day to stay alive. Inna and
Ramon would take care of everything.*

All they had to do was dance.

In a corner of the room, Joseph milled, restlessly. Next to him
Silas seemed anxious, biting a thumbnail.

"Why don't you dance with each other?" Bao had asked.

Uneasy, Silas didn't reply. When he glanced at Joseph, he
only saw the boy's back. Joseph was walking, swiftly and stiffly,
out of the room.

In the hall, pacing, Joseph tried to forget about the dancing,
not wishing to be reminded of the whole silly thing. Of all the

useless artifacts from the past to retain! He was annoyed that not only did his face still feel hot, he couldn't keep from humming the tune of the song being played.

"*'Cause I couldn't take the shame . . .*"

Exasperated, he stopped. To divert himself, he thought of the offer Ramon had made him earlier. The promise of his new responsibilities was so exciting, he was cheered up all over again. Then he felt the cat carrier he always wore on his shoulder shift as he heard the sound of a cat mewing.

Joseph set the leather-and-canvas bag on the ground. Unzipping it, he freed the restless tabby waiting inside.

"Let's go find something for you to eat," he said.

He located the unlit stairwell at the end of the hallway and, together, the boy and animal edged down in the darkness. Once they emerged in the mall itself, his cat followed in her fashion—occasionally wandering off to the side, sniffing around, investigating sounds only she could hear. He noted her pinched sides and bony hips with a pang. Although he managed to get her to eat a few vegetables, Stumpy was starving, he knew. Perhaps with any luck, they would come across a squirrel or a mouse that had managed to find its way inside.

Although he didn't mean to, Joseph soon found himself heading in a new direction. He rounded a corner, then another. Within minutes, he found himself on a completely new hallway, where it was mostly dark. As he passed one unfamiliar store after another, each with metal gates rolled down and fastened to the ground with a padlock, he realized that he was lost. Feeling forlorn, Joseph stopped in his tracks.

"Hey there."

Joseph turned and saw someone stumbling toward him through the dim and silent hall, holding aloft a lit torch. It was Ramon, who had apparently grown tired of the party, as well.

Joseph felt self-conscious to be found lurking around in the dark. But the old man, who smelled a little like the intoxicating liquid that the adults had been drinking, didn't seem to care. When he drew closer, Joseph could see a foolish grin on his face.

"There's only so much dancing a man can do," Ramon said. "Am I right?"

Joseph found himself nodding with vigor; he couldn't agree more. Then he felt Ramon's hand drop heavily onto his shoulder and shake it once, hard.

"Sometimes men have to attend to more important things," Ramon said. "Right?"

"Right."

"Feel like getting to work already?"

"I do!" The truth was, there was nothing he would rather be doing at that moment.

"I thought so. You've got a good mind."

"Well," Joseph got up the nerve to say, "not like you. You're a real historian."

Joseph's sincere flattery seemed to decide something in Ramon's mind. Rifling through his pockets, the man brought out a set of keys.

"Come in," he said. "I'll show you my other archive."

Ramon handed his torch to the boy before bending to

unlock a door. Then, squatting with much effort, he grabbed the bottom of the gate and attempted to lift it.

Joseph grew concerned. "Do you need any help?" he offered, but the man waved him off.

"I'm fine, I'm fine," he wheezed. "I'm not that old."

Finally, with much groaning and cursing, Ramon succeeded in rolling the metal gate up, which screamed and rattled in its rusty track.

Joseph and Stumpy followed as the older man entered a dusty space filled with one desk and many file cabinets and shelves. Ramon moved to the desk and stuck the torch in a metal bracket. Then he patted the swivel chair before it.

"Take a load off," he said.

Joseph eventually realized that this meant he should sit down. Meanwhile, Ramon was rummaging through some high shelves, grunting to himself. He returned to dump several flat wire baskets onto the desk. As he leaned over Joseph, the smell of his drink was overpowering.

"Here you go," Ramon said, with obvious pride. "You can see the kind of thing I've been up to. I'm going to need a little help putting them in order."

They were records, and the amount of information they represented was dizzying. Each page was nearly black on both sides with tiny, terse descriptions, numbers, dates, and times: *ounces planted/yield percentage. Six kilograms radishes. Twenty-one kilograms potatoes. Thirty-six liters of water. Compostable remains. Vol. of compost tea in milliliters.*

The accounting it represented wasn't just thorough; it was

overwhelming. Eight baskets were piled on the desk, and there were clearly many more, filling up nearly an entire wall. The words and numbers began to swarm in front of Joseph's eyes, like ants.

Then Ramon seemed to get inspired.

"Hold on," he said. "I'll get you the original notes, which were all handwritten and crude. Maybe that would be a good place for you to start."

Ramon stumbled away. Joseph heard the older man rifle through file cabinets on the far side of the store as the torch-light threw crooked shadows against the wall. Ramon made a lot of noise: closing some drawers, opening others, catching his fingers in one, cursing, slamming it shut.

Utterly confused, Joseph picked up one sheet and then another. Wanting to make a good impression, he seized an entire basket in the impossible hope of skimming its contents before the man returned. In his haste, his finger hooked the one beneath it, causing it to tip and begin to spill its paper. Joseph lunged to save it and, as a result, knocked the stack to the floor with a clatter.

Luckily, Ramon was either too groggy or making too much noise to notice. "Be right there!" he called. He sounded the most jovial he had been since Joseph and the others had arrived.

Filled with fresh panic, Joseph crouched low to the ground, wringing his hands over the mountain of paper. He was about to stuff the whole pile into the wire baskets when he realized that they were now completely mixed up. Frantically, he picked up a few sheets, checked the dates, and stuck them into one of the containers. Then he scooped up another handful, and another, and another, trying to put them into some semblance of order.

Records were still scattered all over the floor and Ramon would be back any second now. Nearly fainting with terror, Joseph had begun cramming papers into their bins any which way, when his eye fell on one sheet.

He stopped to read it.

Repurposing of visitors . . . Capture and corralling . . . three male, one female . . . thirty-three kilograms. Forty-eight kilograms. Forty-one kilograms . . . Breaking down of carcasses . . .

Joseph's gaze skittered down the page, not making sense of what he saw. Yet as he read, a strange, unpleasant feeling began to steal over him and he could feel the skin of his neck prickle.

Bone racks . . . Maturing chops . . . Slaughtering . . .

"Here we go!"

Ramon was stumbling toward him. He was carrying an unwieldy armful of folders, files, and other bits of paper.

With an impulse that went against everything he believed in—honesty, respecting other people's property, and the sacredness of printed material—Joseph grabbed the sheet of paper and stuffed it into the pocket of his jacket. Then he took the entire remaining stack of records off the floor and hoisted them onto the desk.

Ramon appeared at his shoulder. "Hey," he said. "What happened here?"

Joseph struggled to come up with an explanation. But

Ramon had already opened one of his notebooks on the surface before them.

"Now you'll see," he said, "these records go back several years, when I cleverly went from longhand to a kind of shorthand I devised myself. You see, these symbols over here . . ."

In all the excitement, Joseph hadn't noticed that Stumpy, still hungry, had ambled across the store and out the door.

Silas had drifted away from the dancing, too. Though he couldn't admit it to anyone, if there had been enough girls, he might have given it a chance. But dancing with Joseph? Probably not.

There was nothing to look at in the hallway outside the party; so he, too, headed for the windowless stairwell and descended to the lower levels. He walked through the dim floors of the mall, the soles of his new sneakers squeaking on the marble floor. Idly, he peered in at shuttered stores—CHANEL, COACH, BURBERRY, LULU GUINNESS—and examined the endless items on display: handbags, watches, scarves, overcoats, wallets. Reaching the street level, he decided to go even farther, down the final set of stairs.

Silas and the others had not yet been shown around this section of the complex. In the scant light, he saw that the basement floor had much the same layout as the ones above: an open area, lit by the waning light from far above and ringed by what looked like restaurants: PRET A MANGER, JACQUES TORRES CHOCOLATE, HARRY & DAVID.

He tried to peer past the metal gate that guarded the giant

doorway of one store. He could see a glassed-in counter, a cash register, and what seemed like crude bedding on the floor. But just as he was about to turn away, Silas noticed a reflection in the counter and whirled around.

Joseph's cat was roaming the basement by herself.

It was an unusual sight. The animal was rarely out of her carrier and always stuck close to her owner. Silas thought he ought to at least follow her. If nothing else, he could do Joseph a favor and keep her from getting lost.

"Hey," he said, snapping his fingers. "Come here."

Stumpy paid no attention to him. She slunk low to the ground, darting forward and then freezing in place. She was clearly stalking something hiding in the murky shadows.

Silas didn't want to ruin the tabby's hunt by scaring away her prey. Besides, he thought it might be fun to watch her catch something. So he moved after her slowly and kept his distance. Whatever she was pursuing seemed to be heading farther into the darkness, and soon Silas found himself far from the metal staircases.

At last, he saw what she was chasing, sniffing at the foot of two metal doors. He smiled. *Well, what else could it have been?* It was a rat, large and grayish brown.

Silas wondered how there managed to be vermin in such a pristine environment. There had to be food somewhere nearby; the rodent was surprisingly fat. Stumpy was frozen in place with a paw raised in the air, with only the tip of her tail twitching. When the rat nosed the ground, she crept forward two paces, then stopped again.

Silas held his breath as the cat coiled herself like a spring. She shimmied her hindquarters once, twice, three times. But in that moment, the rat glanced up, its beady eyes perceiving the threat. Even as Stumpy launched herself at her prey, claws extended, the rat was scrabbling at the impossibly narrow threshold, flattening itself enough to slide under the door and disappear.

Stumpy examined her paws, which had closed on thin air. The appalled expression on her round face seemed almost human, and Silas laughed. Then he glanced up and noticed the doors under which the rat fled.

Unlike the rest of the immaculate building, they were badly dented and scratched. There were letters on one of them, which he sounded out with difficulty: TO GARAGE. He pressed the metal bar handle, but it was locked.

Then he heard people approaching.

From the far, dimly lit end of the hall, he saw silhouettes heading his way. Two older men were wheeling a large plastic can on a hand truck and chatting with each other. Even from where he stood, he could see the pistols at their belts.

There was no real reason to fear them. Yet Silas obeyed his instincts, which were overpowering. He grabbed the startled cat, which gave an indignant mew. Then he fled to a shadowy corner across the hall and hid in a doorway.

Sure enough, the guards were headed toward the dented twin doors. When they got there, one took out a huge key ring and fumbled with it until he was able to unlock them.

"Shh," Silas whispered to the protesting Stumpy.

In the meantime, the other guard had wrenched the lid off the barrel and pulled from it a black plastic bag, knotted securely. He disappeared in the room and when he returned moments later, empty-handed, his partner handed him another bag. Maybe six in all were brought into the room, one by one, before they were done. Then the guards shut the doors and locked them up again.

It seemed to be a dirty, unpleasant task. *And strangely*, thought Silas, *it was one they hadn't asked their guests to do.*

The two men walked away, the empty plastic container now rattling before them. Once he heard their footsteps fade, Silas placed the cat down and stepped out.

Silas knew he could go back upstairs and no one would know where he had been. But by now, his curiosity was too strong.

The animal at his heels, Silas stepped toward the door. From his sock, he retrieved his thieving tools, which were two slim pieces of metal. He slid one into the lock, and jiggled it until the tumbler turned. Then he took the other one, a thin yet unbendable steel hook, and inserted it. Patiently, he attempted to tap the lock from inside. It took longer than he expected; after a while, he started to sweat and his hand to shake. Impatient, Stumpy began to cry next to him.

"Okay, okay," he whispered. "I'll get it."

At last, he heard a click.

Checking behind him, Silas pushed the metal bar and stepped into darkness. The sound of the door opening echoed, telling him it was a cavernous place, even as the stench of the room hit him. He clamped the crook of his elbow over his nose and tried not to breathe.

Stumpy had her own agenda. Rushing past him, she darted into a black corner. Silas heard a tussle, a squeal, then nothing.

It was impossible to see. Silas reached behind him and pushed the door further open, allowing in more light.

There seemed to be an underground mountain range in the garage. Shadowy, hulking forms surrounded him on every side; immense heaps of garbage sorted by type: empty cans, bottles, discarded clothes. These were dwarfed by piles of black plastic bags, filled with human waste and in some cases spilling their foul contents onto the ground.

All around him were the active sounds of rats: squeaking, battling, tearing open bags. As he picked his way through the mess, Silas was astounded that such squalor existed mere floors below great luxury.

That was when he saw it on the floor.

At first, Silas was not sure what it was. It was small, the size of two fists, and its pale material caught the faint spill of light from the hall. Then as his eyes adjusted, he was able to make out more details. They made his stomach lurch and his blood feel like ice.

Empty sockets. Teeth. Nasal bone.

It was a human skull. And small enough to have belonged to a child.

NINETEEN

Overcoming his revulsion, Silas made a quick decision and picked the object up. It was surprisingly lightweight, as dry as a piece of old wood and so small, he could carry it tucked under his shirt. Then he looked around for Stumpy.

She was crouched behind a pile of garbage bags, devouring the remains of a freshly killed rat. He tried to lift her, but when she tensed up and growled, he relented and set her down again. It was, after all, the first real meal she had eaten in days. But Silas was uneasy about remaining much longer; he didn't like the possibility of the guards returning and finding him. He was relieved when the cat finished eating, licking her jaws and letting out a tiny belch.

"Let's go," he said.

Holding her, Silas picked his way back to the open door. When he pulled it shut after him, he was glad to hear the lock click.

But in his eagerness to get away from the hellish room, Silas did not look to see who might be watching. He bounded up the narrow staircase that led from the basement level, taking two steps at a time. He was halfway up when a harsh voice boomed from above.

"Hey . . . you! What were you doing down there?"

Two adult faces were staring at him over the railing several flights above. Even from that distance, he could tell they were furious.

Moments later, the clatter of their footsteps running down the metal stairs began echoing throughout the marble atrium.

But no one was there to hear.

By the time the men reached the basement level, Silas had already sprinted down the hall to the enclosed stairwell. Still clutching the protesting cat, he raced to the third level before disappearing into the expanse of the mall.

Michal spun in a circle, her dress glinting in the torchlight.

Much to her disappointment, the dancing had ended half an hour earlier. Now, she and Skar were alone in the store that was their room, SUNGLASS HUT. As she had been so often lately, Skar seemed preoccupied and thoughtful, sitting on the edge of her cot and chewing her thumbnail. But Michal continued to dance alone, admiring herself in one of the many mirrors that adorned the walls of the store.

The adults had not allowed their guests to drink any of the intoxicating liquid. Still, Michal felt as free and loose as if she had finished an entire bottle by herself.

"'*Cause I couldn't take the shame,*'" she sang. Then, with a smile, she opened her arms to her partner. "Come on . . . dance with me again." But although Skar returned the smile, she shook her head.

Michal sat next to her, her face flushed. "What's wrong?"

Skar didn't answer at first. "It's Esther," she said. "I'm worried about her."

Michal flopped onto the bed and raised her arms above her head. Earlier that afternoon, Inna had asked Bao to take Michal and Skar to a jewelry store on the third level. Once there, the girls were allowed to select as many things as they wanted: emeralds, sapphires, rubies. Now Michal admired the glints of colored light that glanced off the gems in her rings and bracelets and played across the ceiling.

"What do you mean?" she asked, not really paying attention.

"I don't know," said Skar. "She seems different."

"Different? Like how?"

Skar searched for the right words. "Esther is very loyal. But that is only after you have earned her trust, with actions. It is unlike her to give it away so quickly, without even questioning the other person's motives."

Michal was puzzled. "Who are you talking about?"

"Inna."

Her partner's bluntness surprised Michal. "Don't you like her?" she asked, sitting up. "I think she's nice."

Skar shook her head.

"It is not a question of liking. Esther is our leader, and I am speaking of her judgment. She trusts Inna, even though the woman has not yet earned it."

Michal wrinkled her nose. "But she gives us so much nice stuff." She shook her arms one last time, making the bracelets jangle. "She said we can have whatever we want. All we got to do is ask."

Skar sighed. "True," she admitted. "But we don't know who Inna is . . . not yet. Not really. And each day, Esther's trust in her grows and grows."

Michal put her arms around Skar's neck. "You sound like you don't trust *Esther*," she said. Then another thought came to her. "Or maybe you're jealous," she added in a teasing voice, "because Inna likes Esther more than she likes you."

Skar smiled and was about to reply when something darted into their room.

It was Joseph's cat, Stumpy.

As the animal disappeared behind a display case, Silas appeared at their doorway. He was ashen-faced and breathing hard.

"What are you—" Michal started to say, but Skar, realizing that something was wrong, had already leaped to her feet.

"Stay here, in case anyone comes," she said to Michal. Then with a glance into the hallway, Skar grabbed Silas by the arm and pulled him deeper into the store.

Ducking behind a counter, the two were hidden from view. "Are you all right?" she asked. He nodded, unable to speak. "But someone is chasing you. Who is it?"

Silas caught his breath. Then speaking in whispers, he started to tell her what had happened.

Skar stiffened and held up her hand, silencing him. Seconds later, they could hear footsteps approach and stop in the doorway.

"Did you see anyone come by here?" said a man's voice. A murmured reply came from Michal, and after a moment, the footsteps continued on their way.

"What did you find in the garage?" Skar whispered to Silas, once she knew they were safe.

Without saying a word, he untucked his shirt and pulled something out.

"Maybe it's an animal," he said in a low voice. "I don't know enough to tell."

Skar held up the object and turned it around, examining it. With her finger, she traced the empty eye sockets, the delicate jut of bone at the nose, and the teeth, which were mostly intact. Then she shuddered.

"No," she said. "It's not an animal."

Michal had joined them and when she saw the skull, she gasped.

Skar looked grim as she turned the object around. "And that's not the worst part. You see this?" Holding it up to the torchlight, she indicated where a section of bone had been smashed away in the back. The jagged hole radiated into fine cracks.

"Whoever it was," she said, "somebody killed him."

In the party room upstairs, all that was left was the beautiful wreckage of the table: dirty plates and goblets, crumpled napkins, empty bottles. Yet there was still so much food—not only figs, berries, and grapes, but also more-familiar treats made of packaged ingredients. Gleaming silver trays and bowls were stuffed with salted flatbreads dripping honey, sugary porridge, candies, and plastic containers of soda.

Esther stood alone at the table, nibbling a crust. The only other person left was Eli. He was watching her from across the room, but he was too shy to approach.

In truth, he was still dazed from the dancing. He liked it more than he had expected, a lot more.

Holding Esther and moving with her, feeling her body pressed close, her hand enfolded in his—it had unearthed all the old emotions and made them even stronger than he remembered.

And, unless he was crazy, he thought she had felt a flicker of something for him, as well.

Could it be true? Maybe at long last, after all the loss and struggle and pain they had both been through, he and Esther were finally ready to meet in the same place.

If that were so, Eli thought with a new sense of gratitude, *it was because of their hosts.* Inna and Ramon had introduced them not just to music, dancing, beautiful clothes, and fine food, but something rarer. They had taught them that they were entitled to pleasure, as well as something few of them had ever fully known in Prin.

That thing was happiness.

Though he had eaten less than an hour ago, Eli realized he was hungry again. As he filled yet another plate, marveling for the hundredth time at the opulence of the banquet, a funny thought struck him. The adults never ate with them; they always stood to the side at mealtimes, watching as their guests ate and then finishing up what little was left. Yet they had never once stinted on what they served.

"It's almost like they want to fatten us up," Eli joked to Esther.

But the two had no sooner sat down and started to eat when something made them look up. Joseph had entered the room, looking pale and unsteady on his feet.

"I—" he started, then stopped. "I've been looking for you."

Esther had already crossed the room. "What's wrong?"

He found the nearest seat and sank into it. He was panting and blinked a few times.

"It's all right. Just calm down." Esther knelt beside him and smoothed the damp hair from his brow. "What's happened?"

"I wanted to get away from where I was."

She spoke as if addressing a panicked child. "Where were you?"

"I was reading some of the . . . records. The ones that they keep. Inna and Ramon and . . . the others."

"And what did they say?"

"They seemed to . . ." Joseph had regained some of his composure. "They seemed to refer to . . . how they've survived. What they . . . what they eat."

Esther was losing patience. "We *know* what they eat. You remember their garden? They grow it all themselves."

Joseph swiveled and stared her right in the face. "That's not all."

Unnerved by his intensity, Esther felt a prickling sensation at the base of her scalp. Then she dismissed it. Joseph was forever worried about something. In fact, he was already fussing with the leather carrier he always had across his shoulder and which now hung open, empty.

"Where's Stumpy?" he asked, his voice rising with panic. "Has anyone seen her?"

"I've got her."

Silas stood in the doorway, the cat struggling in his arms. The second the animal saw Joseph, she pulled herself free, leaped to the floor, and sauntered over as if nothing out of the ordinary had happened. Joseph reached down to scoop her up.

Skar and Michal were with Silas. Now the variant girl stepped forward, holding out an object. When they saw it, everyone grew quiet.

"What is that?" said Eli, drawing closer.

But even at a distance, Esther didn't need anyone to tell her. She had seen dead bodies before—skulls and bones worn down by the elements, the freshly dead consumed by flies. Corpses still wearing the tattered remains of jeans and T-shirts.

"We think it was somebody young," Silas said. "I found it

where they bring the garbage. I don't know how many others they got down there."

"This is what I meant." Joseph spoke in a soft voice, rocking his cat. "This is just what I meant." He fumbled in his pocket and pulled out a crumpled piece of paper, the one he had stolen. "Look," he said.

Esther stared at the writing. Although she didn't know most of them, a few words were clear to her, enough to make a terrible kind of sense. As she struggled to comprehend it, she realized that the others were looking at her, waiting.

"It can't be true," she said, at last. "I don't believe it. Inna wouldn't . . . she just wouldn't."

Doubt seemed to ripple across the room like a wave. Esther saw it flash across their faces, even Skar's, and for a moment, she was angry.

"Where's Kai?" Joseph asked suddenly.

"Inna has him." In an instant, Esther became defensive, and then hostile. "Why? Don't you trust her to—"

"And your rifle?" Skar asked.

Esther began to answer, then stopped. It occurred to her that she had no idea. "I . . . they must have taken it somewhere. For safekeeping."

Even to her own ears, her words sounded foolish. Then she shook away the doubt: If she entertained it, all certainty and safety would come crashing to the ground.

"Why don't we ask Inna about this?" Eli spoke in a neutral, reasonable voice, as if he understood how difficult this was for her. Esther shot him a glance of gratitude.

"All right," she said. "And you all come with me so you can hear for yourself."

Inna and Kai weren't on the roof or in the dark stairwell. Nor were they in the eating area lower down, or in any of the other places they had visited earlier. Now Esther and her friends stood in the vast central atrium on the ground floor, uncertain where to look next.

Esther knew it was ridiculous, but she was starting to feel a twinge of anxiety.

Then Skar glanced up. "Listen," she said.

Cocking her head, Esther couldn't hear anything at first. Then she detected the faintest, high-pitched thread of noise, coming from somewhere in the darkness farther up. Because the enormous space seemed to both magnify and disperse the sound, it took them several minutes to pinpoint where it was coming from. By the time they made it up to the third floor, they finally knew what it was.

It was music, unlike the kind they had danced to, with a thin, metallic sound that was both pretty and eerie. The tinkling noise came from a distance, where they could see a light flickering from a storefront.

It was a shop none had entered before, full of bright colors, small pieces of furniture, and stuffed animals. At the back of the room, a lit torch was set in a wall bracket; and by its light, Inna sat in an armchair with Kai in her lap. He was wearing a crisp, new pair of yellow overalls, with a red-and-white-striped shirt, and tiny blue sneakers on his feet. As he wrestled with a cloth bear sporting button eyes, he laughed at the odd noises that came out whenever he squeezed it. Other toys, some of them still in their boxes and covered with plastic, lay scattered on the floor around them.

On a low table nearby was a strange object. Two small ceramic children approached a house made of candy and other sweets. As they spun in a slow circle, the tinkling music poured from it, repeating again and again.

At the sight of Inna and Kai, Esther felt as if a vise had been released from around her heart. She turned to Skar.

"See?" she whispered. "He's fine."

Inna looked up and smiled.

"Look," she exclaimed. "He's grown so much these past few days, he already needs new clothes." She stood him up in her lap, holding onto his hands. "Doesn't he look handsome?" Kai laughed, bouncing up and down, as Inna hoisted him into the air and set him down. Then he tottered to a playpen that had been set up steps away.

"Now," she said, smiling, as she turned to Esther and the others. "What can I do for you all?"

All at once, Esther felt foolish standing there and preparing what she was about to say. If it were up to her, she would have turned around and gone downstairs again.

Yet her friends were still frightened and suspicious behind her; she could feel their eyes locked on her back. Esther took a deep breath and began.

"We found something downstairs," she said. Inna cocked her head in polite interest. "In the parking garage."

The woman laughed. "I'm sorry you went down there!" she exclaimed. "It's incredibly filthy. That's our least favorite job, dealing with the garbage . . . nobody ever wants to do it and it does pile up." She paused. "So what exactly did you find?"

Esther swallowed. "A skull," she said. She was aware she was blushing. "We think it's human. A child."

Inna wrinkled her nose, thinking.

"Well, I suppose that's possible," she said. "The Insurgents are always trying to break in. Occasionally, they manage to slide through pipes or break through a vent. If one of them made it as far as the garage, I suppose he could have gotten trapped down there and then starved to death. It's horrible to think about." She made a face and shuddered.

But Esther forged ahead. "We also saw something in your records." She glanced at Joseph, who blanched and seemed to shrink as she spoke. *He wasn't making this any easier,* she thought with exasperation. So she simply blurted out what she had to say. "Do you eat babies?"

Behind her, someone drew in a sharp breath and there was a desperately uncomfortable pause.

"You mean like Kai?" asked Inna, astonished. "Am I going to eat *Kai?*" She burst out laughing. "No! Oh no, no, no, no. Of course I'm not going to harm the baby. What an idea!"

She rose and then bent down and picked him up from his playpen. "Here," she said, "just look at him." She nuzzled his neck as she brought him over to Esther. "He's in perfect health . . . absolutely perfect."

Kai clung to Esther's shirt, burbling, and grabbed her hair.

It was obvious he was in better shape than he had ever been in his life: clean, well-fed, and full of energy.

"Satisfied?" said Inna, and Esther nodded, abashed.

"You see, he's not like the rest of us," continued the older woman as she smiled down at him. "We're all contaminated by the water and the sun and the soil, no matter how much we try to keep them away . . . we're garbage, really. But babies are different. They're pure . . . untouched. With any luck, Kai will live to be seventy, eighty years old. And he's going to regrow the Earth."

Esther was trying to follow what Inna was saying, but her words were too confusing. The woman seemed to be thinking aloud, no longer acknowledging there were even other people in the room. *It was*, Esther decided, *time to go.*

"See?" she said to the others. "I told you they don't eat children."

With Kai at her shoulder, Esther turned to leave. But the older woman roused herself.

"Oh," Inna said, "I didn't say *that*."

"Stop!"

Aras had no choice but to comply. With difficulty, he pulled Pilot to a halt. If he was about to be attacked, he thought with grim resignation, at least he wouldn't go down without a fight. His dog was already growling and straining at the lead, his body tensed to spring.

The two had crossed a bridge late that morning. Over the past two days, Aras had not run into anyone to ask directions.

He had done his best to calculate the distance and could only hope it was Mundreel. Yet as they made their way through the echoing streets, he could hear no one; the panting of his dog was the only sound. At the command, Aras couldn't help but be filled with relief, as well as illogical hope.

But when the voice called again, closer this time, he realized with a sinking heart that it wasn't Eli or Silas; it belonged to someone he didn't know. And there was more than one. He could hear the sound of several bicycles, only a block away and approaching fast. Even with his sight, it would have been impossible to flee. And so Aras waited, outwardly calm yet prepared to set his dog loose.

He heard bikes skidding to a halt—three, possibly four, it was hard to tell. Then a boy spoke.

"Leave Mundreel." Aras figured him to be maybe fifteen or sixteen. "Ain't safe here."

Aras nodded; at least he was where he intended to be. "Why?"

"The ones inside," the stranger said. He spoke with assurance; Aras figured he was the leader. "The ones who got and we don't. They hunt us. Like we was some kind of—"

He was interrupted by the blare of a siren. It was impossibly loud, drowning out their voices and echoing through the silent streets.

"They seen us!" Someone else, a girl, screamed over the din. "You got to come before they start shooting!"

"But why—"

Aras felt himself pushed into some kind of wagon. Having

no choice but to trust these strangers, he pulled his dog along with him. No sooner were they inside than the vehicle took off. Aras lurched to one side, nearly falling to the ground, as the wheels rattled over broken pavement. He thought he heard the distant crack of a rifle.

After several minutes, the vehicle braked; around them, Aras could hear other bicycles skidding to a stop. When he and Pilot emerged, he heard people milling about and murmuring: many more, perhaps dozens. They were now inside a large space, and the smell of smoke hung heavy in the air. *An encampment*, he decided.

"You lucky this time." The leader's voice came from close by. "Most time, they just shoot to kill." There was a pause, as if the boy were appraising him. "I'm Gideon. Why you here?"

Aras detected wariness in his voice. "I'm looking for people." Pilot had stopped straining at his leash, although the guide could tell he remained alert. "Seven of them. One's a baby."

"Was they led by a girl?" spoke up another voice. "Thin, and her hair stick up?" At the description of Esther, Aras felt his chest tighten.

"That's them," he said. "You know where they went?"

"We tried to save them," another boy said. "But we was too late. They got them."

"Got them?" Aras's reply was sharp. "You mean she's—"

"Don't know," said Gideon. "But no one git out alive."

Aras recalled the words of the dying child he had met on the road and a chill fell over him. "Tell me about this place."

"It's near where you was. They take folks. Strangers, mostly, who don't know no better. And ain't no one see them again."

Aras's mind was racing. "Is there a way in?"

Aras could hear the boy spit on the ground. "We been try-ing a long time. But ain't nothing work." There was a pause. "You got an idea?"

Aras heard the calculation in the boy's voice. Unless he was mistaken, there was something shrewd beneath Gideon's apparent crudeness. Aras wasn't sure if he trusted or even liked him, and the last thing he wanted was to get involved in some-one else's fight. Yet he also knew he was alone in a strange city, facing an unknown foe.

He would need all the help he could get.

As if he could read his mind, Pilot stood and pushed his muzzle into the boy's hand, whimpering. Aras crouched down to scratch him behind the ears.

"It do seem a shame," he remarked to his dog, "to come all this way for nothing. Right, boy?"

TWENTY

ESTHER WAS DRAGGED AWAY BY THE MAN CALLED TAHIR.

There was no fighting him; although his hands were soft and scented, they were like a hawk's talons gripping her arm. Glancing over her shoulder in despair, she could only watch as her friends, escorted at gunpoint, disappeared into the darkness.

Tahir forced Esther around a corner. She thought she was perhaps being kept separate from the others because she was their leader; now she was brought, alone, down to the basement level. She still found it difficult to walk in the red shoes Inna had given her; she stumbled and nearly fell down the narrow metal stairs.

"Don't try anything," snapped Tahir as he yanked her back.

At the bottom of the steps, the man led Esther through the cluster of abandoned restaurants on the underground level. Then Tahir let go of her arm and shoved her, hard. As she landed on her hands and knees, she could hear the squeal of the rusty metal grille being pulled down behind her, followed by the click of a key in the lock.

"Get used to it," Tahir said. Then he turned and soon the sound of his footsteps faded away.

The moment she was alone, Esther ripped off her shoes.

Then she unfastened her bracelet, one Inna had given her, and smashed it to the ground. The gifts were a torment, a terrible reminder that she alone was to blame. For Esther had acted no better than a little child, impulsively and without judgment. Her face burned with shame when she realized why.

Inna had seemed like a mother.

And because of that, Esther had guaranteed the deaths of herself and her friends.

There was only one comfort: Kai wasn't among them. From what Inna had said, Esther didn't think there was any threat to Kai, no possibility he would be killed and consumed, like them. It was a small relief, yet a real one.

By now, Esther's eyes had adjusted to the faint spill of light that came from the atrium and through the gate. Gazing around, she saw she was in what was once a restaurant, with matching tables and benches made of fake wood bolted to a grimy tiled floor. The ground was strewn with trash and a dank smell arose from what looked like a filthy pile of bedding in the corner.

Children were kept here before me, Esther realized with a dull shock. She thought of the small skull and felt sadness and fury in equal parts.

Esther forced herself to focus: She had to find a way out. Using her sense of touch and the dimming light, she searched the walls and floor for any vents she could pry open, any hidden storage spaces, any weak places in the plaster. She could find nothing. Then she checked the metal grille, looking for loose slats, something she might be able to use as a weapon. But whoever had been there before her had clearly tried the same thing, and in vain. The entrance and walls were marred with the fading scratches of someone else's fingernails.

There was no escape, and no way to protect herself when her captors came for her. Yet for some reason, Esther found herself thinking of her childhood in Prin.

No escape, no protection.

The words reminded her of one of the many games she used to play with Skar, the all-day competitions that took the two girls across the tangled ruins of Prin and deep into its outskirts. Although the contests changed from day to day, the rules were always brutal, simple, and, for Esther, nearly impossible. She had lost many, many times to her best friend. Yet over the years, the games had made her fast and strong while also teaching her the skills of stalking and escape that all variants learned when they were very young.

A faint clanging noise brought her back to the present.

Someone had begun descending the metal stairs to the basement.

No escape, no protection.

Esther had only a few moments to think.

What could you do if you had no means of escape and no weapon with which to defend yourself? When you had absolutely nothing, what could you use against your enemy?

The answer came to Esther in a flash: *You could use surprise.*

She gazed at the doorway. The entrance took up most of the wall that faced the central court. Fake wooden trim ran around it, with perhaps a two-foot gap above it to the ceiling.

That was the part that caught Esther's eye.

She took a moment to grab a piece of bedding, a foul-smelling sheet that she draped around her neck. Then she approached the door and examined the trim.

The bevel was shallow yet had a sharp angle, which allowed her to take a firm hold. Pulling hard and hoping it wouldn't break away from the wall, she lifted one foot and set it on the trim, just below her hands. Treating the plastic strip as a kind of ladder, she managed to inch her way up the side of the door. When she could go no farther, she clambered onto the section that ran across the top. Crouching low, she braced herself against the ceiling as she looked down over the entrance beneath her feet.

All she had to do was wait.

She smelled it first: the aroma of cooked vegetables. Then Esther could hear footsteps growing closer. There was the jangle of keys and the sound of one being fit into a lock.

"Come and get it!"

It was Tahir. She heard him grunt; she figured he was kneeling to raise the gate. It screamed in rusty protest and she could feel the reverberations travel up the wall and into her legs as she silently undid the sheet from around her neck.

She could see a tray being slid inside. Then silence. Esther didn't move.

"Hey," Tahir said. "Where'd you go?"

Esther tried to quiet her breathing, which was coming quick. The man cursed.

"Where are you hiding, sweetheart?" he asked, and made the endearment sound ugly.

There was a click; and then a faint glow of light spilled into the dim interior of the restaurant. Esther watched as it wavered, exposing first the bedding, then the piles of trash, then the area underneath the tables.

Tahir cursed. Then she heard and felt him push the gate higher.

Esther saw the top of his head beneath her, shifting back and forth as he held a lit firestarter, still trying to see around the room. She waited for the right moment. Finally, he stopped rocking.

Esther dropped onto him.

She aimed both feet at the top of his skull, hoping to maximize her meager weight. Combined with the element of surprise, it worked as she planned: He fell as if clubbed, hitting the ground with a crash. In an instant, Esther wadded up one end of the sheet and stuffed it into his mouth. He wasn't quite unconscious; he blinked once or twice, his eyes not focusing. But she had already used the rest of the cloth to bind his wrists and ankles.

It wasn't perfect, she knew; but there was no time to tie him more securely. She grabbed the key ring from his belt and the communication device that emitted an occasional squawk. His handgun, however, gave her more trouble. As she struggled to free it from its leather holder, something kept it in place and she had to leave it where it was.

She didn't think to take Tahir's firestarter, a decision she would soon come to regret. But for now, all she knew was: *She had to get to the others.*

Esther bolted from the restaurant. Then, with a leap, she grabbed the gate and yanked it down. Fiddling with the keys, she finally found the one that locked it.

Then she took off.

Esther raced through the hallways and up the staircase, her bare feet silent on the cold marble and metal surfaces. She ran the way Skar had taught her years ago: zigzagging like an animal from one safe place to the next, keeping to the deepest shadows possible. As she went, she kept her ears keyed to any sound. She knew it was only a matter of minutes before Tahir worked himself loose and called for help.

There were dozens if not hundreds of possible places where her friends could be hidden. The adults had isolated her; perhaps that meant the others were locked up together. That was her only hope. Yet as she worked her way through the ground floor, checking each store, the cavernous darkness gave no clue: no voices, flickering lights, telltale shadows, or sounds.

Desperate, Esther stood still in the middle of the central atrium, feeling the silence and empty blackness weigh on her like a mountain. Then she heard something.

It was a skittering sound, coming fast out of the dark, nails sliding on marble. A hulking dark form, low to the ground, rounded a corner and bore down on her, breathing hard.

Terrified, Esther recoiled, her hands held uselessly in front of her to fend off whatever it was. A scream boiled up in her throat as the thing leaped at her, nearly knocking her off her feet.

As she staggered backward, Esther found herself gripping fistfuls of coarse fur. Then the creature thrust forth its face and, moments later, she felt an immense, warm, and wet tongue lick her face.

To her shock, Esther realized it was Pilot. And the moment she recognized him, she became aware that someone followed close behind.

"Aras?" She could not disguise the hope in her voice.

The click of a firestarter provided a brief flare of light. To her disappointment, it revealed two strangers, a boy and a girl.

"You alive," said the boy. He was pale-skinned, ginger-haired, and his bony frame was swathed in black tatters. With a shock, Esther recognized him as the leader of the group that had chased them their first day in Montreal. *The Insurgents*, Inna had called them. "Where the others?"

Esther hesitated, her guard up. "That depends. Who are you and how did you get in?"

The girl spoke. "There's a metal door in the ground. When you break through, you in the basement. More of us are coming."

The firestarter had evidently grown too hot and the boy let the flame go out, plunging them into near blackness again. "I'm Gideon. We here to help. We try when you first come."

Esther was still wary. "And where's Aras?"

"The boy that can't see? He say the dog find you." In the darkness, it seemed as if he smiled. "Say you the only one it won't kill."

Esther smiled, too, her mind spinning.

"We try to get in for years," said Gideon. "Your boy say how to do it. So now we get your friends and go. That it." He paused, and then he spoke with bitter relish. "This place ours."

Everything was moving too fast for Esther. She wasn't sure if she trusted Gideon and his plans. Yet she had few choices open to her and even less time.

"Last I knew, Inna had my baby on the third floor. But we got to find the others first." As she spoke the words, Esther was struck by the hopelessness of their situation. No matter how confident Gideon seemed to be, the three would be attempting to search a massive place she knew only slightly, and in near-total darkness.

Then she felt something soft and moist on her hand. It was Pilot, nuzzling her. At the touch of his velvety nose, she had an idea.

In the darkness, she fumbled in the pocket of her skirt. From it, she took something out. It was the leather necklace

Skar had given her, which she still carried for luck.

She offered it to the dog. "Find Skar," she said. "Take us to her."

At first, Pilot only looked at the object. Then he sniffed it, with greater interest. At last, he looked up at Esther, his tail wagging.

"Let's go," Esther said.

The dog took off so quickly, he nearly yanked the lead from her hand. Esther had to run blindly, a strange and unnerving experience. Yet once she decided to trust Pilot, she found she could go almost as fast as she could fully sighted.

The Insurgents rode behind, following by sound as the animal led them through the darkened halls. They carried their bicycles up one set of metal stairs, then another.

It wasn't until they were on the second floor that the dog slowed to a trot. He paused and raised his head, to smell the air; then he put his nose to the ground. Sniffing the marble floor, he walked down the hall and came to a stop in front of a shuttered store.

He sat, looking up at Esther, and whined. Esther approached the grille. The store looked locked and deserted, like every other storefront they had passed. But when she peered in, she saw silhouettes moving around further back.

"Skar," she whispered. "Eli."

In a flash, her friends emerged from the dimness and huddled close to the grille, their fingers curled through the slats.

"How did you get here? And who's that?" Silas indicated the two Insurgents who lurked in the shadows, still on their bicycles.

"They took Eli." Skar pressed her lips to the grille so she could speak in Esther's ear. "Because he's the biggest. Did you see where he is?"

Stumpy, held in Joseph's arms, was hissing at Pilot. "Isn't that Aras's dog?" asked Joseph.

Esther only nodded. She couldn't waste time answering any more questions. She was already fumbling with the key ring as she tried first one and then another in the lock that held the gate secure.

"We got to go," Gideon whispered, balanced on his bike.

But there were several dozen keys in all, and Esther had to try each one in the lock. The first nine keys didn't fit and she willed her hands to stop shaking. As she tried the tenth with no success, she heard something that made her heart sink.

It was the distant sound of shouting.

She assumed Tahir had worked free of his bonds and was calling for help. It would only be a matter of seconds before all of the adults would come after them.

"Hurry," breathed the Insurgent girl.

Esther worked her way up to the fourteenth key, then the fifteenth and sixteenth.

The seventeenth key slid in and turned with a clunk.

As Gideon and the girl pulled the gate up, Esther had already moved on down the hallway, searching for Eli.

Like Pilot, all she had to do was follow her nose. The faintest aroma of vegetables and sugared fruits wafted from down the hall and grew stronger the farther she went.

Eli was the biggest, Skar had said, which made a terrible kind of sense.

He would be the easiest to fatten up.

She found him huddled in another darkened store. "How did you get out?" Eli whispered. There was no time to reply. By the time she was able to free him, the communications device in her pocket had started to crackle. From it, they could decipher a few phrases: "Escaped." "Heading upstairs." "Unarmed."

The others were waiting for them. "This is Gideon," Esther said. "He and his friend can lead you out of here, but you got to hurry."

Michal spoke up. "What about you?"

"I got to find Inna. And get Kai back." Before the others could object, Esther cut them off. "This was my mistake. So I got to make it right."

"At least take one of us," said Eli. "That way, you can—"

At that moment, brilliant light flooded the hall, silencing him. The giant glass stars that hung high above burst into electrical flame, illuminating the darkest hallways and deepest corners.

Everyone shrank back, wincing and exposed as they blinked in the shocking brightness.

"Lights on so they can shoot," Gideon whispered. He seemed distracted, Esther thought, as he gazed around at their opulent surroundings; she remembered he had never been inside before. "Can't outrun or outhide them now."

Silas was ashen-faced; and, beside her, Esther could sense Joseph trembling. Michal clung to Skar in silence.

Then Esther gazed down at the dog panting by her side.

"We still got one thing," she said in a soft voice. "Pilot can see in the dark. Or near enough."

"But how—" the Insurgent girl began. Esther cut her off.

"We got to get rid of the lights. Turn off the generator somehow." She turned to Joseph. "We can do that, can't we?"

"Yes," he replied with hesitation. "But—"

"Just for a few minutes," Esther said. "So you can all escape. And I can get to Kai."

"I'll go," offered Skar. "Just tell me how to do it." But as she spoke, Esther saw the color drain from Michal's face. Michal tightened her arm around Skar's waist as Skar covered the girl's hand with her own.

"No. *I'll* go."

It was Eli. He no longer had a partner or anything left to lose. The thought pulled at Esther's gut, but she shook off the feeling. "Thanks," she said.

"It's like a truck," Joseph offered. "It's parked inside on the ground floor. We saw it on the far exit, opposite from where we came in the first day."

"But be careful," Esther said. "I don't know if anyone will be posted, but guards are on the lookout for all of us."

"Right," Eli said, his voice unwavering.

Joseph took Eli aside and, as quickly as possible, told him in whispers what to do once he made it to the generator. After a few moments, Eli nodded and took off.

As he rounded the corner, Esther tensed, waiting for the sound of gunfire.

It didn't come.

Gideon spoke. "If we gonna do this, we got to move."

Esther nodded. "Wait for me with them outside. Don't come back in. I'll come to you."

The Insurgent leader didn't reply; in fact, he acted as if he hadn't heard. He and the girl took off with Skar, Silas, Joseph, and Michal close behind. Instead of using the same staircase as Eli, they were apparently going to use one on the far side. A *smart move*, Esther had to admit, *in case anyone gets caught.*

She waited until she was sure they were safe, and then she took Pilot by the lead.

"C'mon, boy," she said.

TWENTY-ONE

IT WOULD HAVE BEEN HARD ENOUGH FOR ESTHER TO MAKE HER WAY undetected through the brightly lit District had she been alone. But now, she was accompanied by a large, shaggy animal that panted, yanked on his chain, and whimpered. One time, he even sat down and scratched himself vigorously, making his collar jingle.

"Hush," she whispered to him for what felt like the hundredth time.

Esther was trying to remember the way to Inna and Ramon's rooms. She thought she was on the right track, when she realized she didn't see any of the familiar stores. She spun on her heel and cursed to herself when she realized she was on the wrong floor. Girl and beast had been trading positions of power; right now, it was Esther's turn, and she feared her instincts weren't good enough.

Her only chance was to avoid drawing attention until Eli could turn off the power.

Esther peered around a corner and saw two adults no more than a few feet away walking in the opposite direction. One of them carried a rifle. Her heart thundering, Esther shrank inside a doorway. Stroking Pilot and praying that he remained silent, she waited until they had passed.

Up ahead, she saw a set of metal staircases.

Esther was convinced this was the way to go. Yet the stairs seemed miles away, across a broad and open expanse at the end of the hall. Everything was still pitilessly bright. Light reflected off store windows and bounced off gleaming railings and the polished floor. There was no place to hide.

Esther again peeked around to check if the coast was clear. She couldn't see anyone, yet there was no way to know for certain. With a sense of fatalism, she gripped Pilot's lead and stepped into the open.

"*Hey!*"

Esther flinched.

Two women were at the end of the hall. One was speaking into a communication device. The other was pulling a weapon from her belt.

There was no other choice. Esther began to run for the stairs, dragging the dog with her.

Then a shot rang out.

* * *

Eli looked at the incomprehensible machine.

He had a vague idea of what generators were. There had been one in Prin, he knew, that provided the Source with its electricity. He, along with everyone else, had been forced to spend most of their waking hours harvesting gasoline in order to keep it running.

This one was immense. It was, as Joseph had said, a truck, parked on the main floor against one of the exits. Eli eyed it with caution. The humming noise it produced was so loud it was impossible anyone could hear him approach, but a quick glimpse reassured him that it was unsupervised.

The thing was made of tan-colored steel and covered with a bewildering assortment of pipes, boxes, and joins. The smell of grease, hot metal, and fuel hung heavy in the air. Eli stepped around it until he found an open panel on the side. As Joseph had told him, there were many glass dials, switches, and wires in here. These were what he was supposed to focus on.

Eli tried to remember the rest of Joseph's instructions. There were two ways to disarm the system: He could either try flicking a few buttons or pull out the long, rubberized line that led to the wall. But if he made a mistake, Joseph had added, he might burn to death; he wasn't really sure. In any case, he said, Eli couldn't be too careful.

The dire warning made it hard to remember his instructions, so Eli decided not to heed it. It had been difficult enough making his way to the ground floor without being seen; there had been adults everywhere, running from store to store and searching each one. He had done it for one reason alone: Esther was depending on him. That was the only thing he cared about.

His heart was beating so hard it hurt.

Eli saw one switch on the side of the contraption that seemed to fit Joseph's description. Yet actually touching it made Eli anxious. He extended his hand and, at the last minute, drew it back.

Of the many wires, one stood out. It was a thick, gray cord that snaked forward, leading down the hall and disappearing into the darkness. Could this be the one Joseph had mentioned? The casing was made of a familiar material, rubber. The remnants of rubber he had seen in Prin had never been dangerous.

Eli fingered the front of his denim jacket. He had liked it ever since Inna and Ramon had given it to him; and it was what he had been wearing when he danced with Esther. But he took it off and wrapped it around his right hand, to give him extra protection. Then he grabbed the cord and gave it a yank.

It was no good. The cord didn't budge. He would have to use two hands.

Eli took a deep breath. Then he threw aside the jacket and grabbed the line with both sweating hands. He braced one foot on the wall next to the machine.

Then he pulled as hard as he could.

As she ran, Esther saw a bullet whiz past her, going so fast it was a blur. Up ahead, there was the resounding crack of breaking marble as it struck the wall. Then it ricocheted off and smacked into the wall on the other side before bouncing off and hitting a display window, which shattered in a burst of broken glass.

Pulling the confused dog along, Esther veered first to her right and then her left, zigzagging as she continued her sprint toward the staircase. She hoped a moving target would be harder to hit than if she took a straight path. But she knew she was only buying herself a few precious seconds, and in her mind one thought kept repeating itself again and again.

What was taking Eli so long?

Ahead, the staircase seemed impossibly far away. And even if she made it there, Esther realized she would be offering her unprotected back to the gunman as she raced toward more adults undoubtedly waiting on the floor above. Esther was running straight into a trap of her own making.

She heard a second shot. But she never saw the bullet.

The hall had been plunged into darkness.

The relief Esther felt was so great, it was like a physical shock. She heard the bullet ping off a wall in front of her and gutter out, as the first one had. She didn't think there would be a third.

In the distance, Esther heard one of the guards curse.

Esther called to Pilot under her breath, clicking her tongue in the way she had heard Aras do so many times. Obeying instantly, the dog began to lead her straight across the hall, quickening his pace. Within moments, Esther bumped her foot against something: It was the bottom step of the staircase. With one hand on the banister, she held on tight as Pilot headed up.

In blackness, they reached the third floor. Esther had a clear picture in her mind of its layout and with the dog's help, was able to navigate back to the store full of children's clothing and toys. When they rounded a corner, Esther saw that she was right: Candles flickered in the distance and she could hear the murmur of faraway voices. As she drew closer, Esther melted into the shadows by the wall and listened, trying to identify them.

Outside the storefront marked PRADA, the older woman was pacing, agitated. Esther wasn't certain, but she thought she was holding something in her arms. Was it Kai? Next to her was an armed guard.

With the dog by her side, Esther moved forward as silently as she knew how. Yet Pilot's nails clicked on the hard tiles and the guard looked up.

"Who is it?"

Esther held her breath. Next to her, Pilot began to growl. It wasn't loud, but it sent a vibration rippling through the darkness.

The guard spun around, raising a rifle to his shoulder. "Who is it?" His voice was shaky now.

Pilot's snarl grew louder. Panicked, the guard fired at the sound, and Esther ducked. The noise brought others racing from different parts of the hall. In the confusion, Esther saw the candles in Inna's room go out.

The noise seemed to madden the dog. He leaped forward and Esther, unprepared, let go of the lead.

The animal vanished into the darkness. Moments later, a man screamed; there were the sounds of struggle and loud growling. Then came a piercing yell, which echoed as it faded. An instant later, an explosion from the ground floor far below seemed to shake the entire building. It was followed by a deathly silence.

The lights went on, everywhere.

Esther had known it was only a matter of time. Still, the few precious moments of darkness had not only saved her life, but also allowed her to come this far. As the dog bounded back to her, wagging his tail with incongruous happiness, Esther slipped with him around a corner. She watched as Inna, carrying a lit torch, hurried into the hall. She headed for the stairs, her expression grim.

Kai wasn't with her.

Esther blinked, dismayed.

Where was Inna keeping her child? She had no idea. Yet every minute she hesitated gave the older woman the chance to get farther away.

Esther tried to remember the commands Aras had given his dog. She tried a different one now, giving a low whistle and jangling his leash. "Go," she whispered. "Follow her." Pilot took off and Esther went with him. Within moments, they had crossed the wide hallway and caught up; she could hear footsteps on the staircase above them.

For all her craftiness, Inna knew nothing about tracking and stalking. Unlike Esther, she had never needed to hide from others or avoid detection. So her footsteps were giving her away as they clattered up the metal stairs.

Even without his dog, Esther thought with disbelief, *Aras could track Inna by how much noise she made.*

The woman's steps were slowing down and her breathing was loud and ragged; it was easy to put on speed and catch up. Yet by the time Esther reached the top, Inna had already disappeared. Esther hesitated. There were numerous stores Inna could have hidden in. But then the bang of the metal door at the far end of the hall once more gave Inna's location away.

She was heading to the roof.

As Esther and Pilot entered the airless cement stairwell, she could hear the clatter of Inna's footsteps several stories above. She doubted Inna was armed; in fact, the older woman seemed to be spooked and not thinking properly. By fleeing to the roof, Inna was in essence putting herself in a corner. Still, Esther knew it was foolish to underestimate her enemy; even the most cowardly animal could be vicious when trapped. As she mounted the final flight, Esther put herself on guard against a possible ambush.

Yet when she pushed open the door and stepped out into the suffocating humidity of the roof, she was stunned by what she saw.

Inna was gardening.

At least, that's what it looked like. Halfway across the roof, the woman was leaning against a trellis dense with foliage, reaching up to prune it with a pair of shears. After trimming a branch, she would step closer to examine the vine before making another cut.

Esther stared at her. It would have been impossible for Inna not to have heard the door. Yet, other than a faint flush along her cheeks, the older female seemed perfectly at ease.

A whistle, so faint it was barely audible, arose from the open door behind them. Pilot jerked free. Even as Esther grabbed at his chain, the animal was escaping down the stairwell, as if he had been summoned below.

"Pilot!" she yelled, but he was already gone.

When she turned back, Bao was approaching from across the far end of the garden, Kai in her arms. The boy was holding a handful of grapes, stuffing them in his mouth. He smiled at Esther; yet when Bao set him down, it was toward Inna that the child stumbled. The older woman greeted him with a hug, then dismissed Bao with a nod of thanks.

Esther was alone on the roof with Inna and the little boy.

"Would you hand me that?" Inna said, indicating a flat wicker basket. After a moment's hesitation, Esther did.

Inna placed several withered vines in it. "You have to prune away the old growth," she explained as she continued to trim. "Otherwise, it steals nutrients from the new. And you need to distribute the weight by making sure there are only so many buds on each vine." She counted under her breath, then made another cut. "Did you know that?"

When Esther didn't answer, Inna smiled. Her expression was pinched. "No . . . I didn't think so."

Esther started to speak, but Inna cut her off.

"You see, this didn't just happen by magic." As she gestured at the roof, the flush on her face deepened to two red spots on her cheeks. "I suppose you think that we just walked in and found everything waiting for us. But believe me, everything—the water, this farm, our electricity, our standard of living—is here for a reason. And that's because we studied how to make it happen. And we worked hard."

Inna was becoming agitated, punctuating her sentences with snips of her shears. "But you wouldn't understand," she said. She was sweating now, her hair flopping forward into her face. She pushed it away with one hand and kept clipping. "You're just a child, and what we're doing here is grown-ups' work. And yet you have no problem coming here and judging us. As if you even know what we've had to do in order to survive."

"I *do* know. The children—"

"There are sacrifices!" Inna exclaimed. "None of us want to do it . . . we *have* to! We have to do it in order to live!"

Something in the older woman seemed to break. Dropping the clippers to her side, she turned to Esther with a beseeching expression.

"Don't you see? You and your friends have spent years in the outside world. It's only a matter of time for you. All except for Kai, of course." She had pulled the boy to her and now held him close. "And the baby, too."

Esther blinked. "What baby?"

"Why, yours, naturally. The one you're carrying."

Esther was struck silent.

Could it be true? Although she now suspected everything the older woman said, Esther thought of her fatigue, the nausea. She tried to recall the last time she and Caleb had made love. Was it in Prin? No . . . it was while they were traveling with the others and they spent the night under the highway bridge. It was true she had not had her monthly blood in a while, but she had never paid it much attention.

Having a baby, she now realized with the shock of a thousand emotions, *was completely possible.*

Esther was trembling. "I thought it was something else."

"That's why I had you separated from the others." Inna was gazing at her with what seemed genuine warmth. "I'm going to take care of you . . . and then the two little ones. After you're gone."

She rose and came closer. Esther was so stunned, she allowed Inna to wrap her arms around her. For a moment, she was amazed by the fleeting yet powerful sensation she once again had of security and trust within the soft embrace.

But a sound snapped her out of her reverie.

Across the roof the door opened, and several adults came spilling out, weapons drawn. Ramon was among them and, with a start, Esther noticed he was carrying her rifle.

More than fear, she was overcome by anger. She yanked free of the older woman.

Esther was furious at not only Inna, but herself—for allowing herself once again to be so easily manipulated. She seized Kai, who let out a squawk of protest. Then she took a step backward, her eyes darting around.

There was no escape. She and Inna were against a wall. There was only one door, and it was crowded with armed adults. Esther was glad that all of her friends were most likely outside by now, safe and free. Yet she was outnumbered, unarmed, and alone.

The heel of her foot banged against something.

It was a bucket, one of the containers used to catch leaks. It sounded no more than half full of water, poisonous rainwater that hadn't yet been processed. Esther thought of the ending of *The Wonderful Wizard of Oz*, and how Dorothy killed the wicked witch. Even as she heard the water slosh, Esther pushed Kai to the side. Then she grabbed the bucket by the handle and hoisted it up high.

Inna was staring at her, puzzled. She recoiled as realization struck of what Esther was threatening to do; and her expression changed to one of pure contempt, a patronizing smile on her face. She was about to say something, but Esther cut her off.

"Your weapons." She was speaking to the others who now stood clustered around the door, confused and motionless. "Throw them away."

The adults looked at Esther as if she were joking and then at Inna. She was standing close to Esther, much too close to escape; surely, the older woman had calculated the space between them and realized it was impossible to run.

Inna's lips were pinched together in a thin line. Then she spoke. "Do as she says."

"Out there," ordered Esther.

The adults exchanged a baffled look. Then one stepped forward and hurled his rifle at the transparent wall closest to him with all his strength. Glass exploded as the weapon crashed through and sailed outside; moments later, they could hear it smashing on the pavement far below. Then Bao threw a handgun after it, and Tahir and the rest of them, in a noisy shower of flashing metal and shining splinters. The last to go was Ramon. Keeping his eyes on Inna the entire time, he tossed Esther's rifle off the roof and it disappeared.

Hot air gusted in through the shattered glass walls.

Esther and Inna stared at each other. The bucket had grown heavier; as Esther shifted it, her palms sweaty, the water sloshed again, nearly spilling, and Inna jumped back. Her face was now filled with terror.

The truth was Esther had no intention of killing anyone. But Inna didn't know that.

"Look," said the older woman. She sounded desperate, even as she tried to project an air of calm. "No more guns. That means we're equal now, you and I." She licked her lips and swallowed hard, her eyes bright. "Maybe we can come to an agreement."

In spite of herself, Esther almost laughed. "You mean if we live here with you? We already tried that."

"No," Inna shook her head. "I know that's over with. But there must be *something* we can do."

Esther hesitated. She didn't trust Inna and realized the older woman was saying whatever she could think of just to stay alive. Yet what she said made a kind of sense. Esther thought about it a long moment. Then she spoke.

"If I let you live . . . will you teach us?"

Inna looked uncomprehending. "What do you mean?"

"You know." Esther thought of all the adults had accomplished, what they had built from nothing. They had years of valuable experience and knowledge between them, decades' worth. "We'll let you stay here. But only if you teach us what you know."

Inna blinked, rapidly. Her eyes flickered to those of her partner. He gave a faint shrug, as if to say, Why not?

"So is it a deal?" Esther lowered the bucket, extended her hand and waited. An eternity seemed to pass before Inna nodded.

"It's a deal." The woman looked older now, much older than Esther had ever seen her. And yet she seemed relieved, too. She was about to grasp Esther's hand, when something made them both look up.

The noises were faint, yet impossible to miss, rising up from the cement stairwell: shouting and cheering mixed with the sounds of glass breaking and heavy objects being toppled. Esther became aware of the smell of something burning. Only then did she notice wisps of smoke that seemed to be rising from the building beneath them. A faint tremor passed through the roof once, then twice.

The Insurgents had arrived.

They had not stayed outside, as Esther had asked. Instead, with no one to stop them, they were taking over.

"I see," Inna said, her eyes narrowing. She had already withdrawn her hand.

"No." Esther was confused, appalled. "I told them to stay away. I told them to—"

"Very clever. You lure us up here and convince us to get rid of our weapons. All the while your friends are breaking in, to destroy everything. It's brilliant, really."

"No—I didn't. You have to believe me . . ."

Inna reached forward. Before Esther could stop her, she plunged one hand into the bucket, her bracelets clanking against the metal. Scooping up a handful of its water, she dragged it across her own face, leaving a shining trail that dripped from her forehead, ran across her eyes, and into her mouth.

"My terms," she said.

Across the room, the others gasped. But Inna ignored them. Still poised and collected, she turned to the person most familiar to her.

Ramon stepped forward. He took Inna's wet hand and raised it to his lips, kissing the palm. Then he too brought it to his face and brushed it there, letting the poison drip into his eyes and mouth.

"I . . . please." Esther was so stunned, she could barely speak. "Stop. You don't know what you're—"

But Inna didn't stop. She turned to the other adults, who quailed as they clung to one another, shocked.

"Your turn," she said.

No one moved. Incensed, Inna grabbed and twisted the bucket out of Esther's grasp. Then she hurled the contents, dousing them all.

As they shrieked, Inna threw the empty receptacle onto the ground, where it clanged with finality. Then she took hold of Ramon's hand and started for the exit. No one made an effort to stop them.

Bao wept openly, trying to dry herself off with her scarf. The others stood as if made of stone, disbelief written across their faces.

As Kai cowered behind her, Esther stared at the ones left behind. But she couldn't stay. The sounds of destruction had grown even louder and she had to find her friends.

Holding the child's hand, Esther headed to the stairs.

By the time Esther reached the third floor, the clamor had grown ever greater.

Dozens of Insurgents swarmed the marble halls like an army of vengeful skeletons arisen from the dead. They ransacked stores in a blind frenzy, grabbing whatever they could find— clothes, shoes, belts. Others used torches to set them on fire and the air was full of the stench of burning cloth and leather. Insurgents wrenched bars off the same railings Eli and the others had polished with such care only days before. They used them to smash windows, while others tossed display tables and racks over balconies. The noise was deafening.

Esther spied a familiar group huddled together far below, on the ground floor: Skar, Michal, Silas, and Eli stood by an exit. To her vast relief, they all seemed safe. But even as she realized that Joseph was not among them, Esther became aware of a commotion coming from the second floor.

She thought she recognized her friend's voice.

With Insurgents running past her, Esther fought her way through the crowd and down a flight of the metal steps. As she moved, she was met by billowing waves of smoke. They filled the mall floors, rolling toward her like a thick, white carpet. Choking and coughing, she kept following it until she saw where it was coming from.

It was a store that was completely ablaze. Silhouetted

against the flames was Joseph, trying to get in.

Esther sprang at him and grabbed him by the arm.
"Joseph—no!" Although smaller than he was, she was much
stronger. Yet Joseph fought her with a ferocity she didn't know
he possessed.

"The records!" he kept shouting. "The records! I have to
save them!"

She finally succeeded in pulling him away. He was trembling, his face wet with tears. Although the fire was already
beginning to die down, nothing was left inside the small enclosure other than charred embers and giant pieces of soot that
wafted through the air.

"Now no one will know." Joseph spoke with a grief Esther
had not known he was capable of. "No one will know . . . except
me." Like Inna, he too looked suddenly older than his years . . .
and afraid.

Esther put her arm around him, although she knew well the
limits of comfort. Then she retrieved the cat carrier that had
been pushed to the side. Handing it to him, she led the weeping boy away from what had once been the library.

It was only when she caught up with the others that she
understood what had happened. *Gideon had deliberately ignored her
instructions. Once Aras had shown them the way in, the Insurgent leader had
taken full advantage of it. He came in through the basement, as directed, and
then opened the main doors to their friends outside.*

"They don't aim to harm anyone," Eli said. He was watching
the destruction with interest, even excitement. "They even let
Inna and Ramon go past them and leave."

Esther glanced up sharply. "Did she say anything?"

"Just good-bye."

Esther gazed out the revolving doors. But if she was expecting to see Inna and Ramon, she was mistaken.

Someone else was standing across the street. It was a thin, dark boy with long hair and sunglasses. Sitting by his feet was an animal that seemed half wolf, looking up at him with an expectant expression.

Esther pushed past Insurgents, squeezing and shoving her way through the mob that clogged the entry. Once outside, she raced across the street, only remembering at the last second how much Aras hated to be snuck up on.

"It's me," was all she said.

And then she was in his arms.

The first crop of radishes, their tops lush and leafy, was almost ready to harvest.

Standing over them, Esther felt a wave of pride she didn't know was possible. For six weeks earlier, the flourishing garden that surrounded her had been nearly destroyed.

When the Insurgents had invaded, one of the last things they did was ransack the roof. Once they realized that the plants growing there were edible, they had plundered it: eating what they could and fighting over everything else. They upended planters, smashed glass panes, and trampled fruits and vegetables. It had been impossible to stop them.

One thing that escaped the rampage was a large cabinet in the corner. The Insurgents knew nothing about the tens of thousands of seeds, safely locked up behind its metal doors. And for that, Esther was still grateful. It had taken Silas nearly an entire day to break into it.

Esther had only learned about the seeds much later, from Bao and Uli. They were the two adults who had asked to stay. Esther alone had promised to take care of them in their final days, for others were too afraid to help. In return, they talked.

As the disease took hold and they began to sicken, Bao and Uli shared all that they knew. In failing voices, they described how to plant and compost; how to tame the sun's rays; when to reap; and how to prepare and preserve what they harvested. And they also talked about the past: not only the world they had once known and the marvels it held, but their own lives, as well. Intrigued, Joseph dared to join them; his face wrapped tightly with a scarf against infection, he stood at a distance, scribbling down as much as he could. *The tales they told*, he thought, *were as magical as anything found in Oz.*

Esther, Aras, Skar, Silas, Michal, and Joseph were able to repair the ruined garden. Following the adults' instructions, they replaced broken panes of glass, fixed the leaks in the draining system, and tried to replant everything that had been eaten or destroyed. At first, Gideon had mocked their efforts. Yet now, weeks later, Esther and her friends were ready to reap the rewards of their hard work.

"What am I holding?" Aras now asked as he brushed his hand over the lush greens, grazing hers.

"Beets. Radishes. Squash." Esther guided him from one container to another, then paused. "Our future." She interlaced her fingers with his.

The two were still not partnered, although they had grown closer than ever. Aras had asked her, shyly, the first night they were together; and Esther had spoken the truth.

"I still need time," she had said.

It wasn't the memory of Caleb that held her back; it was the knowledge of what was growing inside of her. Esther wanted to be certain that her unborn child had all of the energy she had left after taking care of Kai and the others. Yet more and more, she realized she was being foolish. Being with Aras only made her feel stronger, not weaker. The happiness and peace she felt in his presence was like a living thing, flourishing deep within her.

She almost said something to him now, almost accepted his offer, then stopped, for a faint cheer had risen from the open stairwell.

She knew it was Gideon, who often spoke to his people. His speeches were cold and crudely worded, invariably about his hatred of the privileged few and his belief in the common person. Esther agreed with him in principle—she had seen what had happened under Inna. Yet she wondered how Gideon meant to carry out his beliefs.

After the rebellion, Gideon had approached Esther and proposed that the Insurgents move in with them, and initially Esther had been all in favor; she knew that, properly maintained, the District could support hundreds in comfort. But it was growing clearer every day that there were huge differences between the two groups.

Letting go of Aras's hand, Esther went to the stairwell and headed to the mall level. Gazing down from behind the brass railing, she saw that a crowd had gathered to hear Gideon speak.

His tone today was even more aggressive than it had been before. And standing in the front row was Eli. Since Esther's new intimacy with Aras, Eli had become distant to her, even cold.

On the fourth floor, Esther felt torn between two worlds. Waiting for her above was Aras and the sunlit garden. And below her was something she didn't understand, something she found disturbing.

She knew what she had to do. Esther walked across the tiled floor and started down the stairs.

She wanted to let them know, without a doubt, who was in charge.